'A gripping story of love, los[...]
Country and To[...]

'Another fascinating, moving story from the author
of *After the Party*' *Good Housekeeping*

'This clever novel set across three timelines tells
the story of a family haunted by tragedy. A skilfully
written, powerful drama' *BEST*

'The plot is neat, tight and unexpected but the novel's
deep satisfaction comes from Connolly's total
immersion in historical atmosphere and profound
understanding of human pain' *Literary Review*

'Moving [and] powerful . . . Connolly's vividly drawn characters
grapple with trauma, unkindness and greed in an intriguing novel
where past actions reverberate in the present' *Daily Mirror*

'A ravishing novel from the great family-saga-teller Cressida
Connolly and an honourable tribute to the past' *The Times*

'The novels of Cressida Connolly are a wonderful discovery'
Country Life

'A writer who seems able to peer directly into the human heart'
John Preston

Bad Relations

CRESSIDA CONNOLLY

PENGUIN BOOKS

PENGUIN BOOKS

UK | USA | Canada | Ireland | Australia
India | New Zealand | South Africa

Penguin Books is part of the Penguin Random House group of companies
whose addresses can be found at global.penguinrandomhouse.com.

First published by Viking 2022
Published in Penguin Books 2023
001

Copyright © Cressida Connolly, 2022

The moral right of the author has been asserted

Printed and bound in Great Britain by Clays Ltd, Elcograf S.p.A.

The authorized representative in the EEA is Penguin Random House Ireland,
Morrison Chambers, 32 Nassau Street, Dublin D02 YH68

A CIP catalogue record for this book is available from the British Library

ISBN: 978–0–241–53772–5

www.greenpenguin.co.uk

Penguin Random House is committed to a
sustainable future for our business, our readers
and our planet. This book is made from Forest
Stewardship Council® certified paper.

To
Nicky Shulman
who thought of the magic bean
and to
Tom Phipps
with love

PART I

I.

Spring 1855

After he had sat for a time with his dead brother, William Gale composed himself and took out his small silver pocket knife and with it began to cut. Close to the neck the hair was darkened with mud or blood or some mixture of the two, so William cut several pieces from around the crown, where the hair remained bright. It was soon done. He could have sworn that Algie's body was yet warm, sure he discerned the heat of life through the thick stuff of his coat. But in the while he had attended his brother, the fingertips, the nose and cheeks had with stealth assumed the pallor of death, yellow and somewhat waxen, like a stale candle. As William cut, the head lolled suddenly forward, but William was able to keep possession of his fright at this and did not recoil.

He had seen before what death did. He was familiar, now, with the sudden weight of a human head, cradled in the crook of his own arm, as a man took his leave of this life. This was something he had never hoped to learn. These past months had brought terrible lessons, sights and sensations which could not be unknown, much less forgotten. There was little difference between the weight of a head and that of a 12-pound round shot, for all that one carried all the dreams, memories and most tightly cherished hopes of a man within itself, while the other brought only carnage.

William summoned the presence of mind to judge that their mother would require sufficient of his brother's hair to mount in the glass behind a brooch, and perhaps extra for a locket. He considered too their sister, Caroline. She would be sure to wish to commemorate their brother in like fashion. Then there was Algernon's fiancée, poor Emily Norris. Would their mother begrudge her a lock of Algie's hair, as she had already begrudged her the boy's love? Even as he cut he was sensible of the fact that there could not be more of that hair: what was needed must be now obtained, for there could never be a further supply of it.

There being no clean paper to hand, William took from his pocket the last letter he had had from his wife Alice – a missive which had not pleased him, though he kept it near – and folded the pieces of hair into it. It was a sad and curious thing to consider that those same locks which had shone around a young man's living face only hours before would now sit encased in gold and glass upon the breasts of three women. Though its weight was negligible – little more than a dab of sealing wax – the sorrow it brought would ever more weigh heavy upon them.

His work finished, William lifted Algie's head in both his hands and laid it back gently. With his thumbs he closed the green-blue eyes which would never more open upon a morning, nor look upon a day.

William Gale, at nine-and-twenty, had not been in the expectation of finding himself on the field – or, rather, the rocky hillside – of battle. Yet here he was, some two thousand miles distant from his home. His father, like his own father before him, had after the purchase of a commission been for a number of years a soldier; but the family estate and other interests had drawn each away from a full military life. William and Algernon's father had nevertheless fought bravely in the Peninsular and in the action at Albuera, where an injury to his foot saw an end to his service. It was expected that his sons would also, in due course, serve the 23rd Regiment of Foot. But Britain had been at peace since Waterloo in 1815 and no one in the Gale family had expected William's time in the uniform of the Welsh Fusiliers to be spent away from home.

If the truth be said, William was not a natural officer. Affable, accomplished, handsome, with a strong sense of justice, there was a streak of stubbornness and of pride woven deep within his nature. He had no desire to command men. Military strategy did not absorb him. Such appetite as he had for firearms or for blood was easily satisfied by the modest exertions of the partridge shooting season. He did not care very much for a life among soldiers, preferring his own bed and the comforts of home. He enjoyed also the civilian freedom to express whatever opinions he cared to form. But filial duty could not be lightly dismissed. To serve the Crown was an honour the Gales were proud to undertake. A commission was obtained. Thus it was that, two years later, he had found himself on board a ship bound for the Black Sea. A number of his fellows had sold out, rather than face the skirmishes which may have lain ahead. But this had seemed to William dishonourable. Algernon had joined only at the end of the last year. If William was not by inclination a soldier, Algernon was by temperament entirely unsuited to the martial life. He was dreamy, somewhat slow, with the sweet smile of a much younger fellow.

Here outside Sebastopol, William could not let himself recall the companion of his boyhood, their childish games on the long afternoons; how they had played together, raced together, fished together. He and his brother and sister full of fun at nursery tea, taking their buttered bread and sprinkling tiny amber crystals of demerara sugar upon it, purloined from the sugarbowl, whenever their nurse was not looking. Algie's small freckled limbs, as a child of seven or eight, splashing in the clear brown shallows of the stream. How his teeth had chattered, his lips paled, the first time he had fired a gun. That had been their father's 20-bore, when they had set out to shoot pigeons in the fields one afternoon. Although Algie had not hit a bird, still the force of it, the noise, had shaken him. There came into William's mind those times – oh the pity of it! – when he had remonstrated with Algie, found fault with him for being too slow, too timid, too fond of remaining indoors. Oftentimes the boy had preferred to sit on the window seat in the nursery with Caroline, drawing, than to come outside and play rough and tumble. William remembered the incline of Algernon's head, as he had concentrated on his drawing book. The thought of his youthful seriousness was inexpressibly tender. Yet he must not think of these things.

He stood and stepped back, pausing to be sure that the eyes stayed shut. Here was another thing he had never thought to know: how to close the eyes of the dead. More dreadful still, that it was uncertain whether the lids would remain closed. He had seen before that if they were not weighted down, the lids could rise a little over the now clouded, unseeing eyes, like an ill-drawn blind across the darkening glass of a window. But William had no coins for the task and he had not the heart to find stones. Not the stones of this place of death.

Algie had missed the worst of the fighting, arriving as a reinforcement only in December, some four months earlier. He had not seen the clamour above the Alma River; nor, after the great battle at Inkerman Heights, the fallen as numerous as a whole hillside's worth of sheep. He had not known the increase in weight of a bayonet as hour after hour of fighting progressed. Nor the force required for the blade to do its terrible work, piercing the coats of the Russians, then their ribs: it was butchery. Shot as thick as hail, all but invisible in the fog and smoke, until it found a man's flesh.

Yet there had been beauty. Frequently at night William had watched the shells flying in their graceful curves and marvelled that destruction could wear so lovely a coat. Seeing a star, it was easy to take it for a shell also and to wonder that it moved so slowly across the blackness of the sky. In the vineyards by Alma, before the fighting began, finches and larks had congregated in flocks. There had been buntings, gold-crested wrens and yellow-hammers. The song of linnets had hung in the soft air. The first sight of the little harbour at Balaklava had been delightful, scarcely two ships' breadths at its entrance, with magnificent high cliffs along each side, higher than any he knew of on the English coast. It had put him in mind of Clovelly.

But a siege was unrelenting work and this was what Algernon had come out to. There was no verdure here at camp; only mile upon mile of mud. In the cold the trampled ground had frozen into hard deep ruts that caused men and horses to stumble. The privations, especially those endured by the men, had been very hard. Every day men were lost in the trenches from grape and shell, but more had fallen from exhaustion, starvation, ague, cholera. Algie had been much afraid, though he had tried to conceal it, even from William. Perhaps especially from William.

He felt tired. His limbs ached from lack of sleep. When presently he emerged from the trench where his brother's body lay, a furore of sound met his ears. Yellow smoke filled the air. There was the smell of burnt sugar, like toffee apples, which hovered wherever black powder had been expelled from the guns. It struck him that all the noise – the cries and shouts of men, the sporadic report of guns, the boom of occasional cannon fire across the ridge – must have been just as loud within the hollow as it was without; yet he had been conscious of none of it. While he had been sitting with poor Algie there seemed to have been no sound at all.

It came to him that he must now write to his father. It grieved him that the news would reach them at home before his letter could, in the lists of the wounded and the dead published in *The*

Times and the *Illustrated London News*. How terrible to thus discover their poor boy's demise! And Lord Raglan's next despatch
would likely be printed sooner than the mail could carry his
missive. How his mother would greet the news he could not
bear to consider. At least he would be able to say in truth that his
brother had died as the direct result of wounds, while fighting
alongside his company. That Algernon's last words had demon-
strated a selflessness which would surely commend him to his
Maker. Gale could say, too, that the boy had died under enemy
fire. Algie had been about to go back to camp after a night in the
trench when a stray shell burst some way in the air and one piece
came down and struck him just below the left shoulder. There
had been a great deal of blood, the wound too deep to staunch
the flow of it. The fellow beside him told William that Algie
had surely been insensible as to the severity of his injury, for he
was reported to have said: 'If there is anyone worse hit than me,
he had better be taken first,' the lad having seen that there was
only one stretcher at hand. He was not heard to speak again.
During all the time it took for someone to run back to camp and
fetch his brother the bleeding had gone on. By the time William
arrived at his brother it had stopped.

When it had fallen to him to write other such letters to the
families of his special friends, his pen had faltered. *'We are all in
great affliction at the present time, Death having snatched from us one
whom we all loved. We struggle to conceive how the sad news of such a loss
will be met at home, by those whom poor so-and-so held in the dearest
regard . . . Your son, from the day he joined the 23rd, proved himself to be
a credit to us, and a most determined soldier. I have every reason to believe
that he is now in that place where you would not wish to have him back
from.'*

But how to lessen the great blow to a father or a widow when
a man had died not from gallantry, not among the flash of bayo-
nets and the terrible glory of battle, but from cold or sickness,

lying groaning like a beast in his own ordure? This was how his dear friend Lockwood had met his end. The cholera. He had known that his time was coming: he handed his pocket watch to Gale. It had been his last wish that William should visit his widow and the two little daughters he was to leave behind, to offer them some crumb of comfort. It was a meeting William did not anticipate with any gladness, for how could he in honesty convey the facts of Lockwood's death in such a way as to ameliorate their loss? They would ask questions and how was he to answer so as to preserve the honour of his friend? The press were heartless, listing the cause of death next to a fellow's name: debris, dysentery, diarrhoea. Did the men who compiled these cruel lists never consider the mothers, the sisters, the wives whose dreadful shock and sorrow were by their cruel enumeration made so much the heavier? If their men were to be taken from them, would it not be kinder to allow them to cherish the hope that each had died a hero? Small wonder the press were not popular here.

Algie had done his best, but his brother knew that he had not shown dauntless intrepidity. His face had often had the look of fright upon it. The sight of blood had always alarmed him, from his boyhood. When at home as a lad of eleven or twelve he had cut his hand while whittling he had cried out: 'Don't let me see!' and shut his eyes, holding out his arm for their nurse to attend. The boy had come as one of some two hundred and thirty reinforcements, many of them too young to be of much use. They were not hardy. One officer had joined straight from his lessons at Winchester School, having asked leave of his headmaster. More than forty of their number were dead of cholera before Christmas.

There were times when Gale wondered how noble a cause this Crimean affair could truly be said to be. Many times. He had not been alone in the view, which he had formed while camped at

Varna, that the Turks were a horrid set of people to fight for: in the early days, many had averred that they would gladly go over to the Russians and help them against this wretched nation, if that were only the policy of England. In any case, their masters at home seemed to be bitterly inept. The Commissariat was almost criminally inefficient. Supplies were utterly inadequate, if they came at all. During the long months of the winter, watching men die from sickness, fatally weakened by the lack of food or warmth or shelter; seeing horses eating each other's tails in the cold for lack of forage, he had privately questioned whether this was a campaign worth the fighting. It was a question which was not resolved by hearing some of the younger men call out for their mothers in the hours before death, with nothing to help them.

William had seen sights no civilized man should witness. He had seen men's bodies hanging from the branches of trees, like broken umbrellas. In the height of battle men and horses had fallen in swathes, like grass before a scythe. The numbers seemed impossible. After Alma he had seen a wounded Russian, offered an easeful sip of brandy from an Englishman's flask, reward his helper with the blade of a bayonet. And it had been sickening to a man's soul to witness the women who appeared like vultures after each battle, shears in their hands, harvesting gold braid and buttons from the bodies of the still unburied fallen with no more pity than if they were shearing sheep. Down by the harbour, now, those same women sold snuffboxes carved from the bones of the dead horses.

And how were they rewarded for their courage, those who lived on to fight again? It was reported in the journals at home that the men were often drunk, but William knew that they were very much more often hungry, and cold besides. Illustrations in *Punch* or the *Illustrated London News* showed men in fur caps and great sealskin coats standing before little wooden huts, warming their hands by merry braziers. In truth there was often no wood to get up for building shelters, nor even for a fire to heat a pot: the men lived on biscuit, the officers on ham. When there was a fire, there were not enough mess-tins to go round, for most of the men had thrown their camp-kettles away on the march after the battle of the Alma River, supposing more would be sent out. They slept on, or more generally in, the wet ground, some – like Gale – in bell tents, others in holes in the ground, lined with sailcloth. Men's toes came off from frostbite; even their very feet. When at last came hay and oats for the horses, vegetables and provisions for the men, all lay rotting in the mud close to the harbour: the mules to fetch up stores were all dead, the ways impassable from constant freezing rain. A consignment of much-needed boots were all in too small a size to fit the men. Accordingly, no man nor officer was ever buried with his boots on, their seniors looking away while the men removed the boots from the dead. The Government sent out not the tea which all desired, but coffee: unroasted beans which they had no fire to make good. The pallid beans could no more be made into a reviving drink than could the soil they stood on.

All of this had led William Gale to question the wisdom of the politicians at home and of the generals here on the campaign. It was much discussed that Lord Cardigan had departed with indecent haste from the ruinous Balaklava affair during which such numbers of the Light Brigade had fallen. It was said that he had made for his yacht, with a French chef, safely anchored in the bay. His supporters insisted that he had stayed by the camp fire consoling those who remained of his men, for all of that sad night. No one knew what to believe. Gale fancied that their Commander, poor old Lord Raglan, recognized the fruitlessness of the affair and that this accounted for his protracted absences from the encampments of men. When he did ride out, there were some officers who were said to run away to avoid having to salute him. It was whispered that he had been heard to refer to their allies the French as the enemy, a remnant of his Waterloo days. Nevertheless, word of his acts of kindness spread through the camps and he was generally much liked. It was known he had sent blankets and even lent his own rubber sleeping bag to a corporal's wife, who was giving birth in the snow. He wrote warm letters to the friends of men whose lives had been taken. The story of how he had lost his arm at Waterloo and never once cried out as the surgeon removed it was oftentimes retold. He had endured in silence, only broken in order to ask that a ring his wife had given him be retrieved from the lifeless hand. Such courage was admirable, albeit now at some remove in time from the present. William was in any case grateful to Lord Raglan, for it had reached his ears that the old man had made special mention of his actions at Alma. This would likely bring him a decoration.

Yet for all his private reservations as to the wisdom of the campaign, he would not concede to Alice.

It was most confounding that the qualities which had at first drawn him to his wife were now those very self-same traits which so much vexed him. He had liked her spirit, her independence of thought: she had seemed very alive to him, when compared to the docile young women he had met before. Her parents had both died before she came of age: she had had no father to check her. She spoke her own thoughts, gleaned from her own reading, where most of the young ladies of his acquaintance seemed only to parrot the opinions of their older brothers or fathers. Alice laughed frankly, where propriety had it that young ladies more properly hid their amusement behind their hands, or the flutter of a fan. If she did not possess a certain womanly softness, he had not at first rued its lack. To those who cared for her, Alice was deemed captivating; a flame of a woman. To those who did not, she was thought to want the reticence becoming of her sex.

It was not in any case only Alice's character which he had admired. Her neck was pale and slender and there was a little dark mole upon it, just below one ear: he could still remember how he had thought to have been driven to madness if he could not kiss her in that place. The particular tilt of her head spoke to him of merry complicity and a delightful sense of mischief. To marry her – to possess her – had been the one object of his life.

But a Radical! There was no crime in a woman holding an opinion, provided she kept it to herself; but it was unseemly, at best, for the wife of an officer to speak out against the campaign in which her husband was actively engaged. It was impossible. A man's prospects would be dashed if it were to come out that his wife held such views. Promotion would be out of the question. Discretion was essential. Some dreadful stories confided within private letters sent back from Crimea had been finding their way into the press, to the contempt of the commanders here. It simply did not do.

In Alice's last letter – those pages which now enfolded the locks of poor Algie's hair – she had described a meeting she had attended while up in town, a meeting at which the Member of Parliament for the West Riding of Yorkshire, Mr Cobden, had spoken. The Liberal Cobden had become notorious. In truth, William did not find himself in disagreement with every one of the man's views, for all that he was himself a traditionalist and, by birth and belief, a Tory. He privately acknowledged that Cobden's notion that the British should have sent only naval vessels to oppose the Russians and no soldiers whatsoever was not unsound, especially given the parlous conditions in which the men on land had found themselves over the past winter. Cobden's views on British society and its urgent need of reform were another matter. Gale had hardly known how to respond to Alice's letter. To think of his wife going out in the evening, unchaperoned; consorting with heaven knew what kind of people! Mercifully this gathering had taken place in Holborn: no one in the Gales' circle could have seen her there. She was all for Cobden, who, said Alice, had called the British 'the most sanguinary nation on earth'. The politician had gone on to pronounce that this thirst for blood was fuelled by an irresponsible aristocracy. It was his conviction, furthermore, that the campaign against the Russians should be halted forthwith. He called on Government to cease the war on the grounds that Turkey needed no protection from Russian force. It was in Cobden's view certain that the Mahometans could not prevail. He was convinced that over time that faith would wither and die, and Turkey would come to be governed once more by Christians. This William Gale did not believe.

Alice wrote that she had lingered, after the Peace meeting, to speak with one or two of those other ladies present. They told her of an occasion in January in Trafalgar Square at which a group of agitators – not all of them males – had borne placards and banners with Stop the War emblazoned upon them. It was thought that some one and a half thousand had participated; and upon a Sunday. A service in the church of St Martin-in-the-Fields had had to be halted, because of the commotion without. Snowballs had been thrown at omnibuses and even in the direction of the constabulary. Alice had been told that the ringleaders had appeared before a police magistrate at Bow Street and each had been fined forty shillings, or fourteen days' imprisonment. Gale considered the punishment woefully insufficient. It was clear to William that such people were little more than rabble. Interrupting worshippers at prayer! Parliament was the proper place for debate, not the public streets and squares of London. And such gatherings were most certainly no place for a woman. For Alice to describe this with evident approval was quite wrong.

It struck him, not for the first time, that the campaign here was a more tolerable thing for the unmarried. Those who had wives at home only pined for them and fretted about their welfare. In his case there was the further concern that his wife might by some rash words imperil the family name; or indeed compromise her husband's advancement. These were fears he must perforce keep to himself. And then knowing the comfort, the warmth and the tender pleasures of a married bed, as he did, made the cold nights especially hard to bear. He missed Alice, the weight of her arm around him as she slept, the quiet sounds as she turned in the night. She was a much more gentle presence beneath the counterpane than the animated face she showed upon the day would have indicated.

He was fortunate here at least in his tent-fellow, Derrington, who was an amiable fellow and hardly snored. Derrington had been one of a group from Gale's other companies with whom he had found himself at Varna, last August. How distant that time now seemed! Men who had been there before his arrival had had a bad time of the cholera; a dreadful fire had ravaged through the town and much of the camp, taking supplies in its flames. Lord Raglan's entire travelling library had been incinerated. But the little town itself, its green wooded coasts, the bay full of vessels: all had charmed him. In order to avoid the fever they had moved camp again and then again, the horses – some eighty-five in all belonging to their regiment – picketed in rows in the rear of the tents. One such encampment found them beside a lake, and after they had bathed in the mornings, the subalterns often amused themselves hunting the wild dogs that were about the place. Races were put on. When they were closer to Varna, those who knew how to swim rose at six and went out in little boats to bathe. The days at Varna had been spent most agreeably, getting up parties to go quail shooting in the hills on the sturdy local ponies, or rowing about the fleet. In the evenings there had been to-ing and fro-ing between camp and the yachts and steamers ranked in the bay, for dinners and easeful sitting with glasses of port afterwards, beneath the stars. After a great ball at the French Ambassador's, all the talk was of Prince Napoleon, who had been seen there: it was said that he was dressed like his uncle and resembled him to a wonderful degree. A few fellows had sisters or cousins who had come out, so there was occasional pleasant company at table. The warm air hung heavy with the scent of Turkish tobacco and cigars.

Sailing from Varna towards their goal had afforded Gale some of the greatest spectacles of his life. At about one hundred miles from Sebastopol the fleet – some one thousand strong – had had the order to cast anchor. On every side were ships, and such ships! There was the *Trafalgar* and the *Himalaya* and the *Golden Fleece* and countless others besides, four-masted ships and steamers and transports and rafts, siege-trains and magazines and steam tugs; all stretching away in every direction for what seemed to be miles into the distance. They lay entirely out of sight of land. Providence had seemed to favour their designs, for there was uninterrupted calm over those days while they waited in the Black Sea: not so much as a breath of wind disturbed them. During the clear nights the waters were splashed by stars. In the evenings all the bands played, their gay music echoing out across the still, dark water. Gusts of men's laughter rippled sometimes across the deep. The lamps on each vessel had shone with such brightness, like brilliants laid out against a jeweller's black velvet. The sight was so affecting that he had almost fancied himself in the midst of some highly lighted town. '*It was more like the view from one of the London bridges at night than anything else,*' he wrote to Alice. '*A lovelier sight you cannot conceive.*'

Derrington had been by his side then as they looked out across the illuminated fleet, its brilliance doubled by the myriad spots of reflected light dancing gently on the sea. Now his friend greeted him as he returned to their tent, the sombre task of attending Algernon's remains completed. He could tell from the younger man's expression that he already knew the worst. 'I daresay you'll be needing to write some letters,' he said. 'I'm going to go and see if I can beg a hen's egg from Bourke, to fortify you.' Bourke had somehow managed to procure three or four hens and had spent two whole days in constructing a miniature camp for them. The eggs secured him extra tobacco, porter and much else besides. As Derrington made off, he felt his eyes quicken: kindness had a way of bringing a fellow closer to tears than any barbarity. He was grateful that he would have a moment alone, to himself. He felt he could not have borne to answer, just now, any questions about his brother.

This morning he had been planning to write to his mother and father about the Tsar's death. The news of it had reached the English through the telegraph, before it could get to the Russians. Lord Raglan had sent Lord Burghersh into Sebastopol, a white flag ahead of him, with the intelligence. It was said that the Cossacks had not believed him, suspecting a ruse until he took out his betting book and offered to wager them £50 apiece that it was so. At this he was given credence. It was rumoured that the Emperor's demise might hasten the end of the war. This was the story William had meant to tell his parents.

Derrington had lately been sent from a London supplier a small campaign table, which served them both as desk and dining table. Upon it Gale had before him several handfuls of the bulbs which he had collected. These were the source of the dearest little white flowers, tiny lanterns which hung at the end of tender green stems, their faces drooping down like shy children. These snowdrops covered the ground beyond the camp, together with crocus and small wild hyacinths. It had become something of a craze, among the officers, to send quantities of the bulbs home. He had thought to enclose some of the bulbs – each no bigger than a peppermint – in his next letters home.

The empty page over which his pen hovered must now contain sadder things. In all his letters home, he had tried to maintain a levity which, to say the truth, seldom matched the circumstances in which he found himself. Only to his father did he occasionally confide the more sober sentiments he was sometimes prey to; even to his wife he had held back from describing the true horrors of this past winter. To his family he outlined the barest sketches of those battles he had participated in and the occasional skirmish, without dwelling on the losses incurred. Such reticence was somewhat in vain, for the wretched *Times* correspondent supplied more unpleasant detail than William ever cared to; and made many errors besides.

The boy's hair he would not consign to the treachery of the seas, but keep with him until he came home. But the letter he must write and with haste, for he guessed there could be no rest for his parents, nor his sister besides, until they knew the end of poor Algie.

My dearest Father,

It is with a grief which cannot be diminished by the certainty of his having been removed to the Heavenly Kingdom, that I now impart to you the Dreadful news, that my brother has in the small hours of this morning met his end of this life. A more distressing intelligence I know it would be impossible for you to receive, than that you should never see again one of those whom we all of us loved dearest on earth. You may be assured that Algie was gallant indeed. He rose this morning still a boy, but by his fortitude and courage he died a man. With his final breath he expressed the wish that someone more severely wounded should be brought back to camp before himself.

The only consolation I may offer is that he knew no suffering. He stood, he fell, all in one instant. Enemy fire took him with such swiftness that he cannot have been sensible of it. His cerement will . . .

Here he faltered. How could he tell his father that the boy lay still unburied, where he fell? That an armistice for burial might be two days off, or more? Nor could he bear to let them know at home that his brother would be buried without a coffin. Lacking timber enough to build shelters for the living, and fires to heat their food, there was no wood spare to make cradles for the dead. At the rear of the camp, where gabions and fascines were in constant production, a mere handful of rough coffins had been nailed together; but these boxes were only for more senior occupants than Algernon Gale. Instead, William would supply one of his own blankets as a makeshift shroud, for he could not let earth fall on the boy's uncovered face.

2.

Alice was in an agitation. It was her habit to keep abreast of the accounts of what was said in Parliament, lest any debate therein should shed light on what was planned concerning the Russian war, for it seemed to her that her husband's fate was just as likely to be decided at Westminster – or more latterly, at the Conference at Vienna – as on the shores of the Black Sea. Thus it was that Mr Cobden's speech of the 5th of June had come to her attention and within it a warning which troubled her greatly. It was that gentleman's contention that any man, if well clothed, well fed and sheltered, may survive a winter. But, he went on:

> The best authorities tell you that it is hardly possible for an Englishman in the Crimea, unless he take every possible precaution, to escape infection in the summer months of July, August and September. You sin against the law of nature if you go out in the sun in the day, and you equally sin if you go out in the night dews. Such, again, is the effect of the climate, that if you partake of new corn or of fruit in undue measure, these things will bring on intermittent fever. Now, these precautions our soldiers disregard, and therefore is it that I dread the months ahead, for all our troops in the Crimea.

She knew it did not soothe her husband for her to express her fears too forcibly, and yet Alice was convinced that she must apprehend him as to the forthcoming dangers of exposure to the hot climate. It was known that there had been greater casualties as a result of infection than of battle wounds. Alice had felt a lifting of disquiet that the cold, wet season was over, with its hostile vapours and fogs. This fresh danger she had not foreseen.

She set about composing a letter in which she hinted at the caution William must now attempt as regards the perilous outdoor heat of the weeks ahead. This she must convey, yet without appearing to scold. She worked hard at her writing. By the inclusion of some mention of his family and of one or two amusing little occurrences of recent weeks, she was satisfied. In answer she received from William:

4th July 1855, Camp before Sebastopol

My dearest One

Yesterday was the funeral procession of poor Lord Raglan and a more splendid sight you cannot conceive. Hardened and accustomed as we all are to death and horrors out here, I shall never forget my feelings as we uncovered our heads to honour the good old man's remains — the simplicity of the gun carriage that bore his coffin, covered with a Union Jack and on it his cocked hat and a little wreath of Eternelles (placed there by old Pelissier) formed the most touching contrast to the magnificence of the pall bearers' dress and that of the numberless staff who followed. One felt that all this wondrous spectacle was a labour of love, not costing a farthing, a whole Army just turning out to do honour to one whom, whatever his shortcomings, all loved who knew. I know that your fellow Cobden spoke in Parliament against Lord Raglan only a month ago, but here the feeling was very different. I think those who served under him are better placed to know the true character of the man. I fear that the failure of the assault on the 18th of last month weighed most heavily upon him and indeed hastened his demise.

For five full miles the way was lined with our Infantry, leaning on their arms reversed, and where we ended the French Zouaves took up, then the French Imperial Guard and at last the French regiments completed the seven miles that the cortege traversed. At Kazatch the cavalry defiled to the left and the artillery to the right, and formed long lines along the sea shore. Then the coffin came straight through the marines and sailors, brilliant in their white dresses, and with their hats off. The boat which bore the coffin went off under a salute of nineteen guns and we were not back here much before 10 o'clock, it having been a fine day and a cloudless, warm evening.

While waiting on the shore I had a good view of our Celebrities here. Omar Pasha looked splendid. It is most curious to imagine his passage from his youth to his present position as Commander of the Ottoman forces here. I expect you know that he was born in Austria, a Christian, and as a young man served as a tutor and a writing master: he is known to have the most beautiful handwriting to this day, and his signature is said to have a great deal of flourish. He is a most intelligent looking old man with a fine, noble head, and his dress was more gorgeous than I can describe: one blaze of gold, and on his Fez was a single great diamond like a star. On any other man one would only have seen the dress. However, you will see all these things much better told in the papers – though with less truth I daresay.

I have been taking advantage of the very lovely weather that we have been enjoying lately by going for long rides into the new territory we have got. (Your warnings as to the dangers of exposure I have not heeded, for I am grown accustomed to the climate here and fear it not.) Arthur Derrington and I rode out to Baidar the day before yesterday and found it a delightful spot, in the midst of a very smiling fertile valley. Quantities of the jolliest children I ever saw were running about, the smallest chaps imaginable wandering freely in little gangs, giving chase to a merry assortment of dogs and the oddly long-legged fowl they keep. They have had to furnish labour and bullocks, indeed all they had, to support the Russian Army, yet they still maintain their friendliness and hospitality. We got some milk there which we enjoyed, the first milk, by the way, that I have tasted for nine or ten months. These little excursions form the bright spots of one's life here.

Might I ask a small favour, my darling? As you already know, my poor friend Lockwood met his end here, leaving a widow and two children: I wonder if you would be kind enough to call on Mrs Lockwood, in Cheltenham? I know your aunt is there and it was my idea that perhaps you might pay the call when next you visit that good lady?

Here Alice put down her husband's letter with a sigh. She knew him to be wilful, for all his qualities; nevertheless she had hoped that he would heed her, concerning the risks of going about in the heat. And was it fanciful to detect in William's description of the little Tartar children some trace of yearning? It had been a grave disappointment to them both – more than a disappointment, a gnawing sorrow – that, after the early demise of one infant, and then a second, no child had been forthcoming. William was especially dear with children: when her own sister visited, with her two boys, William spent almost all his time horizontal on the Turkey rug, lifting them aloft on his feet, so that they squealed with delight. This widowed Mrs Lockwood that Alice was asked to call upon at least had two dear compan- ions to hold close and to remember her dead husband by: if William were to perish, Alice would be left with no one. And now that Algie had gone, Alice felt it more incumbent upon her than ever to keep the Gale name alive; yet while her husband was so far off there could be no hope of an heir.

Alice had plans, in any case, to go to Cheltenham. Her Aunt Felicity had been her father's only sister and Alice was especially fond of her; it was her custom to spend a night or two each month under her roof. Fair-skinned, prone to blushes, her aunt was quick to laughter and to tears; her moods passed with the alacrity of those pillowy clouds at the seaside. She was clumsy, good-natured and saw the best in everyone; as the hymn had it, she was slow to chide and swift to bless. Also, the town was the place to pick up embroidery silk and sheet music and passementerie. Alice liked to have a jumble of things in her work basket and across her desk, cottons and papers and printed pamphlets and paper-knives and drawing things spilling from one table to the next; she was one of those who felt more alive if the tasks before her were half-done than from a thing completed. She enjoyed her visits to Cheltenham. It was agreeable to stroll about there, on a summer's evening, when the bandstands in the leafy parks gave out the strains of brass or silver ensembles and the smell of lime flowers scented the air. There were concerts at the pump room and, nearby, a variety of tropical birds in an elaborate aviary, their plumage as vivid as the bright hues in the low beds of annual flowers which now adorned the pleasure gardens.

It had been here at Felicity's tall house, overlooking a square in which an especially fine weeping copper-beech tree formed the centrepiece, that Alice had first encountered Dr Nolan. He was not prepossessing. A wide nose sat at the centre of a wide face, the effect of both exaggerated by two small dark eyes, like boot buttons. The hair was soft and meagre and of no particular colour: hair the sparsity of which would have been charming on a small child but was, on the top of a grown man, hardly adequate. The scantness of the hair on his head was not, however, equalled by that on his chin. His cheeks were seldom entirely clean-shaven, for he was one of those unfortunates whom nature required to shave twice a day if he were to maintain a semblance of neatness. The effect was as of iron filings sprinkled across the visage: he had been better to have worn a beard. His one advantage was height, for he stood something over six feet tall in his stockinged feet.

Dr Nolan had become quite a favourite of Aunt Felicity's, for he had a fine mind and was lively in conversation. Some of his ideas, regarding advances in his profession, seemed to the older lady to be dangerously modern; but a man may as well keep up with innovations, if he is to progress in his occupation. Secretly, she hoped to find him a wife. In this plan Alice was an enthusiastic accomplice, for she too had warmed to the doctor, who – for he was the brother of sisters – was unusually at ease in female society. But Nolan's attractions, being those of temperament and mind, were not immediately apparent to younger women. Alice herself had been drawn to William Gale by his dark hair, fine colouring and the clarity and force of his blue-eyed gaze: the young women of today were no different in their liking for good looks. In any case Alice and her aunt could summon from their combined store of nieces and cousins no more than four or five suitable girls between them. It came to Alice that perhaps the widow Lockwood could be a candidate. Then too there was Emily, who had been engaged to poor Algie. Almost daily, it seemed, the war against Russia made more widows and broken sweethearts.

Alice scribbled a note to her aunt proposing herself, and a second to Mrs Lockwood. After she had returned home from the latter call she wrote to her husband:

The Grange, Weston-sub-Edge
22nd July 1855

My most dear William

You cannot imagine – or perhaps you can? – how very much I miss you and think of you daily.

I dined with your mother and father two days ago and a most dreary company we would have been, had it not been for the late arrival of your sister, who enlivens any table and who cheered us all with tales from her recent visit to your cousins in Ireland. I think it was in Caroline's mind to bring some small gaiety to her parents, who although they put a brave face on things seem still to be almost ossified by the sad news of Algie. How your sister reminds me of you! The same dear creases about the eyes when she smiles, the same sense that laughter is never far off. So that, even as I was gladdened by her society, nevertheless it made me feel the want of you the more keenly.

Caroline relayed the subject which is the great matter of your cousins, namely the eye-witness story of your Act of Courage at Alma, obtained through Louisa's husband Brevet-Major Palmer. This must seem very long ago to you, who have seen so much in the months since passed, but your Irish relations were yet much preoccupied with it. All were full of admiration and calling you a Hero and a man of singular bravery! This as you may conceive brought great pride and happiness to your Mama and Papa, their sorrows I think altogether forgotten while we all begged Caroline to tell us again the tale of your derring-do, so that we might rejoice in it anew. There was much talk, both in Ireland and at our own table, of you receiving some decoration from Her Majesty. I pray it may be so — but not as fervently as I pray for the campaign to be soon over. Your continued good health is paramount and I earnestly entreat you to take good care of it.

While staying with my aunt I went to call on your Mrs Lockwood, who resides in a charming little flat-fronted house in the direction of the Pittville Park. A more orderly, clean establishment I have never entered: all was gleaming and sparkling, a pretty fan of paper in the shining grate, the air scented with lavender and beeswax. The widow herself has a perfectly round, somewhat shallow face, like a soup-plate. I fancy I should have found her expression — serenely docile, and yet I thought I spied a hint of reproach tucked just behind it — somewhat irking, had it not been for the sad purpose of my visit. I do not doubt that you will think very ill of me for saying so! But my letters would be dull affairs if I never spoke my mind, would they not? The daughters are quite adorable, spotlessly attired and watchful, the younger with a thumb at all times planted in her mouth, like a good cork in a bottle. I daresay they do have toys or dolls with which to amuse themselves, but their mother had clearly tidied these away for her visitor and I feared that my call was most dull for them, so I did not linger unduly. However, I proposed that Mrs Lockwood join me at my aunt's for dinner on my next sojourn, as I felt that you would wish it so.

Alice had pastimes and society enough to fill her days: a weekly drawing lesson from a nice old Italian, who came to her from Broadway; daily calls hither and thither; occasional balls about the county; rides out in the trap, sometimes in the company of her sister-in-law Caroline. These excursions she especially enjoyed, for she and her husband's sister were close; and although Alice was the more outspoken, nevertheless Caroline, too, was an independent thinker who liked to discourse on matters divers.

To disagree was not to Alice disagreeable. So long as civility was maintained, she found debate stimulating to the mind. At her aunt's house in Cheltenham, only the week before, she had caused Dr Nolan to flush quite crimson in the service of offering a spirited defence of chloroform. Her husband's health at the Black Sea being never far from her mind, she often approached the doctor with pertinent enquiries. Alice had read a correspondence in *The Times* which enumerated the demerits, and then in answer the virtues, of that preparation. The French in Crimea used chloroform enthusiastically for amputations, but some of their British counterparts were more wary. A number of eminent doctors had written to the paper, declaring that the depressing effects of chloroform could cause a patient to die; whereas the pain of the knife provided a powerful stimulant and thereby a much fairer chance of recovery.

'I seem to recall, Dr Nolan, that the author of one such criticism concluded that it is better to hear a man bawl lustily than to see him sink silently into the grave,' said Alice.

'If that were true, it would certainly be better; but it is not so.'

'But the great Dr Hall believes it to be the case, does he not?' said Alice.

'The great doctor is not a young doctor. He is fixed in his ways and in this I regret to say that he is, in this one particular, mistaken. Pain is exhausting to a patient and a worn-out patient is the less likely to recover from an operation than one who feels no pain. It is true that care must be taken in the administration of chloroform, but used correctly it is very much to be welcomed. I would even venture so far as to say that in future all surgery will be carried out with the use of it.'

Dr Nolan and Alice had continued in this vein through the

removing of the plates from one course and the serving of the next, so that both quite forgot to turn to their other side, occasioning a series of rebuking coughs from Aunt Felicity. It was with some reluctance that Alice desisted then and turned to lighter talk with the deaf old man on her left. To talk prettily, to wait out a point and not interject, even when an interlocutor touched on subjects close to her own interests and reading; to keep her voice low and to laugh – but quietly! – when a man was not in the slightest amusing to her: these were the sorest social trials to Alice. Since her husband had been away at war, she often found herself obliged to listen to men's opinions about the Russian campaign. It was not the exception but the general rule that they knew less of it than she herself; yet decorum had it that she should not say so. It seemed burdensome to her that such frippish discourse was what was expected of her sex, when she had so many much more interesting things to say. But when she remarked this to her aunt after the guests had left, that lady replied that Alice was fortunate to find herself still young and handsome enough for a fellow to expect a response at all.

'You will find, in time, that nothing more than passing the salt is expected of you at supper. After you attain the age of forty or forty-five years, they simply talk at you, as if you were a wall. You are moved lower and lower down the table, until you find yourself in a huddle with a retiring cleric, an impecunious elderly cousin and a deaf aunt. Supposed gentlemen show more consideration to a horse than they ever do to a woman of any vintage. When you are my age you will look back on all the young men who tried to flirt with you with something like affection, I assure you, however foolish they appear to you now.'

'But I don't want to flirt, Aunt! I want to talk,' said Alice.

At this her aunt only smiled.

3.

4th August 1855, Camp before Sebastopol

My own dearest

Many thanks for your letter which I received this morning whilst playing a cricket match on the hill against the Cavalry, who by the way managed to beat us most sadly. We have got up a cricket club and when not in the trenches we play – there is to be a match of Etonians v. Harrovians next week. It has not been perfect cricket weather, for it has been very wet; however, we must not be downcast. Our valiant Lord Raglan would no doubt have said: 'I have the honour to inform you that the Weather still continues favourable.' I am sorry to hear you also have so much wet. I hope the harvest will be safely brought in.

The other great sport here is to ride out to see the villages, or to picnic at the Monastery. We start out at about 12 and each takes his share of food and drink – my own supplies lately augmented by your most welcome box, for which I thank you – and when we arrive we put the Hock and other pleasant drinks into a well to cool and wander about, having tethered our horses. We dine under a tree, looking out across the sea. Last week Derrington had a box he'd sent for from Fortnum and Mason, with chocolate and tea and preserved cherries and pâté, which he kindly shared at one such picnic. We are able now to get a few fowls and geese and various fruits, such a pleasure after the winter of ham and biscuit.

These diversions provide us with something to do, for a siege is a dreary thing and the trenches are not hospitable, albeit that we are not yet up to our knees in mud and water as we were in the winter, despite the recent rains. I have never in my life formed such a high appreciation of trees and vegetation as in this camp, where we want for green leaves, every bush and sapling having been uprooted or broken. I look vainly for a tree out of my tent door, but see only dust or bare, wet earth and soldiers, all of which I should like never to see again. If Providence brings me safe home to you, I shall plant trees.

The Tartars are very nice people, the most civil I ever met with. One meets them out in the villages and upon the roads. Their vines have been dreadfully depleted by our work and all the more so by the Russians. Some of their number are beginning to come back from Vermutka and Kutchut Miscomea, from which they were driven by the Cossacks in the winter. The road all day is covered with wagons and arabas of women, children and Tartars, bringing everything they had with them: a far more affecting sight than any trenches or Mamelons, because this is the effect of war on people who have nothing to do with it and are now probably beggars for ever. God forgive any man who having once seen it, wishes to take part in another War!

I will as you suggested in your last letter look out for your sister's friend Brookes, though one might live in a vast camp like this for ten years without meeting a fellow. We can ride 20 miles through camp from one end to the other, and about the same distance back by the rear line. I would have a better chance of bumping into him on the streets of the city of Gloucester than I do hereabouts.

I remain your devoted husband
William Gale

The Grange, Weston-sub-Edge
12th August

My dearest William

I am just home from Cheltenham, where my aunt and myself went to a concert for the benefit of the nurses at Scutari, at the Pittville Pump Rooms. It was a lively programme, with piano duets and songs — as an encore they played *The Girl I Left Behind Me*, to great applause – and we much enjoyed the evening. Our friend Dr Nolan accompanied us, one on each arm, across the park. I can see why people choose to live in town, it is so agreeable to be able to stroll everywhere. You may imagine also how much I like to peer into people's rooms, especially just as dusk is falling, when they have lit their lamps but before they have thought to draw their curtains – it is so interesting to see how their houses are furnished and to spot peculiarities, a caged parrot apparently gnawing its own foot in one window and a sad-looking lady dressed all in green framed in another, standing staring out as if lost.

Present at the concert was my aunt's friend Miss Sanderson, who you may recall is a most independent soul. On a London sojourn earlier this summer she had been to a meeting of the new Administrative Reform Association, at the Drury Lane Theatre. Who do you think she heard give a speech there, but Charles Dickens! She told me all about it, during the interval. You will not approve, for the Association has been founded by that Radical Layard, but perhaps you will soften a little when I tell you that Mr Dickens was apparently moved to join by the failures of the Commissariat to our soldiers in the Crimea last winter. Miss Sanderson said that he spoke with great feeling about the thousands of thousands of the bravest men that ever England has bred, lying newly-buried. Apparently the Great Author had never given a political speech before, but my friend reported that he spoke with great authority, learnedness and wit. Everyone cheered throughout and shouted 'hear'. His name will surely lend sway to the Association.

My sister is coming tomorrow and I shall be glad of her company, for I am lonely without my William. We thought to take a picnic up to Meon Hill if it goes on fine. Do you remember when we were there, four summers ago? When we lay on the soft turf, with the sweet smell of gorse all around us. What a glad day that was, under the June-blue Heaven.

How I wish this war would be over! I pray God will keep you safe and bring you back to your loving

Alice

12th August, Camp before Sebastopol

My dearest Wife

You must not be jealous, for I have a new and delightful companion and she is almost as pretty and quite as headstrong as yourself. She is the funniest kitten that ever was seen. Even now she is attempting to assist me by getting her tail in the ink.

One of the men was thoroughly spooked the other night. He fancied he saw a young woman – in a diaphanous dress the colour of pearls with long golden tresses, no less – gliding towards the river. He was convinced it was an apparition. The Tartars say there is a Nymph of the Tchernaya, who haunts those reaches by night and each morning returns to a tree before transforming herself into a serpent. I was reminded of Keats' Lamia! In any case, there is much talk about the camp of this ghoulish lady and what she might portend. Some of the turns in the Tchernaya allow for a swim of a few yards and this has been an occasional pleasure of mine.

A few days ago I was riding with Herbert along the front of our camp, when up jumped a hare – away went Herbert, and away went I. We had not gone far when we saw a very smart-looking French officer with a beautiful dog; we gave him – the dog – a shout and off he went after the hare, leaving his master with his mouth open in utter astonishment. We crossed the ravine at the head of the camp and galloped away towards the Second Division in hot pursuit. Unfortunately the men saw the hare coming and ran out to head him. We shouted to them and got the hare safe away through the crowd, but our fine dog took fright and turned back. Still on went Herbert, on went I – we had a splendid run down the Inkerman Heights. At last the hare lay down, Herbert jumped off his horse and picked him up. Next day we gave a dinner-party and had delicious hare soup.

There are rumours that the Russians intend to attack us. They certainly seem to have more ammunition than ever.

Ever your loving
William Gale

28th August 1855, Camp before Sebastopol

Alice my dearest one

It is curious that you should write of Henry Layard, for just as our last letters were crossing – perhaps at Marseille, or at Malta – we heard of the death from disease here of his brother, Arthur Layard, of the 38th Regiment of Foot. It is true that for the surviving brother I have very little respect, albeit that his excavations at Nineveh proved so fruitful and of such interest; however I had rather he had kept his head buried in the sands of Persia and kept it out of politics. Particularly I do not thank him for his crass disdain for our poor Lord Raglan. It is said by people higher up than myself, with some cause to know of what they speak, that the Queen herself opposed his appointment to the War Office, on this very account. To incur the displeasure of the Monarch in whose name your own brother is at war is no cause for pride. Now that the poor boy has met his end, I should hope his brother will hang his head in shame. Certainly he would not have made a popular choice here. I am disappointed that so great an author as Mr Dickens would allow himself to be taken in by the prating of such an evident rabble-raiser as Layard. That your friend Miss Sanderson should swallow it all up like a goose thrown scraps in a farmyard comes as no surprise to me.

It is excessively hot here now and we are constantly under arms, for it is thought the Russes may make a further attempt at any time. Accordingly we turn out at two o'clock in the morning to receive them. You will have read in the papers about the French and Sardinian rebuff of their earlier attempt at the Valley of the Tchernaya, which it is now said resulted in some ten thousand dead. Our allies' losses were light, the Russians slaughtered. Tell my father I will write to him about it in detail when I have more leisure. We have known for some little time of the arrival of large reinforcements in the Enemy's Camp and have been expecting some attack on our trenches. When one gets up near to the wounded enemy one sees how ill clad and haggard they seem, altogether a worse sort than our foes at Alma and Inkerman. They are more like the *peasantry of the countryside than soldiers; perhaps indeed that is what they were formerly.*

There was a great mishap in these parts, which caused the loudest explosion I have yet heard here. A shell from the Russians blew up the principal magazine of the French, and I am sorry to report, all who were close by. The noise was so great it was as if Vulcan himself had set up his celestial forge directly above our heads.

Soyer who has set up here gave a demonstration to Generals and Staff &c the other day, showing us how to make our rations into delicious dishes. I was there and he certainly made very nice ragouts and soups, but I fear it will be a long time before we can do it for ourselves. His dishes had the additional advantage of being washed down with iced champagne.

Always your loving
William

10th September, Camp before Sebastopol

My dearest Alice

The Siege is over. You will I think have read that the French took the Malakoff and we followed suit by the storming of the Redan. Our loss was frightful, over one hundred Officers; and the bodies of men were five deep all around the Redan. The affair was so bloody and so difficult there were those – newer arrivals, mostly, and very young – who ran away, though I would entreat you not to advert to this to anyone except my parents. The papers love nothing more than to report on English drunkenness or desertion and by this they do a great disservice to the vast majority, who have worked nobly in the most trying circumstances imaginable. In any case, it is done. The Russes have sunk their remaining ships, all except the steamers and of course have destroyed their bridge across.

I got knocked over by a ball in my arm, mercifully not my right one or I should not be able to write you this letter. I have had no fever and the pain is bearable but it is not known thus far whether I shall regain the use of it. I attempt to wriggle my fingers but the hand is as still as a bunch of white radishes. If Peace will come it will be a small price, cheaper certainly than another winter in the open trenches.

The silence seems so odd now. Instead of the constant rattle of musketry and roar of cannon, everything is quite quiet, except an occasional boom of a gun from the north side to remind us they are still there. I doubt if they will stay the winter. Pray tell my father that I shall send him a fuller report of the Redan skirmish when time allows.

Ever your loving
William

4.

For Alice there had never been such a joy as to have her husband home, and safe. A letter at the start of June had heralded his return, some weeks after the signing of the final peace at the end of March. It was a little under two years since he had set sail, and he would be home in time to see the roses in the walled garden, even if they would be just a little past their best. William was to sail via Malta to Marseille and thence proceed by train, at last traversing the Channel; a journey which would take some two weeks. No sooner had his letter arrived than his wife began to prepare the house for him. The windows must be cleaned with spirit, the furniture with beeswax; the grates blacked, the carpets taken out and beaten. These tasks she left to the household, while she herself took charge of her husband's things. His coats she removed from the wardrobe in his dressing room and brushed, his leather stud- and collar-boxes she buffed, his shirts she had out and took down to the laundry room to be pressed afresh, each to be sprinkled on her instructions with a little rose water. She wanted to provide every comfort for him, after his long ordeal. Housekeeping was not generally to the fore of Alice's mind, but the thought of how dear his home must now be to him was very tender to her. To make him welcome was now her chief preoccupation.

The one matter was if it were incumbent upon her to invite the older Mr and Mrs Gale, and also Caroline, to dine on the evening of her husband's arrival, or whether this might be deferred until the next day. They of course would be most anxious to see him, but she fancied William would be somewhat weary from his journey and benefit from a quiet arrival. He would like a little time, surely, to walk arm in arm around the garden with her. Then too, she hoped that dinner might not be unduly prolonged, so that they could be alone together afterwards, upstairs. She elected to ask them to dine on the following day, once the returning hero had rested a little.

And a hero he was. The news that William was to be decorated with the Queen's new medal had been announced in the *London Gazette* in February and had brought colour to William's mother's cheeks for the first time since the loss of her younger son. The honour was very great. The Cross was to be awarded only for acts of exceptional gallantry and its recipients would be few. News of William's courage at Alma had reached the ears of his family through a number of sources, from one or two invalided officers who had, perforce, returned home; as well as the letters of fellows who had been witness to events, or close to them. Word had spread around the county, so that whenever Alice went about she was everywhere lauded on her husband's behalf. In his own correspondence he had himself been reticent. It was not like him to expand upon any act which would put himself in an especially good light, not least when so many of his fellows had been wounded or worse. All he had vouchsafed, of the battle, was that it had been *the most frightful din you ever heard and as smoky as bonfire night*. He admitted that *the Cossacks took a thrashing, but it was not soon done*. He himself had had *a close shave,* he told her, *but came all right in the end*. She hoped that her husband would elaborate once they had gained the privacy of the tête-à-tête.

All morning Alice fidgeted, even though she knew full well he could not appear before noon. Two or three times she heard the clack of a four in the lane and started out, but each time the carriage had passed before she made the gates. To calm herself she went to the stables which, being empty on account of the season, gave her little reason to linger. Then she went to ascertain the water level in the cistern behind the wall of the glasshouse, where she was met by a toad who was sunning himself on a flat stone by the side of it, next to a patch of rhubarb. Toads were really so very different from frogs, with their warty backs like fallen autumn leaves; it was a mystery to her that anyone could confuse the two. She stood inspecting him for a time. She went back to the house and checked herself in the glass: she looked very much as she had ten minutes before. It occurred to her that the windowsill of William's dressing room was prone to collect flies: she went upstairs to open the window. She came down. It was useless to take up a book, for she knew she would not be able to steady her heart enough to profit from reading. She noticed that the door of the long case clock in the hall was not properly closed: she shut it. There were as ever letters to which she must respond, so she installed herself at the writing table in the library and took up her pen, but no sooner had she written a salutation at the top of a page – the recipient was to have been a kind lady at Winchcombe, who had invited her and William to a tennis party – than ink had unaccountably bled all over her hand and the paper besides and she was obliged to go back upstairs and wash, before it worked its way on to her white cuffs. She checked herself once again in the glass in her room. How was it possible that her glance could be returned to her so levelly, apparently so calmly contained within her form? She felt just now very uncontained, as if her feelings were a bramble spilling over a broken wall, a tangle of leaves and reaching stalks, hidden thorns, bright tiny insects moving among the small white flowers. It was strange to her that her features betrayed none of this disquiet, that her hair stayed close to her head and did not spring out like uncut meadow grass from the sheer force of all her thoughts. That her skin remained impermeable.

And at last he was here. The door opened, boxes were brought in, voices were heard. She felt suddenly shy before him. Was he taller? Or did he seem so because he was more slender than before and his skin darker? His left arm was in a buckram sling, but he was the same, he was her William still; and yet he was not the same. He wore a beard, which much became him, making the blue of his eyes seem paler than hitherto. When she pressed her cheek against his chest the smell she inhaled through his light coat was different, there was smoke in it and something mineral where she expected the old, familiar trace, which had been redolent of saddle leather, gorse-flower. Separating, she held his poor left hand in both her own and laughed that at last his face was less than two feet away from her own; this beloved face that had never been far from her thoughts now breathed the same air and smiled back at her like an answered call.

Through the hours of the afternoon she could not keep from touching him. As they walked around the garden she leaned a little into his side, when they came in for tea she touched his right arm. A stray crumb on his chin she brushed away with her fingertips. Once they were seated her foot reached out towards him as naturally as a flower turning its face towards the sun.

'You will forgive me, I think, if I forbear from retailing all the details of my adventures today? Only I fancy I shall have to go over it all tomorrow, for my father and mother, and I would sooner not try your patience.' At this he grinned widely, for he knew his wife had scant toleration for a thing repeated, and furthermore made little secret of the fact.

Alice's smile was no less frank.

'Nothing you say could displease me in the slightest particular. I am so glad to hear your voice at all that I shouldn't mind if you read aloud to me from a seed catalogue, just to hear it more.'

The tea things cleared away, William stood.

'I have one or two little souvenirs for you, gathered from abroad. I thought I'd go upstairs now and look them out. Will you come with me?' He reached out his good hand and she took it and they climbed the stairs.

She had hoped that their reunion would soon be fruitful, but one month passed and then another, each bringing a little sting of dismay that this was not yet so. If her husband also was regretful of the fact, he made no sign of it. William was in any case much preoccupied: there were estate matters to see to and the taking in hand of a parcel of land which had been given, along with a house, to his late brother. The land was tenanted and it was William's wish to bring it under his own stewardship, while the house was empty and an occupant for it had to be found. Then too everyone for miles about was desirous of seeing the returning hero: each post brought a handful of invitations which it fell to Alice's lot to accept or to decline.

To begin with William had been quite content to give some small accounts of the recent war and the long siege of Sebastopol. Of the local flora and fauna he discoursed a little, describing the terrain as not so very unlike that around and about them: Leckhampton Hill, perhaps, or Cleeve Common; only the far-distant valleys were filled with vines and soft fruit and the tinkling of goat bells, instead of with plump English sheep.

He omitted from his descriptions some of the bloodier aspects of the engagement, although many details had been made common knowledge by the *Times* correspondent. The ladies of the county, when seated beside William, were astonished to learn that the Russians had been so sure of victory at Alma that they had invited numbers of the fairer sex to picnic on the heights, so as to witness the spectacle. Why yes, William assured them: baskets had been brought up by donkey and parasols and rugs besides; champagne corks were pulled and cold legs of chicken produced from folded cloths, while below was carnage. Many pressed him to divulge the details of the action which had won him the Queen's new Cross there, but always he demurred.

'And were you present at the Charge of the Light Brigade?' came the invariable question.

To which William gave the terse reply that he was not. He himself never referred to that day by this name, but always called it Balaklava. Undeterred, his interlocutor would press on: 'What a dreadful thing that was! So many killed.'

Dreadful indeed, he would answer.

'And yet may it not have been avoided altogether, had the order been better given and relayed?'

At which it was his custom to mumble dully in the hope of closing the subject altogether.

But all had more to say. Theories as to whose fault the calamity of the cavalry charge had been were as numerous as sugared almonds; and were passed around with as little reserve. Often a speech informing William of the identity of the correct figure to blame was concluded: 'One gathers that the Russians were so taken aback by the folly of it that they took it that the Lights were in the deeper excesses of drink. In no wise else could the extreme rashness of their courage be accounted for. We read that when the Cossacks took a handful of prisoners afterwards they were apparently so bewildered to find the men sober that they plied them with champagne themselves. One hears that the prisoners were congratulated all round by their captors and treated rather as heroes.'

Oh indeed, said William. He believed he had read the same thing. Manners forbade him, however, from opining that the *Times* correspondent had not made himself universally popular at camp and that a certain scepticism as to the veracity of his reports would not have been misplaced.

'Well yes, of course, you would've. Having been there and all. Well, not at the exact spot, perhaps . . .'

No indeed, said William.

Privately, when he and Alice were installed in the carriage on their way home, he would rail against the common fascination with the ill-fated action.

'Why must people talk only of the wretched Light Brigade, when we have won a fearsome war? Why should the focus of their minds be always on this one action? Three thousand of ours lost their lives at Alma, and less than three hundred at Balaklava. Yet it is always the Charge which holds people's attention.'

Alice was mindful at such times that her wifely duty was to soothe her husband, and as such she made it a rule never to bring up her own reservations as to the wisdom of the campaign on these occasions.

'The bells rang out all over England for the victories at Alma River and Inkerman Heights, and boys were given a day's holiday from school,' Alice told him. 'You must not suppose that these successes went unremarked here at home.'

'Even so,' said William.

'I think, my dear, that Mr Tennyson's poem has much to answer for, in engaging widespread sympathy and indeed outrage; and then as well, you see, there were engravings in the papers. One picture I recall was simply hundreds of cannon balls lying on the stony ground, such a desolate scene it was. One could almost fancy the round shots to have been human skulls. I believe it was titled *The Valley of Death*. Such things work their way into the public imagination.'

'This constant picking over of the carcass of the Charge is most intemperate and wrong-headed. If Mr Tennyson's poem about the Charge of the Heavy Brigade on the same day had been the better verse, we might all have been spared this fuss. I do not care to hear poor old Lord Raglan's name brought into this by people who were quite happily installed at their luncheon tables eating mutton, while so many of us were engaged in war on our country's behalf. I fail to conceive what it is in the British character which makes defeat so much more appealing than victory! The Heavy Brigade did well that same day and one hears nothing of them. At Inkerman men were fighting from five o'clock in the morning until four o'clock in the afternoon. It was common for men to stand in trenches up to their knees in mud and freezing water for twelve hours at a time. Why should people fix on this one event, which lasted only a matter of minutes?'

'I had not thought before of how long it took,' said Alice. She pondered a moment. 'I suppose it was like a flat race, no sooner begun than ended.'

'It was no steeplechase, certainly,' said William, returning to good humour now that he had spoken out.

Yet on the next occasion that he and his wife made a visit, and the time after, the matter of the Charge would once again be raised. William felt it afresh as an insult to those of his fellows who had died, not least poor Algie and his friend Lockwood. If a little pride was piqued in him that an action in which he personally had played no part was the one of which people most often spoke, then he was not sensible of it. A man may be stung and feel it just the same without knowing whether its cause be a wasp or a bee.

On the widow Lockwood it was now his duty to pay a call. His wife's aunt was to give a dinner to celebrate his homecoming, which would bring him to Cheltenham. Alice was full of the notions of some doctor she had befriended and desirous of introducing the man to William. On the morning of their arrival in the town, he took the pocket watch that Lockwood had handed to him, along with the man's buttons, his prayer book, a small packet of letters and a pocket-knife with a mother-of-pearl handle. His sword had already been sent to the widow. All his other effects had been auctioned in the Crimea the day after his death. Such auctions had been all too frequent. To many the affairs were most painful, for the articles put up seemed to a messmate or intimate comrade to be almost a part of the dead man himself. Saddles, bridles, bits, boots, plates, buttons, sheets and bedding all went under the hammer.

Such items as he had Gale polished with his pocket handkerchief before replacing them in the box he had chosen as their housing. Held in his hand they had seemed a pitiable collection by which to remember a fine man. He did not wish the sight of her husband's poor things spread out to be injurious to Mrs Lockwood, so meagre a legacy they made. He had cast about him at home to find some suitable container with which, it was his hope, to imbue them with some little dignity. At last he had assembled them in a mahogany tea-caddy from which he had removed the glass bowl. It was his fancy that the box, with its pleasing proportions, its four balled feet of ebony and the tiny brass scroll at the summit of the lid, bore some resemblance to those grand carved memorials of the previous century.

The Mrs Lockwood he found before him was not at all as sharp-tongued Alice had described her. Rather, the symmetry of her features and the roundness of her face lent her expression an openness which struck him at once as utterly without guile. She was very quiet, whether by temperament or due to the solemn nature of the call William was unable to judge. From the softness of her demeanour and the neatness of her dress, a portraitist might have drawn dainty little feet – the feet of a dancer, or a child – peeping out from beneath her skirts. And yet, as she led the way to the first-floor drawing room, William noticed instead that her feet were rather large and square. The sight of these serviceable, useful feet – feet made for walking and the out-of-doors, feet not intended by nature to be tucked beneath her in some velvet salon – engendered in him a feeling which he was unable to name.

Their interview had barely commenced before the door opened and the two little daughters came in. Mrs Lockwood made to shoo them from the room, but William stayed her: their presence would delay the tale he must impart, of their father's demise. It was a story for which he had no appetite, in no small part because he had strayed very far from the truth when he had written of it to the lady now before him, and must needs continue in this falsehood if her sensibilities were still to be spared.

Both girls were very fair, with their mother's round eyes. The younger came straight away to William and leant against his knee, as if he were a trusted uncle long known to her.

'And what have you been doing this morning?' William asked them.

'I was pasting pictures into my scrapbook,' said the older girl. 'I made the paste myself, from flour. Mama taught me. But Kitty was just playing with her doll, weren't you, Kitty?'

The little child reflected, thumb in her mouth. 'My doll didn't want to put on her outdoor coat. Her name's Evangeline,' she said.

'And what did Evangeline want to do?' William asked.

'She just wants to sit on Mama's lap and listen to a story,' said the child.

'Dolls can't hear,' said the older child at once. William suppressed the desire to enquire whether they were nonetheless capable of expressing their preferences.

'Evangeline can,' said the younger.

'If you would like to fetch Evangeline I should be happy to tell her a story,' said William. 'And I should very much like to see your scrapbook, too. Perhaps we could make up a story from something in its pages, what do you say?'

Both children scampered to fetch their things. Mrs Lockwood turned to William.

'You are too kind,' she said. 'I fear Molly and Kitty may never let you leave, if you indulge them so. Let me go down for some refreshment for you, at least.'

William was left alone to look about him. It was a very pleasant room, with three windows to the ground, furnished simply but with no absence of comfort. On one wall was a pencil drawing of Lockwood, as a younger man than he had been when William knew him. On either side of the fireplace were low cabinets of rosewood, inlaid with brass decoration; there was a highly polished brass fender and a set of fire tongs, shovel and bellows. The metals gleamed brightly in the morning sun. Three or four embroidered cushions of posies of flowers – pansies and dog-roses and small trailing violets – were finely done. He wondered if these were the work of Mrs Lockwood.

Presently that lady returned and her daughters too. The girls settled themselves to either side of William, while their mother took a low chair by the window. A slip of a maid brought in a tray, nicely laid with a threadwork cloth. Mrs Lockwood stood and took it from her and put the things out upon a small table. All her movements were performed with economy and neatness. There was a tall china pot with a squat little sugar-bowl to match and a plate of biscuits hardly bigger than florins. William had been brought up not to remark upon any detail of a repast, but these shortbreads struck him as so delicious that he could not forbear from saying so. Mrs Lockwood smiled.

'The receipt came from my grandmother's house,' she said. 'The flavour is from orange zest, made fine with a nutmeg grater.'

She stood and placed the plate close to her visitor's elbow, so that he might take more as he wished. William commenced to invent a story about a basket of kittens, which he cast upon the waters of a river like so many feline Moses. These unfortunates were obliged to face the perils of inquisitive swans and hungry pike before their timely rescue by a pair of kind fair-haired human sisters, who were able to offer them sanctuary. Kitty sat silently with her thumb in her mouth, while Molly interjected here and there. That a pike might eat a kitten she was not convinced, but William assured her that it was so. He considered adding the fiction that fishermen often found the remains of kittens inside the bellies of especially large pike, but decided withal that this would be an invention more suitable to an audience of boys.

Their story done, and several of the golden biscuits consumed by all three occupants of the sofa, their mother expelled the girls gently from the room. William knew that the time had come to speak of her late husband. Like many of his sex, he was alarmed by women's tears: he was apprehensive of them now. If a fellow protested at such an outburst, he was likely to be upbraided; whereas if he consoled it seemed invariably to bring forth more tears. The one thing for it seemed to be to keep quiet, handkerchief at the ready, to be produced as the storm abated. But Mrs Lockwood only sat quietly, her hands folded in her lap. She did not weep, but nodded gravely from time to time. If any detail of his account rang false with her, she betrayed no sign of it, for which he was also much relieved. At last she received the box from his hands but did not make to open it. It only remained for him to offer her, with as much tact as he could muster, any assistance that it was at his means to provide. It was not easy, to talk of pecuniary matters with a lady. He had already laid the ground by hinting at such an offer by letter, but he felt it was his duty to state the case more plainly, in person.

'My brother has business in Gloucester at the docks and is in a position to be able to help me and my daughters, so I must refuse your great kindness, while thanking you most sincerely. There is one thing I would much appreciate, however.'

'Of course. It is my pleasure to assist in any way I can the family of a man I held in such high esteem.' This at least was true, for Lockwood had been a jovial fellow and a dear one.

'You have been this morning so very kind to my little girls and they are starved, now, of male society. My brother is much occupied and with no father . . . I wonder, if you should find yourself here in Cheltenham, might you consider visiting us again?'

William was most touched by her request. It would be his pleasure, he said.

5.

The injury to William's left hand did not improve. He went to discuss his future with his father, whose own injury had led him to leave the army, as well as bequeathing him a permanent limp. It was decided that William would sell his commission. He was sorry to leave the Regiment, but his incapacity was such that he could no longer load and discharge his Deane Adams revolver, nor otherwise feel himself of use. Through the autumn it became his chief purpose to plan and supervise the planting of trees. A great elm in the park to the front of the house had come down in his absence and it seemed to him now that the right-hand flank of the lawn was too bare and wanted cedars. In the place of the single elm he now installed a short avenue of lime trees, which would make a pleasant alley under which to take shade while strolling on a warm afternoon. By the corner of the house he put in three cedars, pacing out the distance between them and marking the spots with bamboo canes, then standing by as one of the gardeners dug them in. It was confounding that these grew so slowly, but as time went on he could perhaps take out one or two, leaving the best specimen to reach its full maturity. The little snowdrop bulbs he had brought back from the war he planted under the windows of the dining room and his study. These immediate planting schemes completed, he turned his attention to an area on the outlying farm where the ground dipped; he commenced to plant a small wood there. He was satisfied that such a stand of trees would provide good cover for game, as well as breaking up the monotony of the fields. At the foot of the drive he installed a quantity of laurel. He made plans to extend the orchard and replace some of the gnarlier old trees.

Alice was glad that this preoccupation took him much out of doors, for it had come to her notice that if he remained too much inside his spirits appeared to wither. She could not date this shift in him precisely, but by and by she could no longer conceal from herself that something in him was altered. William's nature, hitherto so sanguine, was now subject to vicissitudes which somewhat bewildered her. He was quick to temper: that was new. He had in the past been subject to only very occasional bursts of anger, brought about by an injustice or some grave breach of conduct, and always directed outward, towards the wrongdoer. His anger then had been a welcome thing, like a great thunderstorm which clears the muggy air; yet now small gusts of fury blew through him yet not away from him. These were brought about by what she could not judge nor, worse, predict. More than once he had chided her for the fact that some trifling thing – the letter-knife, the shoe-horn – was not in the place where he expected it to be. He had never been short with her before. And while debate was a sport she enjoyed, incivility, hotness, she did not. Then, too, he appeared preoccupied. Several times she had gone into his study to call him to the luncheon table, only to find him sitting, without a pen in his hand nor a book open at his side. This was most unlike her William, who had never been without occupation.

The matter of the war remained a thorn between them.

William agreed that the Commissariat had been grotesquely maladministered, during the terrible first winter in the Crimea especially. But loyalty to his seniors and to his men forbade him from wholly condemning the campaign itself. Alice continued lively in her poor opinion of the panjandrums of Government, up to and including Lord Palmerston himself.

'It is the contention of Mr Cobden and others besides that

nothing can stop the Russian preponderance,' said Alice as they sat down to lunch one day that autumn. She had spent a stimulating morning reading. 'Did you know that it was estimated that, only two or three years before the war, Russia exported from the ports of the Black Sea some five million quarters of grain of all kinds? And so the calculation was made that if they continued to expand at the same rate as they have over the past five years or so, they would then be exporting fifteen or twenty millions annually. Naturally, they require ports from which to ship this great quantity of cargo. If a country is developing, this is the natural order of things and cannot be prevented.'

'Mr Cobden this, Mr Cobden that! Can you never speak without referring to the man? It is as if he were seated beside you at all times, whispering instruction in your ear,' said William, snapping his table napkin from its silver ring.

Alice looked startled by her husband's outburst. 'It is not only he who has thought to examine the real matter of things. I only mean that Russian exports and Russian expansion are considered inevitable in some quarters.'

'Well then, perhaps those quarters would care to winter out in the rain and snow, dying of cold and hunger and disease; or to survive such privations into the spring, only to be felled by a passing shell? And afterwards, let us hear again from them about the Russians and their marvellous expansion.'

'I believe that a politician may sometimes take a wider view than a soldier, however nobly he has served,' said Alice. She knew she was being obstinate, yet she felt compelled to speak.

At this William's face paled. 'I did not cradle the bodies of my men – and my own brother – in order for you to form such opinions. I will thank you to keep such views to yourself, in the future. You would do better to attend to the management of this household with greater attention. I do not wish it raised more.'

'William, I . . .' said Alice. 'I sincerely beg your pardon.' To restore the peace between them mattered more than what she thought, after all.

'Will you pass me the butter and we'll turn our minds to pleasanter things,' he said.

Their nights together were at least more harmonious, more joyful, than their daily discourse. And at the end of November she was able to tell him, as they lay drowsily together, that she was sensible of the signs that a child might at last be on its way to them.

This intelligence made her husband soften towards Alice. He no longer seemed out of temper. He no longer appeared at the door of whatever room she was in with some small and peevish question, as if hoping to catch her out in some trifling insufficiency. As the weeks passed and the child quickened within her – was it fancy, or did she perceive a sensation like a butterfly beneath her ribs at certain times? – William was more and more his old self.

As her term proceeded, it was Alice's wish to consult with Dr Nolan. She knew him to have attended many a confinement and if he had modern views on the delivering of a healthy baby, she would be more than glad to profit from them. Thus it was that before Christmas she and William repaired to Cheltenham to stay a week at her aunt's.

Gale wrote to Mrs Lockwood announcing their arrival and proposing that he should call. He had in truth neglected to fulfil his promise to her in respect of visiting the little girls, estate matters having kept him at home that autumn. But his thoughts now turned again to his poor friend, who would never see his girls grown, nor walk them up the aisle to the side of their eager grooms. Really it was his duty to maintain an avuncular friendship with the little family. Full of good intent, he sent to his bookseller for something suitable for the children and had back

Lamb's *Tales from Shakespeare* and Macaulay's *Lays of Ancient Rome*. On perusal this latter seemed to him better suited to the taste of boys, for it was all heroics and clashing swords, but it would make a little packet apiece, for them to unwrap.

Mrs Lockwood received him warmly and he found her house more charming in the dingy December afternoon than even it had been in the light of high summer. A fire glowed in the polished grate and the lamps in the first-floor drawing room were lit and shone bright, their wicks neatly trimmed so that the low flames left the glass shining and clear. The trimming of wicks was a special bugbear with William, for the failure to do so caused the glass to blacken and sometimes even to crack. At The Grange he was forever asking for the glass to be taken down and cleaned, the wicks snipped. Alice seemed never to remark this, for all that she daily used a lamp for reading.

Once again Molly and Kitty greeted him without ceremony, but soon clambered on to his knee. They had much to tell: a kitten was now resident in the house and provided them with much amusement, although the animal had scratched when they attempted to dress it in their dolls' clothes, so that they had had to abandon the attempt. In return, William told them about the kitten which had come to lodge with him in his tent in the Crimea and put its tail in his inkwell when he was writing.

'Did our Papa know your cat?' asked Molly.

'I fear he did not,' came the reply.

'Captain Gale is very kind to talk so much of cats and kittens each time we see him,' said Mrs Lockwood.

William was flattered that she should have retained the memory of their last encounter.

'It is true that I do not have occasion to speak of them so often at home,' he said, 'but it is a subject I am content to discuss at any time.' And he twinkled at the widow, over the top of her children's fair heads.

After this exchange, Mrs Lockwood barely spoke more, and took out her work. Every so often Gale glanced across at her and saw that she was attending to what was said between himself and the little girls. More than once a smile lit her features as she sewed. It was most soothing and agreeable to him to be in the society of so tranquil a lady. As before, she slipped out of the room to ask that a tray be sent up: on this occasion a Madeira cake of the softest texture was produced.

When he rose to take his leave of them, little Kitty flung her arms around his knees. 'Oh, Mr Gale, don't go!' she entreated. 'Tell us one more story, please.'

William was late back to change for dinner with his wife's Aunt Felicity.

'The Lockwood girls are most delightful,' he told Alice. 'I think it would be kind to have them out to us so that they might have a ride on a pony. Just around the orchard, on a rein.'

'Of course,' said Alice. 'I'm sure your friend would have been glad to know you were attentive to his family.'

'I do hope so, poor fellow,' said William.

Dr Nolan joined them for dinner, to make up a four; afterwards they would play at cards. Alice prompted him to explain to the others the current ideas for the treatment of melancholia, of which he was an enthusiastic proponent. At Malvern and here in Cheltenham, the waters appeared to have a most benevolent effect: daily and prolonged immersion in the cold waters brought about a great improvement for despondency. It remained to be seen whether such a practice would be of benefit to those unfortunates of unsound mind or nervous prostration who were prone to violent agitation.

'But is there not a danger of your subjects catching cold?' asked Felicity.

'Indeed it would seem that the opposite is the case,' said the doctor. 'It is a most curious thing.'

'And yet we are urged never to set foot outside without a hat and fur muff!' said Alice.

'It would appear that the increase in the circulation of the blood brought about by cold water bathing in some way inures the patient against coughs and colds, just as it revives the spirits,' said the doctor. 'Dr Watson at Malvern has reported excellent results for his hydropathy. But we do not as yet entirely understand the mechanism.'

'In the Crimea the water for bathing was often very cold. Even in the summer it was much cooled by all the rain we had. Once – this was in the weeks before the storming of the Redan – a party of us rode out to the village of Vermutka. It was a glorious, fine day and there was a deliciously cool fountain there. I will not conceal from you that we took it in turns to use it for a tub, much to the astonishment of the inhabitants.'

'Such moments must have been welcome, after all you had endured.'

'They were. Although I fear your ideas about immersion in cold water could not bear fruit where the cholera is concerned.'

'No indeed,' the doctor averred. 'Perhaps you have heard of Dr Snow, in London? It is his contention that the cholera may be passed on by contaminated drinking water.'

'But it is well known to be caused by pestilent vapours,' William objected. 'I have seen it myself, while we were at war. Men were struck down from gaseous miasma. Those who camped close to river courses were most at risk, from the vaporous emanations.'

At this Dr Nolan merely smiled and made a gesture that was neither a nod nor quite a shrug. It had come to his notice that it didn't signify to disagree too far with soldiers.

'It is a pity your Dr Nolan is not more blessed in his appearance, for he is an amiable fellow,' William said as they were preparing for bed.

'Let us call a thing by its true name and admit that he is ugly,' laughed Alice. 'My aunt and myself have tried to think of a wife for him, but young women will be struck by a man's face. I fear they take but one look at him – and vanish.'

'Perhaps we might introduce him to my sister Caroline.' Alice looked doubtful.

'I think Caroline has no interest in securing a husband. I already tried your Mrs Lockwood. I had them both to dine here while you were away, but she barely once looked at him and only uttered please and thank you throughout.'

'She is not given to speechifying, I fancy,' said William.

'No,' said Alice.

'She has a most becoming natural modesty,' he added.

'William! I believe she has turned your head!' teased his wife.

'Not at all. But I am able to judge her pleasant nonetheless.'

So it was that when the snowdrops were in flower the widow brought the two little girls to The Grange for the first time. William took them for a tour: to see the ducks on the pond, the henhouse and stables. The older child, Molly, was much taken with the horses and ponies, but her sister preferred the smaller creatures. She had heard it said that a pony could give a kick quite the equal of a bull and she shrank back when Gale offered to lead them around. Her sister, however, accepted with alacrity and so enjoyed herself that he was quite scarlet in the face with exertion by the time she had done with him. The three visitors stayed for luncheon – at William's insistence the children ate with them – before setting back for Cheltenham before two o'clock, so as to make the journey in daylight.

'Are you a reader, Mrs Lockwood?' Alice enquired.

'I am not. There is always something else to occupy me: making things for my girls, mending.'

'But I am sure you have allowed yourself at least the pleasure of Mr Dickens' works, in *Household Words*? The chapters are not of any great duration, taken one at a time.'

'No indeed. I prefer to keep my hands busy.' And she gave a rueful little smile.

'My wife could expend whole days with her nose in a book or paper,' said William.

'We like stories,' said Kitty. 'Don't we, Molls?'

Molly, who had her mouth full, only nodded.

'You are right,' Alice addressed the girls. 'Stories are one of life's greatest joys.'

'And being useful one of life's greatest purposes,' said William.

Alice, although she found Mrs Lockwood a dull creature, was touched by her husband's kindness to his friend's children and full of happiness that the house was soon to become home to their own family. How fortunate their child would be, to have such a father! Under the care and supervision of Dr Nolan, she allowed herself to hope that the child would be delivered safe and well. William had shown concern that she should no longer be attended by the family doctor, old Dr Aldham at Broadway, but she had prevailed: Nolan was abreast of all the latest medical developments and would look after her and the baby handsomely. Nolan had advised her to rest in the prone position – the feet must be elevated – during the afternoons but to be otherwise as active as ever she was. A daily walk each morning could do her nothing but good. Also at his suggestion, she took a glass of stout before dinner in the evenings, for strength.

The announcement of William's investiture came late in spring, when Alice was in perhaps her seventh month. The ceremony was to take place in the open air, at Hyde Park; the date was set for the 26th of June. It was Dr Nolan's opinion that this would likely coincide with the time of Alice's confinement and that it would therefore be unwise for her to travel to town.

'You must not fret concerning me,' she said to her husband. 'I am well attended by Nolan. Take Caroline with you and your Ma and Pa, then I shall have plenty of accounts of the great glory of it all, which I shall enjoy almost as much as I would have had I seen you receive the medal with my own eyes.'

'I only hope that the child does not arrive in my absence,' said William.

'The likelihood is that it will not,' she said. 'After all, you will only be gone for a day or two.'

In the event he was to stay three nights in London, for there was to be a dinner in his honour given at the Army and Navy Club by the Regiment and another, smaller affair for friends and relations, on the next evening. It was the family's custom to put up with William's uncle, his father's brother, at his house in Cadogan Place: the four Gales travelled thence together, the day before the ceremony.

The days passed slowly for Alice. On the first day of her husband's absence she felt an occasional tightening across herself, as if an inner corset were being pulled and then released, and wondered if she should send for the doctor; but the spasms seemed to pass. Early on the morning of the 26th, however, she awoke in a warm bath. At first she thought she must have passed water in her sleep, but even before the liquid turned cool on her sheets she was awake enough to know what it must foretell. She rang the bell at once to send for Dr Nolan. It would take two hours for him to come, at best: she much regretted having refused his offer to stay at The Grange. And yet she felt a surge of exhilaration that the day had come at last and was glad of this now sacred time alone at the start of it.

★

In London William was taking breakfast at his uncle's in his shirt sleeves. His uniform coat awaited him, perfectly brushed, its buttons newly gleaming. On the sideboard were poached eggs and kippers and sausages; on the table were racks of toast and pots of marmalade and small, ribbed curls of butter arranged upon cut glass circles. Each of these were perilous to the wool of his coat: it would not do for the Queen to find a crumb or a smudge in the medal's way, when the time came. Better to leave off his outer wear until just before leaving the house. Mrs Lockwood had written a note to tell him that she would be in the Park that day, in the hopes of seeing him receive the Cross. He was moved by this kindness and hoped that he would catch a glimpse of her, so that he might thank her for her consideration.

Dr Nolan arrived at The Grange and sprang up the stairs without preamble. Alice had turned very pale and was standing by the window, holding fast to the back of a chair.

'Here we are, here we are,' he said. 'Do you feel the need to bear down?'

She did not answer for some moments while she collected herself and waited for the waves within her to die down.

'No, not yet. Only the pain is very great.'

The doctor came and took her by the arm and helped her up on to the bed.

'Don't be afraid, I am here to help you, and what you are undergoing is after all the most natural thing in the world. It is well to rest a little when the pains are at bay, so as not to exhaust yourself. I will make you up a tincture.'

'I confess I am relieved to see you,' said Alice. 'The sensation was becoming so violent that I feared you would come too late.'

The medals were to be given out in alphabetical order, so that none could claim precedence nor perceive a slight. William was to stand close in line with his fellows, his family to one side.

A great crowd had assembled, the silk of the gentlemen's top hats glinting in the sun, like starlings' wings. A silver band played. The Queen and Lord Panmure and the Prince of Wales, with Prince Albert to one side and Prince Frederick William of Prussia to the other, were mounted, alongside other dignitaries. Equerries stood to Her Majesty's left, one of them bearing the Royal Standard. Guards officers, tall in their bearskins, formed up at right angles to the Royal Party. Each man who was to be awarded took his turn to come to the right side of the Queen. None spoke, awed as they were by the pomp of the occasion and the nearness of Her Majesty. When his time came, William was so immoderately conscious of the smallness of her hands upon his breast that her face made barely an impression.

Dr Nolan applied a soothing compress to Alice's brow with one hand and held both her hands with the other. Her grip was fierce. 'It won't be long now,' he said.

The Queen's cuff was white below the crimson of her coat. Her hands were as pale as unripe fruit. She spoke and William answered her. He stood very still while she stuck the dark medal's clasp through the stiffness of his coat.

Dr Nolan took the infant and washed him in the basin of warmed water which the maid had brought up to Alice's room. He had already cut the cord and delivered her of the weight of what came afterwards, a wide, slippery thing like an ox liver. Alice was shaking and he sent the maid back down to fetch tea for her, and something sweet for her to eat. He wrapped the child in a towel and brought him to his smiling mother's arms.

★

William bowed before his Queen and stood back, the Cross upon his breast. He could not have said whether he had been a minute or an hour in her presence.

Dr Nolan, at Alice's request, took William's own pen, dipped it into the ink and wrote:

A fine and healthy boy has been safely delivered and his mother is quite well. I have the honour to be your obedient servant, Dr Edward Nolan.

6.

William was sitting on the bedroom chair, while his wife – the sleeping child in his cradle at her side – reclined upon her pillows, sipping the restorative beef tea which the doctor had recommended.

'It was a most curious thing that Her Majesty remained throughout on horseback, for her side-saddle inclined her to the left, while she pinned us all to her right. Raby got a fine stabbing when his turn came, but managed to keep his countenance. It's a wonder more of our heroes were not thus lanced,' William recounted.

Alice laughed. 'But I wonder why she did not dismount?'

'We all did. Perhaps it is because the Queen is of such diminutive stature that she did not want to be standing on her tip-toes all morning. Or perhaps it was so that the crowd in the park would be able to make her out. Her mount was the palest of the horses present and I fancy it may have been chosen so as to be discernible by the many who had congregated to see the ceremony. The numbers were enormous: the press are putting the crowd at a hundred thousand. In any case, it was a most delightful occasion and I was glad to see some of my old friends from the Regiment. Even the sun obliged.'

'Oh do let me see the Cross of Valour! I long to hold it in my own hands.'

'It is very plain. The papers have wasted no time in complaining of it: that it is made of only the basest metal and not from gold or silver. They are most indignant on our behalf. It is their view that a decoration so humble is not befitting of the honour it celebrates.'

William came and handed it to her, and stood gazing down at his son.

'Well, it is not ornate, that is true,' said Alice doubtfully, turning it over and then over again. She knew she needs must conceal her disappointment, but this was a very dull article. The ribbon was more eye-catching than the cross suspended from it. Somehow she had expected the weight of it in her hand to compensate, a little, for all the long months of her husband's absence; or at the least to make vivid to her the glory of him in the field of battle. But it was little different from holding a tarnished penny.

'Mrs Lockwood would like to pay you a call – shall you mind? She has something for you.'

'If she does not linger too long I should be happy to see her. But the doctor says I must rest to keep up my strength for nursing.'

'I am sure, as a mother herself, she will not stay too long. She is in any case naturally reticent.'

Alice felt a little prickle of irritation.

'Indeed. I would say mousy.'

William affected not to have heard her. His parents came to see their grandson the next morning and his sister Caroline the next. Alice's own sister came for two nights, leaving her children behind with their nurse, so that their noise should not disturb the quiet of the convalescent. Presently Mrs Lockwood came, bringing a finely worked shawl of her own making.

'How kind you are!' said Alice, touched. 'It is like the most beautiful gossamer.'

'It is a good weight for a summer baby,' said Mrs Lockwood.

'It is lovely and light, certainly,' said Alice. 'Tell me how you are, for I have been abed for almost ten days now and begin to miss the world outside this room.'

'We are well,' said Mrs Lockwood. 'My trip to London was

most welcome and it was delightful to attend your husband's investiture. Such an occasion – the pageantry and the solemnity, both – elevates the spirits.'

'I did not know you had been present,' said Alice. Her voice sounded louder than she had meant.

'Oh yes. I did write to let him know that I would be among the throng – did he not tell you?' Mrs Lockwood's pale round eyes were as expressionless as a doll's.

'It must have slipped my mind. I have had other business to occupy me, as you see.'

Mrs Lockwood looked down at the infant.

'And who does he follow, do you think?'

'He is like my father, I fancy. But it is too early to say of course.'

Mrs Lockwood sat for a few moments in silence.

'I must leave you to rest,' she said.

'William will arrange some tea for you, I am sure. You've come all the way from Cheltenham on this warm day, you must not leave us without taking refreshment.'

'You are good. Yes, he said as much when I arrived,' said Mrs Lockwood.

The child was to be called George, after William's father, and Algernon, in memory of his brother. John, for Alice's father, was to be his third and final name. The baptism took place on a clear, bright day in September; a brother officer from the Crimean campaign stood as one godfather, Alice's brother-in-law as the second. George smiled obligingly, waving his plump, dimpled arms in the Gale christening robe, which was rather too tight. Alice had been dismayed to find, on unwrapping the gown from its calico and paper casings, that there were spots of mildew on the silk. The children she had borne before had not lived long enough to enjoy its use. Perhaps the marks, spotting the front panel of the gown, corresponded with flecks of water from an earlier baptism; or, she suddenly conceived, from some distant child's own drool. She wondered if the last to wear it had been poor Algernon Gale. She rather thought, if her next child was a daughter, that she might commission a new christening gown.

One morning in early October, while the nurse was out wheeling baby George around the lower lawn in his perambulator, Caroline came to call.

'Is my brother at home?' she enquired.

'No, I believe he's gone down to the timber-yard. He is so busy these days, I barely see him. Oh, do stay and wait for him here, an hour with you would be such balm, for my head is full of nothing but lullabies. Should you care for coffee, or chocolate?'

'Nothing, thank you.' Caroline paused to draw in her breath. 'It is in fact yourself I have come to see. My dear, we have an enemy.'

Alice felt her face grow cold, as if she had opened the casement on to a frost.

'William has been to visit me. It seems that this widow has been dripping poison into his mind. He sought to discover from me how frequently you visited with your aunt at Cheltenham while he was in the Crimea, and thereby to establish the nature of your association with Dr Nolan.'

'With Dr Nolan! But William knows the man as well as I do,' said Alice. 'Surely you have mistaken his purpose.'

'He was in an agitation about the doctor. She has convinced him that your relations with him go beyond . . . go beyond fraternization.'

'But this is absurd!' Alice protested. 'I am the mother of a new infant; nothing could be further from my mind than — I hardly know how to put this delicately — fleshly pleasures.'

'I don't know that it is your current virtue which is in doubt. It is the infant himself whom she has most cunningly brought into question. William asked me if I thought George looked to be very much a Gale. When I opined that I thought him just exactly his own little person, he said that this was his point entirely.'

All at once Alice sat down. She felt utterly defeated, her accustomed vitality drained quite out of her.

'How is it possible that he could interrogate an innocent child in this way? Why has he not spoken to me?'

'He purports that Mrs Lockjaw, or whatever the wretched woman's name is, had mentioned that the boy looks unalike to William and that she had then enquired – he thinks in all innocence – whether you had not been friends with Dr Nolan during your husband's time at war.'

'What in the name of Heaven would induce someone to turn a man against his own son, a mere babe in arms? That woman knows full well that I became acquainted with Dr Nolan while William was away: she accepted the hospitality of my aunt and met the doctor at her table.'

'Precisely. I know this also, as does my brother. But she has sown this seed of doubt in him as to the nature of your friendship with the man. I believe her purpose is to create discord between you.'

'But why should she seek to do that?' said Alice.

'You will forgive me if I am blunt, we are friends of long standing and I think I can speak as freely to you as I would if I were ruminating in my own head. I believe she means to take William for herself. She is a widow of no standing: my brother has position and when our papa dies he will have more. He is a hero whose name is known throughout the county and beyond. Her daughters are fatherless: their prospects, when the time comes, would be immeasurably improved by becoming part of a family such as ours. In short, if she became his wife her gains would be tremendous.'

As soon as Caroline issued these words, Alice saw the truth in them. The apprehension was sudden and complete. She remembered her initial distaste for the widow: how she had not warmed to the symmetry and flatness of the face, the lack of animation in the character.

'You are right. I can see that you are right. I begin to wonder whether she had not devised this scheme before she ever met William, but as soon as it became clear to her – when we first met, she and I, after he had written to her – that he meant to take up the role of her protector. And if so whether that was not the reason why I did not find her congenial, for I am generally well disposed to folk, as you know.'

'You are. All your sharpness is reserved for those dearest to you.'

At this they both laughed. The moment of levity was of great relief to both women and went some way towards relaxing their sense of what danger the widow could bring.

'But there is nothing she can do to bring her plan to fruition. I am alive and well, after all, and William would never submit your family to the scandal of a divorce.'

'Of course not. Nevertheless, she is troublesome.'

'I fancy that Mrs Lockwood is of more implacable a nature than her guileless manner suggests,' Alice went on.

'I agree,' said Caroline. 'A woman who is willing to devote so much time to needlework must be very patient.'

The two women laughed again. Each knew the other's work-basket to be filled with unfinished scraps of embroidery, always taking second place to a book or journal.

'That is true. Perhaps she is like a spider. Indeed, the shawl which she brought for George might almost be a cobweb. I think now that I shall not let it near him.' Alice shuddered. 'Then how shall I prevail against her, do you suppose?'

'This is what we must now consider,' said Caroline. 'We are clever and she is not: that must go in our favour.'

'I fear she is more clever than she looks and that she has more influence over William than I had allowed myself to admit. She has been coming here for some time, as I now see insinuating herself. He has grown especially fond of the little girls.'

Alice now stood and embraced her husband's sister.

'I am so grateful for your fellowship in this,' she said. 'Truly I cannot imagine that I would have strength enough to see her off, were I alone.'

The question was whether to apprise William of Mrs Lockwood's campaign. Alice did not want to inflame her husband by casting doubt upon his judgement, for it was a thing upon which he prided himself. His previously erratic temper had improved over recent months, for which she was glad; although she feared that his friendship with the woman – and perhaps especially his avuncular camaraderie with her daughters – was one reason for this amelioration. The girls came with their mother once a week now at his invitation, to sit on the ponies, collect eggs or otherwise amuse themselves. Then, too, Alice had thought that becoming a father had made him gentler.

Conversely, she and Caroline divined that the widow's power, such as it was, would surely be the less were her scheme to become known to him. Alice did not care for concealment, in any case: and so the two women agreed that William must be spoken to. Caroline, having already been subject to his interrogation on the matter of his wife's association with Dr Nolan, determined that it had better come from herself. In this way, the raising of the matter could not be attributed to wifely jealousy or pique. She would tell her brother that she had reflected upon their earlier conversation and had come to the sorry conclusion that the widow was no friend to him nor to his family.

But William would hear none of it. It was his firmly held belief that Mrs Lockwood was a person of the utmost probity. It was not in her nature to make trouble: she was in all things reticent and had spoken only from concern for himself and his reputation. Indeed, he was grateful to her for having brought to his attention his wife's relations with Dr Nolan, which were surely improper. They had consorted for some months during his absence, causing tongues to wag in Cheltenham. The fact that she had forgone the administrations of their old family doctor in favour of this man spoke volumes. But this was not all of his trouble concerning her. Why, at luncheon at Sudeley Castle only the week before last, someone had alluded to Alice's impossible position on the Crimean campaign. It was worse than unseemly for a man in receipt of the Queen's highest award for valour to find himself the subject of gossip in the county because of a wife who could not keep her own counsel. It was intolerable! He had made it evident to his wife that she must desist from her politicking, but still he was visited by rumour.

'William, the widow is taking you for a fool. You know as well as I do that Alice has no feeling for this doctor. If this were so, why would she have been trying to marry him off to every young woman for miles around? You know she even attempted to match him with Algie's poor girl, Emily? Would she not keep him by her, if she wanted him for herself? I would remind you, furthermore, that Dr Nolan is plainness personified: why should she care a fig for him when she has a handsome husband in yourself?'

'She is intemperate in all things,' said William.

'It is true that she makes little secret of her views and that some of those views are not popular. She is spirited. But you knew this when you married her: she has not changed.'

'Well, perhaps I have.'

'I would remind you that marriage is a Sacrament ordained

by God. You must not discard it at will, as you might a pair of old boots.'

'The law would say otherwise. You may have read in the papers that there has lately been an alteration in the law, concerning the dissolution of marriages. If my wife has made a cuckold and a laughing stock of me I should be ill advised to keep her.'

'You are not Henry the Eighth, William! This is absurd. Really you are being uncommonly obstinate. You must cast these baseless accusations from your mind. I urge you to cease all communication with this malicious Mrs Lockson.'

'Lockwood. Her name is Mrs Lockwood.'

'And so her name shall remain. It would do more than displease Papa were you to continue with this matter. It can go no further. Alice is your wife, who has given you a beautiful son: you must turn towards her now.'

For a time no more was heard nor spoken about the matter. William's immediate attention was taken up by the question of what to do concerning his late brother's fiancée, Emily Norris. The girl's father had lost his position at a firm in Cheltenham, it seemed as a result of his propensity for port and Madeira wine. The girl had written to William – no doubt her father had put her up to it – asking if there was a cottage on the estate to which the family might now repair, the lease on their town house being lost because her father was without funds to keep up the rent.

William's mother and father had been against the engagement from the very first. Emily was certainly pretty, but it had been clear to them that the father was a sot and, if this were not disadvantage enough, he came from Trade. There were hundreds of other pretty girls, from good families. But Algernon had been young and tender-hearted and had not heeded them. Now they found themselves in the most unwelcome situation: they were without their darling boy, yet beholden still to the girl and her family.

The senior Mr Gale's reluctant conclusion was that they must find somewhere to house the Norrises. There was an empty cottage to the far side of the home farm which would do. Perhaps it might be that the property was made available for a twelve-month, while Mr Norris sought an alternative. There was a younger brother who was now of an age to begin to make a living; Emily herself might be asked to consider taking up employment as a governess. It did not do to languish. In any case, it was fervently to be hoped that the family would not expect to be sheltered in perpetuity. Certainly there could be no question of their offering employment to Mr Norris. William proposed another solution: that the man be given a sum equal to six months' rent on his current abode, as well as funds to tide him over until employment was found. In this way the Gales need not enter into a long-standing obligation.

The matter was a delicate one. There was much to be said for William's idea, were it not for the fact that the beloved memory of his brother must be considered. While paying off the Norris family was without doubt the more expedient solution, could it be said to be the noblest, the one that Algie himself would have wished? And if word of it reached the wider ears of the county, might it not be whispered abroad that the Gales had behaved sharply?

Thus it was with some unwillingness that it was agreed to allow the Norris family the empty cottage, together with a small stipend to cover their expenses for a year. The boy was to be offered a sum to enable him to train in an apprenticeship and subsequently to purchase a position for himself. The trying question of how the Gales should continue in their relation to the Norrises remained unresolved. Surely they could not call on one another as equals, and yet the Gales did not wish to appear cold or lofty.

It irked William, then, to learn that Emily Norris had been to visit his wife within two days of taking up residence on the estate. She had come to see the baby, his wife explained.

'It is not my father's wish that our house should fraternize with theirs,' said William.

'I could hardly turn her away at the door!' Alice protested.

'I suppose not. But I must ask you, please, not to form a friendship with the girl. Now that they are tenants here we cannot have her forever taking tea in our drawing room.'

'William! You vex me now. I would ask you to consider that had your brother survived, Emily Norris would have had equal standing to my own. It seems unduly churlish to make a scapegoat of her now, when surely your brother would have wished us to be kind to her. Her father's circumstances are no fault of hers, after all.'

'I do not wish to argue every finer point with you, as if we were adversaries in a courtroom. To be frank, your disputatious nature is wearisome to me. Kindly do as I ask and we will say no more about it.'

And with this he went from the room.

Alice was not given to tears, but at this she felt her eyes fill. William had never used to speak to her in this autocratic manner. One of the joys of their courtship, indeed, had been his interest in her opinions and their shared pleasure in conversation. There were many nights when they had stayed up after dining, talking through affairs of the day, or the finer point of a scripture or sermon. Sometimes in their fervour they had allowed the fire to go out, each too caught up with discussion to remember to add a log to the grate. On those evenings when Caroline joined them at The Grange their discourse had been especially lively. Alice had thought herself fortunate to have met such a man. And yet, since his return from the Russian war, he had been more sombre, less readily drawn. It was as if conversation only irked him now. The truth could no longer be ignored: her husband had been out of countenance with her for some time. Their views did not align, they were no longer in sympathy with one another.

There was another thing, a thing which portended such sorrow that she had locked it tightly within herself until her tears released it. To their son William did not show the affection and playfulness she had anticipated. He was not unkind – he was a fine man, after all – but rather uninterested. He glanced into the cradle as if lifting a forcing pot from over a young rhubarb plant, with a certain mild anticipation; but no more. She had noticed that he did not seem to want to hold the baby, but this reluctance she had ascribed to his injury. Now it seemed clear to her that little George did not gladden his father's heart as he did her own. At this apprehension Alice felt more alone than she had since the death of her mother and father. The weeping came with the force she had last known on the evening of the day when her husband went off to war, and for the same reason. William had gone away from her.

7

The death of the older Mr Gale came of a sudden in the spring of 1858. A chill had advanced with alarming rapidity into a fever; his breathing had faltered, then failed. Alice had no heart for a move to the big house, for The Grange had been the home she had come to as a bride and where she had resided since; it was inexpressibly dear to her. Here George had been conceived and born, here she had waited every morning for the post, hoping for a letter from William from the Black Sea. Here she had dreamed of the life they would have together when he returned. She was much attached to the garden and to the green fields and rising hills beyond, which made such a pleasing view through the windows. Her husband prevaricated. It was mooted that Caroline would take over The Grange, while the widowed Mrs Gale would remain at the big house, with her son and his family installed. But the season changed to summer and still no preparations were made for the move. By this delay Alice had hopes that her wish to remain at The Grange might indeed be realized.

George kept her much at home and she did not venture to see her Aunt Felicity in Cheltenham, nor to invite Dr Nolan to call upon them there. In truth Caroline's words had shaken her. As much as she knew herself to be innocent of any impropriety in her conduct with the doctor, still she was loath to pursue a friendship which had been so cruelly misconstrued. In early June, however, she received from him a letter:

32 The Park, Cheltenham, Gloucestershire
3rd June 1858

My dear Mrs Gale

The first birthday of your son must be approaching, for which joyous occasion I wish both he and his Mama many happy returns.

This is to tell you that I have for some time been considering a new life for myself in Australia. A former colleague – a physician I much admire – has opened a practice at Melbourne and writes to suggest I join him. There are great opportunities for the advancement of medicine in that land, opportunities which life here, however congenial, cannot afford. The good denizens of Gloucestershire are traditionalists, but as you will recall from our many stimulating conversations over the course of our acquaintanceship, I am much interested in new ideas. I entered my profession in the hope of improving the lives of my patients and it seems to me that I would better be placed to fulfil this hope elsewhere.

My obligations here continue for a month or two more and I plan to sail in early September. It will be high summer, I think, before I arrive at my destination – to quit one summer only to arrive, at the close of a long sea passage, in the midst of another will be a curious thing. My friend tells me there are all sorts of oddities over there – flora and fauna very much unlike our own – so it may be that the inverted climes will be the least of it.

I hope that we shall have the pleasure of meeting before my time in Cheltenham comes to an end. Please let me know if you plan to come to town, or if I may call on you.

I remain your devoted servant

Edward Nolan

Alice did not at once reply, for she did not wish to displease William. Of Mrs Lockwood she had seen nothing since the troubling events of the previous winter, nor even heard her name spoken. It seemed that William had heeded his sister after all, and abjured the widow's company. Between husband and wife there was now a certain accord: there were no flares of temper on either side, but neither was there the closeness they had once enjoyed. William had gone to sleep in his dressing room when the baby had still been nursing at night and had not since returned to the marriage bed. Delicacy forbade that Alice should question this arrangement outright, but on several occasions she had gone to him and put an affectionate hand on his shoulder, or leant against him as they walked around the walled garden; by these signs she hoped to make known to him that no door would be shut against his return. In a further measure of propitiation, she had tried to temper her views and now kept her own counsel on political matters of the day, where previously she would have shared them with her husband.

Thus she was not unduly perturbed when William requested after breakfast one morning that she come into his study. It was her surmise that he had now come to a decision as to their future residential arrangements. Directly he went to sit in an upright oak carver before the bookcase, and bade her to take her seat on one of the upholstered chairs, to either side of the fireplace, on the other side of the room. This was as he sat when he interviewed tenants; but perhaps it had become his habit to adopt such a formal seating arrangement, with himself at some distance from his interlocutor.

William spoke first, as she had expected him to.

'You will be aware, I know, that we have not been such good companions to each other as once we were. For my part in this I most humbly beg your pardon. I have not meant to make you unhappy.'

Alice was surprised by this, and moved. 'You remain as ever in my heart,' she said. 'If I was not at first sensible to the quieter life you have preferred since the war, I hope I have since made amends.'

William gave no answer.

'It has never been my desire that we should be estranged,' Alice eventually said.

Again he said nothing. The moments passed, seeming to hang in the bright morning air like motes of pollen-dust. At length William spoke again.

'I had hoped that we could continue as we have been, but events have overtaken me. Be assured that I shall not leave you short; you and the boy will be amply provided for.'

Alice could feel her face grow cold from dread.

'But William, what can you mean? Surely you are not planning to leave us?'

'It is an eventuality to which I have given consideration, but it is impossible that it should be I who quits you. As you know, the responsibility of the estate – all the farms – now rests solely with me; there is my mother to be cared for and my sister besides.'

'Well, and we will do so together,' said Alice, though her confidence was faltering.

'I fear that the time for us is gone. Divorce is the only possible solution to the present . . . the present difficulty.'

At this Alice gave a little cry of disbelief.

'But what can your reason be? Such a course would be scandalous for us all! You cannot surely wish to see our names all over the papers, the stuff of gossip and slander. I begin to fear that you have taken leave of your senses.'

'While my father was living there could have been no question of such an action. His good name was more important to me than my own happiness, but such considerations . . . such an impediment no longer obtains.'

Alice did not speak. She had no words to say.

'You read the parliamentary reports, so you will know as I do that there has lately been a change regarding the divorce of husband and wife. It is now possible to petition the court in London directly and I intend to do so without further delay.'

'But I have not been untrue to you, William,' said Alice quietly. 'You know this full well.'

At this she thought she detected the barest trace of a flush come over her husband's features.

'It is my contention that you have . . . you have . . . formed an association with a certain gentleman which transcends the ordinary bond of social friendship.'

'It is true that I like the doctor greatly. He has a lively and enquiring mind and I have a strong respect for him professionally. But that is all. In any case I have not seen him for some months.'

'I would not expect you to say anything else,' said William.

'No indeed, for you know that whatever my failings I do not number the telling of falsehoods among them!'

To this he made no answer.

'Your sister warned me of this. She said your head had been filled with this nonsense by the widow of your friend Lockwood.'

'Sarah Lockwood cannot be held responsible for your own behaviour.'

'Sarah! You are on first name terms then?'

'We are friends, certainly.'

'Perhaps I had better petition myself, in that case.'

'If you were to instigate divorce proceedings you would be obliged to prove that I had mistreated you in some way, that I had been cruel. Since you have already stained my reputation locally by consorting with this doctor, I cannot think that you would wish to bring further calumny on my family name by such a rash and mendacious course.'

'And yet you have no compunction in saying lies of me! Not only saying, but swearing before the justices, I do believe.'

The room seemed uncomfortably warm now. Alice went on.

'Anyway I know of no such besmirchment of you in these

parts. You are well liked and respected by all. As, I hope, am I. What foundation do you have for this charge that I have compromised your reputation?'

At this William sighed heavily. Alice remarked something false in this exhalation, an almost theatrical quality, as if it were for the benefit of some other observer than herself.

'Alice, I will not be swayed. I do not intend to furnish you with a list of the rumours which have reached my ears concerning your conduct. We would do well to guard our tongues, before irreparable harm is caused between us. As I told you just now, it is a source of regret to me to cause you chagrin; but my mind is quite decided.'

'Would that you had been so steadfast in your duty as a husband and father!'

William stood up.

'The child by rights would live with me following our separation, as I am sure you are aware. You must be thankful that I will let him go with you. Now, let us go about our day and speak again when we have had the time to reflect. Decisions will need to be made.'

'And what good will that do?' said Alice, her blood now up. 'It is clear that nothing will make you alter your course. When you propose that we each reflect, what you mean is that I must be quiet. You intend to ruin me and, not incidentally, the reputation of Dr Nolan, who is entirely blameless.'

Alice recalled the doctor's letter and was greatly relieved, now, by the intelligence it brought. At least he was assured of a fresh beginning overseas.

'You say you did not wish to visit this upon your late father, but you show no such compunction, it seems, on bringing it upon your little son. How will it be for him, to have had his mother's good name so compromised?'

At this he made no answer, but only inclined his head slightly in her direction, as if she were a half-remembered housemaid spied across a crowded street.

She could not stay. To be under the same roof as William was now a kind of torture. It was impossible that they should eat at the same table with their accustomed civility, or discuss estate affairs, the health of tenants, the little antics of their son. To see this dear familiar face – so longed for, in his absence – now set in this ruinous course against her was more than she could bear. She could not go to Caroline. Her sister was presently taking the sea air at Lythe, close to Whitby, where her husband had relations. Alice must go, for the interim, to her aunt.

Felicity listened to her niece's account with a grave countenance. At length she suggested that Alice must now make two visits: the first to the kind doctor, the second to Mrs Lockwood. The older lady proposed to accompany her to the latter interview, for which Alice was heartily grateful.

The doctor received her with his usual warmth and called for lemonade to be brought, for the afternoon was warm. But before the maid had come up with the tray, in the midst of outlining to him the events of recent days, a torrent of tears came on.

'I am so ashamed to have brought this upon you, who have never been anything but honourable to me. My only consolation is that your impending departure may save you from the worst of the slander which this action will surely occasion.'

'It is true. I do not think the residents of Montpellier and The Park would seek a physician whose name had been in the papers as an adulterer,' said the doctor.

'No indeed; and I am mortified by it. I can only hope that reports of the case will not follow you to the Antipodes. I have told and told my husband that his accusation is baseless, but he will not hear me. He is quite insensible to my entreaty. He is like a man sleepwalking.'

There was a knock and the lemonade was brought in, causing Alice to halt her weeping. She unfastened her reticule in search of a handkerchief, but found none. The door closed behind the maid and all at once the doctor was before her, a large white cotton square in his hand. Before she could take it from him, he folded it and dabbed at her cheek. He was now so close that she could feel the heat of his breath on her face.

'Forgive me, but I must blow my nose,' said Alice, taking the handkerchief.

She expected him to stand back, but he did not. Instead he put both his hands on her shoulders. She did not find his touch disagreeable.

'Since your husband's course compels us to be frank with one another,' said the doctor, 'I shall now vouchsafe to you the true reason for my departure from here. I have since the first felt an attraction to you which has made me quite blind to the charms of any other woman, for all your kind attempts to make a match for me.' Here he smiled, and Alice could not help but smile back at him.

'Oh, but I . . .'

'Allow me to finish, please. Of all the faces in the world, yours is the one I prefer to see over any other. A day with you in it is for me a glad day. But by that very token, all the days when I did not see you, could not see you, were very flat and dull. By this logic it has been apparent to me that, short of seeing you on a daily basis, I cannot be happy in my present circumstance. This is why I had determined to leave these Isles. I had thought to take leave of you without stating my case; but I must — I cannot not speak — I must take the opportunity to ask you: since Mr Gale believes us to be united by a bond closer than friendship, why should we not now make it so?'

Alice was entirely flummoxed.

'If you were to come with me to Melbourne we might

commence a new life. It has long been my observation that you are in possession of a fine mind. In a new country you might begin again: you might nurse, or write, or otherwise occupy yourself.'

'But I . . . I have George, I cannot take him so far away from his father,' said Alice.

'His father does not in his plan consider his bond to the boy. Why any more should you? In any case, I should be honoured to take over the protection of the child.'

'Dr Nolan. Edward. While I hold you in the very highest regard, I must say that I have never entertained romantic thoughts towards you and I . . .'

At this he came still closer, his hands yet upon her shoulders. Did he smell of bergamot or was it witch-hazel? Alice was aware of the faintest trace of something refreshing and ever so slightly sharp. Or could it be West Indian lime? It was a most pleasing smell. She liked it. This surprised her. But before she had time to think more, Nolan's lips were on hers. This too she liked. In her surprise, she became immediately aware of a new difficulty, completely unforeseen: that of smiling and kissing at one and the same time.

To her aunt she did not relay the details of her perplexing interview with Edward Nolan. She hardly knew what to make of it herself. The sudden rush of delight had quite unseated her. The opinion of another person could not be admitted into the question as yet. She would give herself a day or two in which to privately consider the course he proposed. Felicity was resolved that they should the next day make their call on the widow, a call which Alice did not anticipate with any joy. It could only be a confrontation, unpleasant to all. Alice had no wish to set eyes on her tormentor, yet if the visit afforded a chance to prevent the terrible course on which her husband was now set, she must take it.

But the following morning she received a letter from her husband's sister. Caroline was much agitated to learn that Alice had quit The Grange. It was monstrous that the mother of a young child should not enjoy the sanctuary of her own home. Having spoken at some length with her brother, it had become evident to her that his wife's departure was an event he had not only foreseen, but anticipated. It was surely with this very end in mind that he had not set into train his family's removal to the big house, for he had guessed that Caroline would have offered Alice the shelter of The Grange herself, were she already its occupier.

Caroline had also enquired of him what proof he had for the aspersions he sought to cast upon his wife; whereupon he had claimed to have a witness who had seen Alice and the doctor together during his absence at the war, and on more than one occasion. He had been most reluctant to furnish the name of this person, but she had pressed, and he had by and by named the witness as Emily Norris. This was calumny indeed! Since the girl depended upon William's charity for the roof above the heads of herself and her family, her position was all but impossible. She could not deny him for risk of finding the Norrises out on the very streets. His sister was forced to conclude that his association with a certain lady had caused him to become devious in the extreme. She concluded with the sorry admission that William had sunk lower in her estimation than ever in their lives.

Alice was further sobered by the contents of this missive. Any hope – however faint – she had entertained of regaining the affection and trust of her husband now evaporated. To visit Mrs Lockwood would be futile, if there could be no alteration in William. The only thing that mattered now was that she should not be parted from her child. All at once, with a resolution and purpose she had not felt for some time, she took out paper and ink and pen, and sat down to write.

6 Montpellier Spa Road, Cheltenham
24th June 1858

William —

It has this morning become clear to me that no course remains open to us but to part. Nevertheless I wish to state with all my heart, here in the ink on this page, that this sundering is at your behest. I repudiate your case entirely.

You have since your return from the Crimean campaign been of a much altered disposition, and to this I shall attribute the course you are now set upon.

If you would be so good as to call on me here, I have a proposal to put before you which I believe to be expedient to us both. I have been given to understand that if any collusion between husband and wife should be discovered, no divorce may take place. Therefore I urge you to guard this letter closely, or better consign it to flames.

I remain pro tempore your loving wife,

Alice

There. The thing was done. She sealed the letter and smoothed down her skirt. She smoothed down her skirt again for courage, before dipping her pen once more into the inkwell and beginning a second note, to the doctor. On this page she wrote only three words:

I will come.

PART 2

8.

Cornwall, summer 1977

It was as if he'd never before seen green. There was green of course in the suburbs of Melbourne, in the mothy kind of grass which edged the curbs and carpeted the parks, before it turned tobacco-coloured in the summer sun. There was the deeper, thicker green of the waxy, big-leafed plants people grew around their houses; and then over in the distance was the green-grey of the Dandenong Ranges. But nothing like this. This was a crazy sort of green, shiny and thick as poster-paint, or like the stiff strips of bright plastic grass that separated the cuts of meat in the butcher's shop window at home. Here the sloping pasture caught the light in places, and ruffled and paled in the breeze, like fur. It was everywhere you looked. It was like the green in a cartoon.

As if intuiting Stephen's thoughts, Nick spoke.

'Lovely, isn't it? But you don't get this green without a lot of rain. Like Ireland. This part of Cornwall is green for a reason.'

Stephen kept looking out of the car window to his left and didn't answer. He was appreciating the softness of the hills. Nick was unperturbed by the boy's silence. He'd only just got here, after all, and he was a complete stranger; he was probably shy. Probably hungry, too. Weren't boys always hungry? Stephen was tall and gangly – six foot three, Nick guessed – with longish auburn hair flopping over eyes which were flecked with dark green, like moss agate. As soon as he'd spotted him getting off the train, Nick had thought what a good head the boy had, perfect for a sculpture. His profile was especially fine, with a nose that was just a fraction too big, like an old portrait of a Doge. If there wasn't enough for Stephen to do on the farm, Nick thought, he could get him into the studio to sit for him for a morning.

'I can't remember if you've ever done any farm work before?' he asked.

'Just a little bit. My uncle – well, he's my dad's uncle really – has a farm.'

'Livestock or arable?'

'Pardon me?'

Nick grimaced inwardly. Although he prided himself for being unconventional, no one he knew said pardon.

'Animals or growing crops?'

'Ah. Yeah. Animals. Cattle.'

'Our farm is probably different from what you're used to. It's mainly sheep. Being on a slope, it's mostly grazing land. We keep a few hens, beehives in the orchards. We've got a lot of fruit trees up behind the house. The flatter fields below, closer to the river, are ploughed, but our neighbour – he's what you might call a proper farmer – he sees to the arable side of things. He's got all the machinery. Well, you'll see.'

Stephen just nodded. He wasn't sure what to make of Nick. He wasn't what he'd been expecting. He'd thought, being a farmer, Nick'd be a ruddy type in overalls, with a pick-up truck. Instead he was a little guy, with light denim jeans half-tucked into loose ankle boots, a darker denim shirt which strained a little over the middle and a scuffed leather waistcoat which looked to be a couple of sizes too small. He had pale loose curls at his collar and small, intensely blue eyes. He was like the kind of man who'd play an accordion in a pub, while no one listened. His car stank of acrid smoke, the source of which Stephen soon discovered to be the Disque Bleu cigarettes Nick smoked. The car ashtray was over-spilling. As soon as they drove off from the station Nick had offered him a smoke from the soft white pack.

Stephen didn't really know anything much about these people, beyond the fact that they were relatives. His mum was the one who was big on family history. Apparently they shared an ancestor, his great-great-grandfather on his dad's side. It was a fairly big deal, because he'd been a military hero: his name was in books and stuff. He'd won a medal in the Crimea. It wasn't Nick Clarke who was some sort of distant cousin, but Mrs Clarke. His mum had traced the Clarkes a while back, when she'd been updating the Nolan family tree. She'd written to Mrs Clarke a couple of times and had quite friendly replies about the ancestral connection. He wondered if there'd be any family resemblance.

When he'd decided to come to England, Stephen's mother had written to everyone she could think of – a handful of people – and the Clarkes had said he was welcome to come for a couple of months, if he'd lend a hand with the farm. That was pretty nice of them, it was agreed. They must be decent individuals.

His parents hadn't at first been too happy about the idea of him taking time out to go to England. He'd already completed a year at college, doing graphic design. It would've made sense to see it through before chasing off around the planet. And, let's face it, the course wasn't exactly hard labour. All he seemed to have to do was tracing, measuring, cutting out and drawing. One along from finger painting. Who needed a break from that? It was like wanting to take time off from play-school, basically.

But there was something up with the boy, they could see that. He hadn't been right for a while. Sometimes, when you spoke to him, it took him ages to answer, as if he was on an over-seas phone call with a time delay. His hands were shaky, in the mornings. He was moody. Well, not nasty-moody: Stephen was never sarky or mean, but he wasn't his usual smiling self. It was as if he had a lot on his mind. They didn't know if there was a girl involved. That might be it. Usually he was happy to play with his little sisters before tea in the evenings, but lately he'd shut himself in his room and when they called out to him to join them, he'd answer through the closed door: 'Maybe, in a while.' But the while hardly ever came.

When he'd suggested the trip it was the most animated they'd seen him for months. That swayed them, much as they thought completing his studies should be the priority. And at least he didn't have any commitments: no mortgage, no regular job, no kids. There might never be another chance, and travel was supposed to broaden the mind, wasn't it? Maybe he'd take a different direction when he got back, go into engineering like his dad had wanted him to.

It was great that he had a place to be for the summer. Stephen had stayed in youth hostels in London and Edinburgh for the past few weeks, and with an old colleague of his father's near Birmingham. It'd be nice to be with a family now.

'Cass is at home, but Georgie won't be back until the weekend,' said Nick.

'Ah, right,' said Stephen. Right sounded like riot.

'Break you in slowly!' said Nick. 'Cass'll behave herself, if it's just her; whereas they egg each other on.' They turned off the road and began to proceed up a narrow winding lane. 'There's us, look,' said Nick.

Stephen glanced up and saw a large, square stone house, nestled into the side of the hill. It sat as naturally against the green as a baby in the crook of an arm. There were a great many windows, glinting silvery grey, their glass dissected by narrow glazing bars. Behind the house were low stone buildings and above these, orchards of old gnarly trees rose up towards the summit.

The lane curled and rose before they came to a standstill in the yard at the back of the house. As soon as Stephen opened the car door, a fowl rushed at his ankles. The bird was the shape of a rugby ball, but two or three times the size, with a red bald head and cheeks of the brightest, swimming-pool blue. Its legs were like blackened twigs.

'Christ!' Stephen looked terrified. 'It's a bloody vulture!'

Nick laughed. 'That's just Sadie. She won't do you any harm, her peck's worse than her bite, as it were.'

'What is it?' said Stephen. He looked horrified.

'Guinea-fowl. She's our self-appointed guard dog. Sexy Sadie, she's named after.' Nick was utterly unperturbed by the young man's reaction. Stephen felt almost indignant. Nobody had warned him that England had scary wildlife.

'Are they, you know, native?'

'Lord, no.' Nick laughed and went to open the boot of the car, so Stephen could get his case and duffel bag.

The peculiar bird retreated and the two went into the house, along a flagged path which led to a little side door. Straight away they were in the kitchen. When Stephen pictured Stony Hill Farm, afterwards, it was always to this room that his memory returned. He had never been in a room like it. The kitchen at home was a neat galley, brightly lit with a fluorescent strip. It had a hatch in the wall through to the dining area. There was just kitchen stuff in there: plates and glasses neatly stowed in wall-units, the fridge, a compact electric cooker. This room was full of things that didn't have a lot to do with cooking, and furthermore it looked none too clean. The pine table was covered with papers and books. The whole of one wall was taken up with a dresser whose shelves were stacked with ceramic figures of men and women in historical clothing – later, Stephen learned that these were Staffordshire figures, collected by Celia Clarke's mother. Opposite the dresser was a big range cooker in a tiled alcove, with a patchy old velvet armchair next to it. What looked like a fur rug on the chair turned out to be a dog, which raised its head as they came into the room. There wasn't a lot of wall space left, what with the dresser and the range; but what there was had been rag-rolled in a rich, uneven terracotta paint. A cupboard door had old, curling cuttings from newspapers pinned to it. A thin stream of classical music came from a radio on top of the fridge.

When he became acquainted with the rest of the house, Stephen realized that the kitchen was different from the other rooms. The house was Georgian, it was explained to him, which meant it was a couple of hundred years old; much older than any building he knew of back home. Because of the lie of the land it had four storeys at the farther side and only three on the yard side. The original kitchen had been a narrow, high room down at the end: they'd created the current one from a couple of lean-tos that had been added during the 1920s. It was easier to have it at this side, so people could go straight in with bags of groceries, or to put the kettle on. It had a low ceiling and a snug sort of feeling, whereas the other rooms were very bare and light and sparsely furnished. It was as if this family had never thought of getting comfortable. There wasn't a settee in the whole place. All the seating was hard, with rush seats or unyielding buttoned backs. The downstairs floors were uncarpeted, their bare boards dotted with occasional rugs. The sitting and dining rooms didn't have curtains, just wooden shutters. Nick's sculptures were dotted about all over the house, and there were paintings of wobbly flowers in flowery jugs, or little boats bobbing around on clumsy blue. The room farthest from the kitchen smelled of damp, even in summer. It was on a lower level than the rest of the house, reached by steps down. This was the one the kids used, with a record player and some shelves of books and a table-tennis table. The television was kept in here. It was a much smaller set than the one Stephen's parents had, back at home. There were a couple of divans covered with old checked blankets set at right angles along the walls.

On the first floor was Nick and Celia's room, and Georgie's and Cass's; and on the top floor were four smaller rooms, one of which was to be Stephen's. Nick showed Stephen the bathroom he would use. The tub had long streaks of green at the end where the taps had dripped, probably for ever. There was no shower. The room he was to sleep in had blue curtains and an old carved wooden bed. There was a round, marble-topped table in the window. On a small table by the bed someone had placed a little jar of bright leaves and blue and white flowers. No one had ever put flowers in his room before, not even when he'd had the measles as a boy.

'I don't know where Cass and Celia have got to. Shall we go outside and see if we can find them?' said Nick. 'Or would you sooner have a cup of tea first?'

'Be nice to step outside,' said Stephen.

'They can't've gone far or they'd have taken the dog,' said Nick.

They walked across the yard and through a wooden door into a walled garden. At the far end, bending over something, were two women. The smaller one looked about the same age as Stephen's own mother, with thick hair in a centre parting and very straight features: this must be Celia. Her daughter was significantly taller, with a ripple of long hair that wasn't blonde, but wasn't exactly dark either. As they came closer Stephen saw that she was wearing a cheesecloth shirt with pastel stripes, tied in a knot at the waist. She wore jeans and plimsolls and there were two strands of small, multi-coloured beads around her neck. But the main thing about her was that she was beautiful. She was as beautiful as any girl he'd ever seen before. She had the kind of beauty that you saw on the posters advertising foreign films. She looked sophisticated, not like a country girl; not like someone you'd have the chance to actually talk to. She was the sort of girl you'd expect to just catch a passing glimpse of, in a city street or at an airport.

Stephen hadn't prepared for beauty, he hadn't been expecting it, and the force of it hit him like a physical blow. It wasn't really a nice sensation. He felt a little bit hoodwinked. Nick had collected him from the train and shown him around and everything, but he hadn't warned him of this, hadn't even hinted at it; and now Stephen didn't have time to collect his features and stop himself from gawking at her.

'Hi, I'm Cass,' she said, stepping towards him.

Stephen felt himself blushing and hated himself for not being cool enough to greet her as if she was normal.

'And I'm Celia,' said her mother. 'Everything OK? Get here all right?'

'Yeah. Thanks. It's a beautiful place you've got here.'

Celia inclined her head in a slightly regal way, as if she were accustomed to praise.

'Cass can show you round, show you where you're sleeping,' Celia suggested.

Nick had already done both, but Stephen didn't say so and the older man gave no sign of having heard.

'Sure,' said Cass. Stephen wasn't going to say no: he wasn't going to say anything until he could feel his blush dissolving.

'Right, well, I might grab an hour in the studio, before dinner,' said Nick.

'You two carry on, I'm going to finish training these sweet peas,' said Celia.

Cass began to walk back towards the house and Stephen followed, a couple of steps behind her. She didn't walk like a film star. She had a sort of trudge, head forward, that was reassuringly like a human girl.

'Shall I show you your room, or do you want to see around downstairs first?' she turned and asked him.

'Your dad showed me, before.'

'Oh. Well, we could go for a walk, then? We could go down to the river if you like?'

'That'd be great.'

They skirted the kitchen side of the house and went across an apron of rough lawn to the front. The dog from the kitchen appeared, following them.

'This field is called the snowdrop field,' Cass announced, pointing.

Stephen saw only the thick pelt of bright grass, but he didn't want to reveal his ignorance with a question.

' 'Cause in February or March it's covered with them. I actually don't like them. I don't like the way they face down, as if they're sad. And they make you think it's soon going to be spring when it isn't. Not for ages.'

There was a steep drop from the garden into the field. Cass crouched down before jumping and Stephen followed suit.

'Do you know what that's called?' she asked him.

'What what's called?'

'That thing we just jumped off. It's called a ha-ha.' And she smiled. He realized that she hadn't smiled in greeting, that he hadn't seen her smile until now. Her teeth were smaller than he would have expected.

'Like, ha-ha-ha funny?' he asked, smiling back at her.

'Yes. It's a really silly name, isn't it?'

'Lots of words don't sound like the things they are, I guess.'

'Mm. Like perpendicular. Or rococo.'

'Or, I don't know, rubella.'

'Rubella?'

'My mum's a nurse,' he said, as if in explanation.

They both laughed.

'Lumbago, that's another,' he ventured, hoping she'd laugh again. But the moment seemed to have passed.

'What does your father do?' Cass asked.

'Engineering. Bridges and stuff. Roads.'

'And what about you? What do you want to be?'

Stephen felt shy again. 'I thought I wanted to design album covers, but now I'm not so sure. I think maybe I want to do something I can do in the open. I don't know if I'd be good in an office. Cooped up. Yourself?'

'It changes. Sometimes I think I'd like to be an architect; that's what I've been thinking recently.'

'Your dad's unusual – doing, you know, his figures as well as the farm.'

'He's actually an art teacher. The sculpting is a sideline. And the farm's more of a hobby.'

They came to a band of trees which grew along the river bank. They had to duck beneath low mossy branches to reach the big, smooth rocks at the water's side. Cass's hair was the colour of the shade beneath the trees.

'We sometimes see salmon jump, just over there.' Cass pointed.

'Do you swim in it?' Stephen asked.

'Yes. It's really cold, though. I'll show you where we go, if you like?'

He nodded and followed her back through the trees and along, in the same direction as the water. The river was clear and brown.

'Does your mum work?' he asked.

'Oh, Mum. She does lots of stuff. Sometimes.' Stephen didn't like to ask what that meant.

'Georgie wants never to leave here, but I want to go somewhere else,' said Cass.

'Like a city?'

'I'm not sure yet. Paris, maybe. I'd like to go to university in Paris. Somewhere like that.'

Were there other places like Paris? Stephen wondered but didn't ask what she meant.

'Right.'

'My family can be quite . . . well, you'll see.'

'They seem pretty nice. Easy-going.'

At this Cass laughed. 'People are always easy-going when things are going their own way,' she said.

It took a few days to fall into their rhythm. Nick asked Stephen to take over the care of the hens and collect the eggs each morning. He was set to work, also, repairing the sheep fencing at the top of the orchard. He'd been expecting long hours, but in truth these chores didn't take up much time at all. The hens had to be let out and fed in the morning and then shut up again at night, the bedding straw replaced every few days. They only produced a handful of eggs. There was a small round ironwork basket kept by the kitchen door, for the eggs. It was a French antique, Celia told him, which was typical of the Clarkes: a nice-looking thing, but impractical. It was easy to crack one egg against another, if you didn't put them in really carefully. The guinea-fowl didn't chase him again but, wary, he gave it a wide berth.

Celia was always the first to wake. When Stephen came down in the morning – he tried not to let it be later than 8.30, to be respectful – she was usually alone in the kitchen, standing with her back to the range with a cigarette in her hand, or sitting at the table with a mug of tea. She didn't seem to be occupied with anything, nor to read a newspaper. This was new to him: at home the adults got busy as soon as they'd finished breakfast, and expected the kids to do the same. No one at home left their cereal bowl or coffee cup unwashed on the table. Here things piled up until someone did a sweep and filled the sink. A cleaner came in three afternoons a week. Stephen often chanced upon Celia or Nick on different parts of the property, just standing still, staring into space. This, more than anything else, made him feel he could fit in at Stony Hill Farm. He knew what it was, to want to stop and ponder a while; to be struck by the way a shadow flitted across the trunk of a tree, or to wonder how you'd design something – the henhouse, the stile into the orchard – in a better way. His father had taught him that: whenever you handle something man-made, imagine how it could've been improved. He anyway liked to just take a minute. This was maybe the point of smoking, he thought. A cigarette gave a person permission to pause.

He'd been there for four days before Georgie came home, bringing the London friend she'd been visiting back with her. When he first saw her, he was relieved that she wasn't as beautiful as her sister. He still struggled to meet Cass's eye, still felt himself colour when they found themselves alone together. Her beauty was a barrier to friendship, not an invitation. Whereas Georgie was shorter, with hair that was three shades darker and fell more heavily. He couldn't help noticing that she had big bosoms. Something about her made him guess she could be temperamental. Helena, the friend, reminded him of a girl from home: blonde, wearing shorts made from cut-off jeans. She seemed more like someone brought up on a Cornish farm than either of the Clarke girls did: wholesome and straightforward. She smiled a lot, whereas the sisters did not, which made it hard to know what they were thinking.

At bedtime, the first night that Georgie was home, the three girls congregated in Cass's room.

'When Mum asked him if he's related to Sydney Nolan!' Georgie laughed. 'Poor Stephen, I've never seen anybody look so blank.'

'Well, I wouldn't have known who Sydney Nolan was either,' said Helena.

'Yes, but you're not an Australian whose name is Nolan,' said Georgie. 'He's meant to've been to art school, you'd think he'd have heard of him.'

'Oh come on, give him a chance. He's very sweet,' said Cass.

'Oooooh, Cass!' Her sister pushed her on the shoulder. 'Sticking up for him!'

'It's nothing like that,' said Cass. 'I just think he's a nice person. Harmless.'

'Do you think Mum's only just noticed that he's called Stephen Nolan?' said Georgie.

'Probably,' said Cass.

'You'd think she might've found out his name, before she asked him here for weeks at a time.'

'Well, I quite fancy him,' Helena announced.

'You don't!' said Georgie. 'Really?'

'Yes, really. Don't pull that face! He's lovely looking, hadn't you noticed?'

'All I noticed was the red hair. And the accent,' said Georgie.

'I like the accent,' said Cass.

'And I do,' said Helena.

'It makes you think he's being funny, even when he isn't,' said Cass.

'It *was* funny when he said that thing about how near the public swimming pool was to his house – the thing about the bee,' said Helena.

'*It's just a bee's dick away,*' mimicked Cass.

They all laughed.

'Well, you're here for long enough – you could seduce him,' said Georgie. 'He could be your summer paramour.'

Helena giggled. 'I just might give it a go.'

9.

There was a dinner party planned for the second Friday of Stephen's stay. A new history teacher had been appointed at the school where Nick taught, and had lately moved to the area with his wife. Some old friends would join them, with their son and daughter. They would be twelve, which meant using the dining room. The girls drifted in and out with flowers and greenery for the table while Celia rooted around in cupboards and found the gold cocotte dishes which she planned to use for the first course, baked eggs. Then she sat down, to write a list.

'I'll make my famous coq au vin, shall I?' Nick volunteered.

'Famous with who?' said Georgie. Her father stuck his tongue out at her. His tongue was oddly small and blunt, like a species of lizard.

'People'll have to ask, which came first, the chicken or the egg?' asked Celia.

'Ha bloody ha,' said Nick.

'Dad! That's a bit rude,' Cass remonstrated.

'Shall we bother with pudding tomorrow, or just have cheese?' said Celia, unperturbed.

'Oh no, let's have pudding as well. Might as well do it properly.'

'I'll do it,' said Cass. 'I'll be in charge of pudding. Dad, can you buy some cream, when you go to town later?'

The Clarkes did not as a rule eat anything sweet after a meal, which was new to Stephen. At home they generally had ice-cream, or a fruit pie for dessert; trifle on special occasions.

'Anything in particular you'd like me to do?' he asked.

'Could you lay? The table I mean?' said Celia. 'Then we won't have to think about it later.'

'Sure,' said Stephen.

'There are napkins in the drawers of the sideboard in the dining room,' she said. 'And we use the raffia mats. Oh, and Georgie, can you take the side-plates through? The majolica ones, you know.'

'No,' said Georgie.

'Yes you do! The green ones that look like leaves.'

'Oh. OK.'

'She's always especially useless when she has a friend staying, have you noticed?' Celia remarked, to no one in particular.

The history teacher and his wife arrived first and were introduced. Stephen never caught their names. The wife was pretty, with freckles and a small nose. They'd moved from East Anglia and were in love with the hills here, the walking. As Nick was refilling their glasses their other friends appeared: the adults in early middle age, a daughter of about thirteen and, lastly, a boy in his late teens. Stephen sensed the change in Cass as soon as they walked in, when a sort of stillness settled on to her. It would have been imperceptible to any other onlooker, but Stephen had made himself a connoisseur of Cass. He had been studying her out of the corner of his eye, looking whenever he knew she was absorbed and would not notice. He knew now what she looked like when she was reading, when she was exasperated, when she was about to contradict something someone was saying. He knew that the right-hand side of her face was ever so slightly more beautiful than the left, when viewed in profile; he knew that she moved the tip of her left thumb over the philtrum of her lips when she watched TV.

Now he understood why she'd suggested making an ice-bowl for tonight's pudding and had devoted so much of yesterday afternoon to it. She had gathered young vine leaves from the dilapidated greenhouse, and small blue flowers and daisies from the garden, and then she'd gone through all the mixing and serving bowls to find two that fitted into each other with a suitable gap. On the kitchen table she had poured water into the space between the bowls, then fixed the small one in place with masking tape she'd fetched from her father's studio, so that it wouldn't bob up. She'd pushed the leaves and flowers ever so gently into the water. Then, holding the bowls with both arms, she'd asked Helena to open the chest freezer in the outhouse. Stephen had never seen a bowl made of ice and couldn't imagine that it could be worth all the faff. You wouldn't want to eat it, after all; it didn't have any flavouring, it wasn't like ice-cream. But now he realized that she'd made it to impress the visitors' son. It was a sort of offering. A crystal chalice.

This apprehension occurred in a rush so that Stephen barely had time to take in the names of the new arrivals. Hamish and Lucy were the youngsters, Bruce and Carolyn their parents. The mother looked tired. The father was wearing orangey corduroys which were deeply ridged at the ankles, but had worn smooth over the knees and groin. Bruce and Nick made guttural, semi-animal noises at each other by way of greeting, instead of words. From this Stephen guessed that they were better friends than their wives. The history teacher looked on, a fixed smile on his face. Stephen at once felt sorry for the girl, Lucy, because she was younger than everyone else. Not so much younger as to be a pet, only young enough to feel awkward. She reminded him of Hazel, the older of his own sisters. She had the same look, half timid, but with a little hint of determination about her mouth.

At the table Stephen found himself seated between her and Helena. Nick at the head closest to them had the history teacher's wife on his right and Carolyn to his left; their husbands sat on either side of Celia at the far end. Hamish was in between the

Clarke sisters. Stephen tried to draw the younger girl out, but she answered only in monosyllables and did not return a question. Helena joined in, papering over the cracks by laughing a lot and saying 'Exactly!' at almost every word Lucy uttered.

As soon as the eggs were finished, cigarettes were lit.

'We always go in for inter-course smoking in this house: no waiting till after we've eaten,' Celia announced, to mild laughter.

'She always makes that joke,' Helena whispered. Stephen responded with a smile, while straining to overhear bits of what Nick was saying to the history teacher's wife.

'. . . I'm a very sensual person myself, that's why I can recognize it in you . . .'

'. . . I'd love to know when you were born, because I'm guessing that you'd have your moon in Virgo . . .'

'There's a secret creek not far away, I could show you if you like . . .'

If Nick had been single, Stephen would have been impressed at a bloke flirting so openly. Although getting into horoscopes was a bit corny, even for a teenager; leave alone a man of Nick's age. As it was, he felt a deep embarrassment. What if his daughters heard him? He didn't seem to have a thought for that. He was a married man, a dad.

When Cass stood and began to clear the plates, Stephen got up to help, as did Helena. Georgie was holding Hamish in conversation and didn't join in. Cass set down used crockery on the kitchen table and picked up the big bowl of new potatoes that were being kept warm on the top of the range. She smiled faintly as they passed. Helena brushed against him as they both moved to pick up the larger of the two casserole pots and he felt a little jolt of involuntary desire. Where did that come from? He didn't even fancy Helena, or he hadn't thought he did. Not that she wasn't pretty. Technically, if you saw the three of them lined up in a photograph, you might even have thought she was the prettiest. But the Clarke girls just had something, something else about them; and it was more intense because there were two of them. He wasn't sure if he really even liked Georgie, there was something in her, a flicker of spite perhaps, that he didn't trust. But still.

In the end room where the television was, there were art postcards propped up along the bookshelf. One of them was a picture of a young man leaning into a pond full of topless girls. It was as if the artist had caught the youth just before he toppled into the pool; as if the girls were tempting him in with their beauty and their silent, watery pleading and the gorgeous paleness of their naked flesh. The girls in the painting looked really similar to Cass and Georgie – the one on the left was especially like Cass – which was maybe why they liked the picture enough to display it in the first place. He'd turned it over to see who had painted it: J. W. Waterhouse, *Hylas and the Nymphs*. The nymphs were eerie because they looked so like one another. There was an otherworldly quality too, to the Clarke sisters. It pulled at you.

Back at the table, he glanced across at Cass. He hadn't had a chance with all these people around to consider what he felt about her liking Hamish. He wondered if everyone else knew that she liked the boy, or whether it was just he who'd noticed, because noticing things about her had become what he did with his time. He wondered how long she'd been interested in Hamish and whether Hamish reciprocated her feelings. Surely he did? He couldn't help hoping that she didn't actually love him, that it was just a crush.

Down at the far end of the table, Bruce was remonstrating with Celia about something. It had probably started as a jest, but now the volume and insistency had the taint of anger. Celia's features looked slightly smudged; from too much red wine, Stephen guessed. She tended to get that look, in the evenings.

'. . . because it's the modern personification of the Mithraic, that's bloody why! It's an essential expression of man's relationship with the barbaric divine,' Bruce said.

'It's just disgusting cruelty, the lowest form of bloodlust. They're all peasants anyway, the Spaniards. They don't know any better,' said Celia.

The rest of the table fell silent.

'But all festivals and rituals need peasants. Bums on seats. You wouldn't want to be too elitist, would you?' sneered Bruce.

'Are you on to bullfighting?' Nick called down the table. 'Oh, do let me join in, I love a good fracas.' He smiled at the history teacher's wife with a slight flourish, as if he were offering her a nosegay.

'Bruce thinks it's fine that they taunt and torture innocent animals,' said Celia.

'Well, they're Roman Catholics. They're used to blood sacrifice,' said Bruce.

'And what do you think?' Nick asked the history teacher's wife.

'God, you're crass,' said Celia. It wasn't clear which of the two men she was addressing.

Georgie stood up and pinged her glass with her spoon. 'OK everybody, it's time to cool it. And what better way than with delicious fruit salad chilled in a magic bowl fashioned from our finest Cornish water.'

'What fun!' said Carolyn brightly. 'Let me help clear while you bring it in.'

'We don't want any plebs here, do we?' Bruce shouted.

'Oh, shut up, Dad! You always have to have the last word,' Lucy called out. It was the most animated she'd been all evening.

Stephen helped Carolyn clear the main-course plates, while Georgie went out to fetch the pudding.

'Are you OK?' Stephen asked Cass in a low voice, when he came to her place.

'Fine,' she said, tightly.

Georgie reappeared with the glass bowl on a platter. 'Quick!' she called out to no one in particular. 'It's so slippery I'm afraid I'm going to drop it.'

The glass bowl was surprisingly large. It was beautiful, the vine leaves and flowers clearly visible through the frozen water. Everyone looked up and stopped talking when they brought it in.

'Look at that,' said Stephen. 'Nice one, Cass.'

'*Nice one, Cyril, nice one, son . . .*' the history teacher sang, then looked around expectantly, as if he was expecting the others to join in. But no one seemed to recognize the tune.

'What a lovely thing,' said his wife. 'I've never seen one of those before.'

'Lovely,' echoed Carolyn.

Stephen looked at Hamish, willing him to comment on the bowl, to praise it and by extension the maker of it, but he carried on smoking his Rothman cigarette and said nothing.

Cass said, 'Shall I bring it round, or leave it on the sideboard, so people can help themselves?'

'Put it on the side, it's too slippery to pass,' said Celia.

There was murmured assent. Everyone's voices were quieter now.

'Hang on, I've got a bottle of pudding wine somewhere,' said Nick. 'That Sauternes that whats-her-name brought, last time.'

He left the room and the history teacher's wife now addressed Stephen.

'So, whereabouts are you from?' she asked.

'Australia,' he said.

She grinned. 'Yes, I gathered that. But where? I've got family in Adelaide.'

'Ah, that's a long ways off,' said Stephen. 'I'm from Melbourne. Well, the suburbs of Melbourne it is, really.'

'Well done, Rosanna,' Celia called out. 'None of us have got round to asking him that, have we, Stephen?'

Stephen smiled. 'It's called Croydon. The area where we live.'

'Croydon!' Celia said.

'You heard of it?' Stephen asked her.

Celia had an odd smile on her face. 'No. It's only that there's a Croydon here, too. Somewhere on the way out of London. Ghastly sort of place, ribbon development. Crematoriums. Like Slough, but the other side.'

'*Come friendly bombs and fall on Slough!*' said Nick, appearing back in the room with the bottle.

'You see! That's just what I mean,' said Bruce. 'Celia pretends to be a lefty, but really she's the most frightful snob.'

'Says our friend the rich landowner,' Nick countered.

'A lot of Australian places are named after English places, as a matter of fact,' said Stephen.

Georgie stood up and pushed back her chair, which grated on the floor in protest at her abruptness.

'Who wants to come and listen to some records?' she said.

'But we haven't finished,' Celia protested. 'At least finish your pudding. There's shortbread to go with it, look. Someone hand it round.'

The history teacher talked about the bats in his garden – 'I thought they were nocturnal swallows, at first, because they fly so low' – while everyone else ate the fruit salad in silence.

Then Hamish stood, and a fraction afterwards Georgie. Cass and Helena and Stephen followed suit.

'You coming?' Stephen turned to Lucy.

'Yes please,' she said, grateful to get away from the grown-ups and their unfathomable talk.

They went into the end room. Hamish took an album from the box next to the gramophone and set it on his knees. He brought out a little plastic twist of what looked like treacle fudge, as well as Rizlas, a lighter and his own cigarettes.

'Oh great, I was going to ask you to roll a joint,' said Georgie.

So Hamish was that guy, Stephen thought. There was always one, at every party back home; not especially good-looking, not especially good to talk to; the guy who produced the dope, the one who the girls always fancied. The one with the battered Zippo cigarette lighter from which he was expert at commanding flame, but which invariably refused to light in anyone else's hands. Stephen wondered if these people practised their lighter skills in the mirror, back in the bedrooms of their suburban homes: flick, strike, flare; one seamless motion which made momentary Jim Morrisons out of them all. And how come the lighters were so battle-scarred, as if they'd been dented on some epic motorcycle adventure, as if their just-out-of-school owners were the stars of *Easy Rider* and not boys who rode everywhere in the back seats of their mothers' Toyota Corollas?

'What shall we put on?' asked Cass. 'Genesis, or Emerson, Lake & Palmer?'

'*Selling England by the Pound*?' said Hamish.

'Yeah, classic,' said Georgie.

Cass appeared to have been struck dumb.

'I hate my dad sometimes,' said Lucy. 'He's so . . . he just thinks it's so clever to annoy people.'

'Your parents are really different from mine,' said Stephen.

'In what way?' asked Helena.

'Well, we don't really talk like that at home. It's more about what we did in the day, what we're planning to do tomorrow. Little stuff, practical stuff.'

'Georgie's parents are really cool,' said Helena.

'Until Dad comes in here and puts on *Tea for the Tillerman* and starts singing along at the top of his voice,' said Georgie. She looked at Cass and they both laughed.

'I reckon Dad thinks he looks like Cat Stevens,' said Cass, joining in at last.

'Steve, you want some?' said Hamish, in a strangled, holding-his-breath voice, proffering the joint.

'Sure,' said Stephen.

The time began to drift. They played both sides of the Genesis and then one side of something else, before Hamish said it was a mood-killer and chose the next album himself. The one he selected seemed much gloomier than its predecessor, dirgey and tuneless, but the three older girls nodded along to it anyhow, with what looked like conviction. No one put the records back into their covers, but left them out on the table top next to the gramophone. Stephen fought the desire to prevent them getting scratched by at least reintroducing them to their inner sleeves. Away from the adults, Lucy became more and more talkative. She told a long story about how someone at the local riding stables where she worked on Saturday mornings had been mean to her, but the others weren't really listening. Hamish didn't seem to pay Cass any attention; it was Georgie he mostly interacted with. You couldn't really call it conversation. She would say something like 'I love this track' and he'd agree. Once he asked her to pass the ashtray. Cass looked more and more pained, Stephen thought. It was almost a relief when Hamish stood up and said, 'Cass, you coming?' and without a word she followed him out into the corridor. They heard the garden door open and shut behind them.

'I'm going to go through to the kitchen and see if there's any more booze,' said Georgie.

Once she was out of the room, Helena came and sat next to Stephen on the divan. She leant against him. She could feel her bosoms flattening against his arm.

'Ooh, I'm actually quite stoned,' she said. The idea came to her of pretending to fall asleep, half on top of him; but she couldn't be sure he'd realize this was a come-on. He might just lift her legs on to the divan and put a rug over her and leave her to sleep it off. He was that sort of person. He'd probably take her shoes off, first. And in any case, Lucy was still in the room, prattling now about a boy at school who'd given her a gonk and whether that might mean that he liked her.

'Do you have gonks, in Australia?' Helena asked him. It suddenly seemed incredibly funny to imagine: gonks at the Sydney Opera House, or on the Barrier Reef. Gonks in the pouches of kangaroos! Gonks held aloft by koala bears. Laughter frothed in her. She tried to communicate these comical images to Stephen, but he only looked puzzled.

'Yeah, we have them,' he said. 'My sisters have them, on the ends of their pencils and stuff. Bigger ones too. You can win them at fairgrounds.'

Helena couldn't stop laughing.

'We have all the same stuff you do, pretty much,' Stephen said. 'It's not a desert island or anything. It's a helluva size.'

Lucy's mother Carolyn came into the room.

'You ready?' she asked her daughter.

'I am, but Hamish has disappeared somewhere,' said Lucy.

'Oh, Hamish,' said his mother, as if she'd forgotten about him.

' 'Bye, then.' Lucy turned to Stephen.

'Yeah, 'bye,' he said. He looked at his watch and was surprised that it was after one o'clock.

Georgie came back into the room just as the others were leaving. 'Couldn't find any. There's some spirits on the drinks tray, only nothing I like,' she said. 'But it's freezing in here – shall we go through to the kitchen and warm up a bit?'

Helena and Stephen stood. Stephen went over to the record player and switched it off at the wall.

He glanced in at the dining room as they trooped through. The two lamps on the sideboard were still glowing and he went in to switch them off. At home the last person up always turned everything off. Between the lamps the remnant of the ice bowl was revolving very slowly on its platter, propelled by its own melting. It sat in a puddle in which some of the leaves and flowers, released from their icy casing, were now darkening. He lifted the platter and brought it through to the kitchen, careful not to slop water on to the floors as he went, although no one would have noticed if he had. Celia was still up, sitting at her usual spot at the table, smoking. She had a glass of whisky in front of her. Georgie went to put the kettle on, while Helena stood at the range, warming herself.

'Oh, well done, Stephen. Just bung it on the draining board, will you?' said Celia.

'Should I put it back in the freezer?' he asked.

'No, not worth it.'

He would have liked to have saved the bowl, but he did as she said. Georgie made a pot of tea, pouring out a mug for her mother first.

'Anyone seen Cass?' she asked.

'No. Probably gone to bed,' said Celia. 'That man was quite hard work,' she added.

'Bruce?' asked Georgie.

'Oh God no, not Bruce. That teacher. He barely said a word all evening.'

'His wife was a nice lady,' said Stephen.

'Bad luck to be married to a bore like him then,' said Celia. She began to laugh, pleased with her remark.

'Oh, Mum,' said Georgie, half-reprovingly.

'I'm going up,' said Helena, having gulped the last of her tea. ''Night, everyone.'

In the car, as they were negotiating their way, drunk, down the lane, the history teacher's wife had said, 'Never again. I never want to set foot in that house ever again.'

'Oh really?' said her husband. 'I thought they were rather

entertaining. We'll probably have to, anyway, because he teaches at the school, remember? More or less runs the art department, apparently.'

'That man is really awful. He's all puffed up with himself, like some horrible little Puck in boots.'

'His wife was quite fiery. I don't know how much of it you could hear, down at your end, but she gave their friend Bruce quite a tongue-lashing,' said the history teacher.

'He seemed pretty dreadful, too. His wife looked exhausted. Probably from having to live with him.'

'The daughters seemed nice though. And it's an amazing house, you must admit.'

'The house was nice. And the handsome Australian boy.'

'What's he doing there?'

'I didn't get around to asking.'

'I wonder if they'll all be like that. The rest of the staff, I mean.'

'I shouldn't think so. I hope not.'

In the other car, Carolyn was driving.

'You should've gone to look for Hamish,' she was saying. 'Now I'll have to go back and fetch him tomorrow.'

'I don't know why you couldn't have looked for him. Anyway, I can get him if you can't be bothered.'

'I was in the middle of a conversation with the teacher's wife.'

'Yes, she looked interesting. Didn't catch her name, did you?'

'No.' Carolyn sighed. It was predictable that Bruce would describe a younger, pretty woman as interesting.

'Typical of Nick to put her next to him,' said Bruce.

'Well, he couldn't very well not,' said Carolyn.

'The Australian boy was nice,' said Lucy from the back seat.

But her parents were thinking their own thoughts about the evening and neither of them answered.

★

Stephen didn't draw the curtains in his room. He liked sleeping with the window open, and the curtains too. He wondered where Cass had got to. Of course she would have a boyfriend, he should've known that as soon as he first set eyes on her. But no one had mentioned Hamish, that was what had thrown him; if he'd known, he could've got himself ready, psyched himself up. He wasn't sure what he'd have prepared himself for, though. He wasn't sure, either, whether it made things worse or better that Hamish was so ordinary. If he'd been the best-looking guy ever, or the cleverest or the funniest, at least then he'd have been worthy of Cass.

He'd think about it in the morning. For now he was tired. He lay, looking at the milky softness of the moonlight which fell across the carpet, drifting towards sleep. And then the door opened and there was a figure in white standing in the patch of moonlight, matching it; and the arms rose, lifting the filmy whiteness of her nightdress up and over so that it fell away.

'Budge up,' said Helena, lifting the covers and sliding naked into the single bed beside him.

'Hi,' said Stephen, opening his arms to take her in.

'Hi,' she said.

10.

One morning early, when it was just he and Celia in the kitchen, Stephen asked her about the little glass-topped table on the landing outside his room. The table was in the shape of a clover leaf and had two compartments or shelves, both topped with bevelled glass, in which a number of old medals lay. Their ribbons were frayed and looked faded; the velvet lining each shelf – perhaps once a rich, sunny yellow – was now as pale as unsalted butter. It was mottled, slightly bald in patches, like a patch of dried-out, badly mown grass.

'That's a fair old number of medals you've got in that case upstairs,' said Stephen.

'What?' said Celia.

'The table up on the floor where I'm sleeping. The one with the medals.'

'Oh yes, you mean the trefoil table. It's rather pretty, isn't it? I think my great-great-grandmother had it made specially for her husband's medals.'

'Mum mentioned that someone in the family had won a medal, one of our ancestors, if that's what you'd call him. It's a pretty big deal, isn't it?'

'William Gale, you mean. He won the Victoria Cross, which is the highest medal there is. His set are on the lower shelf and then there're some First World War ones from my father's side of the family on the top. The VC is the dingiest-looking one, oddly enough. They were made of base metal on purpose, so they wouldn't have any value. The value was all in the honour of the thing. It was to discourage soldiers or their widows from selling them.'

'Do you know how he won it? Must've done something pretty spectacular.'

'I'm not entirely sure. Battles aren't really . . . I can't pretend to be very keen on military history. It's meant to be an important one, I do know that much. The medal. Because of being one of the first, you see. It came to me when Mummy died, the little table. It used to be in my father's study, at home.' She sighed.

'Yeah, I don't know much about your wars and stuff. Still, it's great to know someone related to us did good. When was the Crimean war?'

'I don't know that they're our wars, particularly. I can't quite remember the date. Victorian, in any case. Obviously.' Celia was already bored and well on the way to becoming irritated. She didn't want to have to give a history lesson, at this hour of the day. And she felt slightly caught out for not being surer of dates.

'I don't know a lot about that. Nothing, actually.'

'Well, you'll know about Florence Nightingale. It was the one she nursed in.'

'No.'

'You must've heard of Florence Nightingale! Everyone's heard of Florence Nightingale!' As Celia spoke, Georgie came into the room.

'I don't recollect hearing that name.' Stephen's neck had gone pink.

'The Lady with the Lamp,' said Celia. 'Georgie, do you know, Stephen here has never heard of Florence Nightingale!'

'So what?' said Georgie, lifting the lid of the bread crock.

'It's not a thing we study in school,' said Stephen. 'Who was she, anyhow?'

'Well, she . . .' Celia found quite suddenly that she could re-call absolutely nothing about Florence Nightingale.

Georgie interjected. 'Didn't she clean up the hospitals? Wasn't it that they all used to die from their wounds going gangrenous in the heat, but she invented disinfectant. Or carbolic soap, or something. Cass did a mini-project on her, do you remember, at school? We could ask her.'

'Yes, yes, carbolic. I think that was it,' said Celia. But she wasn't sure.

'Oh. Right,' said Stephen. He didn't want to annoy Celia by asking any more questions.

Celia could be friendly, but she had a harsh side and you never knew when it might come out. She seemed to pick on Georgie in particular. Generally it was when she'd been drinking her red wine: her eyes would get a glassy look and sometimes there'd be a dark line, like a scab, along her lower lip. But she could be a bit sharp at any time. Nick was safer. As long as he was talking about himself – inviting you to share his wonder at himself, really – he was all right. Georgie was more like her mother, but she could also be unexpectedly kind. She thought more about other people than Cass did, even though Cass was a gentler soul.

A couple of times Nick had invited Stephen into his studio. He'd begun to sculpt a bust of his head, but it hadn't developed as he'd wanted so he'd abandoned it and done some drawings instead. Lord knew if he ever had an exhibition of his stuff, or sold anything. It wasn't clear to Stephen what the Clarkes lived on, money-wise. It was a big place, for a teacher: huge, if you included the outbuildings and the land. They called it the farm, but it wasn't a proper farm: they certainly didn't live off the land or what they grew on it. Neither of the girls had holiday jobs and apart from gardening Celia just seemed to float around. Their cars weren't new and they didn't seem to go out to fancy restaurants or anything; if there even were any fancy restaurants in this part of the world. But even so: four people living a life of leisure on a teacher's salary just didn't add up. Stephen asked Helena about it, one night when they were lying in his bed. They never spoke before they made love, too hungry for each other's bodies to waste time on words. But afterwards they often stayed up late, talking in whispers, even though they didn't need to. There was no one else on the top floor of the house to overhear them, but their hushed voices gave them a feeling of delicious complicity.

'Celia's the one with the money,' said Helena. 'Or what's left of it. Georgie told me that Celia had thought there'd be more; when her mother, the girls' granny, died there turned out to be less of a legacy than she'd been expecting. Old money always runs out, that's what my mother says. Celia's grandfather was a lord, or something. That's where the posh furniture comes from. And the china. You know, those plates with gold rims and crests and stuff.'

Stephen had never heard his mother or father mention any lords, so he supposed this must be on the other side of Celia's family, nothing to do with the Nolans.

'Was this house his place, then?'

'No, she and Nick bought it when they were first married. There was some sort of trust that Celia got on her marriage. They'll tell you, if you ask: they're proud of what a bargain it was. It's a long way from anywhere, down here. If it was in Surrey or somewhere it would've cost them a fortune.'

'So how come Nick works, if they're loaded?'

'They're not really loaded. They get a special rate for the girls' school fees, because he teaches there. Anyway, he likes it. He likes getting all the attention from the pupils, the girls especially. He's a bit of a cult figure at school. He takes everyone to the pub in Truro and buys them ciders. Lets them smoke in art classes. Does an autumn trip to London, to the Tate and the

National Gallery. You can imagine how he likes standing in front of some huge old painting, explaining it to everyone. Most summers he takes a group out to Italy, to see the pictures. He does Rome one year, Florence the next, so the A-level students can go on both. He hasn't done it this year, I'm not sure why not. Maybe there weren't enough pupils doing art history.'

'Have you seen his feet?'

'No! He always wears those little boots, doesn't he?'

'In his studio the other day he had bare feet and some of his toenails were painted, different colours.'

'You're joking!'

'No. Honest truth.'

'When you say "some of them", what do you mean?'

'Well, you know, some of them. Just two or three on each foot.'

They both began to laugh. 'Do you think Celia does them for him?'

'Ew, creepy,' said Helena.

'He's actually really nice,' said Stephen.

'Yeah, he is. I've been coming here since me and Georgie were first friends, when I came to the school four years ago. He's always really generous. They're great, the way they never interfere, they just let you do what you like. Compared to my parents. I can't move at home without my mother asking me where I'm going or what I'm doing.'

'How come you go to school so far away from where you live?'

'I had older cousins who came here. My mother thought it'd be more fun for me than being an only child in London. She's at work a lot.'

'Do you get, you know, lonely?'

'I did at first. You get used to it. Cass and Georgie are lucky, they're day-pupils.'

Helena was meant to be going back to London, but she kept putting it off. Her parents were divorced and her father was taking her – together with his two younger children from his new marriage – to the South of France: she'd have to go in time for the trip. But for now there were three days in a row when the sun shone and it was hot; real summer heat, the kind of hot that Stephen recognized, when the backs of your knees stuck to the sticky plastic of the car seats.

'You should've been here last summer, in the drought. It was boiling,' Georgie told him.

'It was the best summer ever,' said Cass.

'We all know why *you* thought it was,' Georgie taunted.

Stephen, always alert to signs which might help him to decipher Cass, pricked up his ears.

'Shall we make our way down then?' said Cass, ignoring her sister's remark.

They were going to swim in the river for the first time since Stephen's arrival. The four of them trooped down the snow-drop field, not saying much. As on the first day, they followed the narrow path along the bank, winding in and out of the dappled shade of the trees. Today there were clouds of midges dancing near the surface of the water. At their swimming place a knotted rope swung out from a high branch across the water. The river curved here, and the water deepened around it. A few feet further along there was a gap in the trees where the flat rocks at the water's edge had been paled and warmed by the sun. They left their clothes here and their towels; except Georgie, who carried on a way along the path.

'Where are you going?' Helena called out to her.

'I want to skinny dip – I'm going to get in down here.'

'She's got the curse,' Helena whispered to Stephen.

'Pardon me?' said Stephen.

'Her period.'

Stephen recalled that girls at school had sometimes given in a note to the teacher to get off swimming: it was rumoured that you couldn't swim at that time of the month. He wondered if it was because there'd be blood in the water, or whether it was that the girls got cramps. The thought of Georgie menstruating in the river stirred an unfamiliar feeling in him.

It didn't occur to him that Helena's recounting of intimate details went two ways. After the third night Helena had spent in Stephen's room, Georgie couldn't wait any longer to be told what she called 'the gory details'. Helena had had her morning bath and was getting dressed in Georgie's room.

'Well, are you going to leave me in suspense for ever . . . what's he like?'

'Not like you'd think. He's pretty fantastic, actually,' said Helena.

'How come? Does he recite Shakespeare's soliloquies while he's fondling your tits?'

Helena threw her hairbrush in Georgie's general direction. 'No!'

'What, then?'

'He's really good at it.'

'No!'

'Yes. And he's got a big knob.'

'Like how big?'

'Big.'

'Blimey. I wouldn't have guessed that somehow.'

'I know.'

They both pondered the mystery before them.

'I mean, how does he compare to Danny Gillespie?'

Danny Gillespie had been in the year above them at school – the same year as Cass – but had left at the end of the Easter term, less than halfway through A-levels, because his parents were moving back to America. By some kind of odd, unspoken osmosis, he had been selected by almost every girl in their year as the boy to take their virginity. The girls who wanted to lose theirs, in any case; which was only a handful. As the two oldest in their year, Georgie and Helena had been the first. Danny Gillespie was mild and sweet-looking, with a nose like a button mushroom, and his accent was a turn-on. But it was tacitly agreed that he wasn't the sort of boy you'd fall in love with.

'Oh goodness, so much better. No comparison. Better than Piers, too. And I thought he was pretty OK.'

Georgie had not much enjoyed her two-night stand with Danny Gillespie, the second evening an attempt to improve upon the rather sore and unsatisfactory event of the first. She had not repeated the experience with anyone else, but Helena had gone out with a boy called Piers who was the brother of a London friend, and she claimed to have slept with him several times.

'He's really natural and gentle and just . . . just lovely, actually.'

This revelation had caused Georgie to re-evaluate her opinion of Stephen. Shy, smiling, red-haired Stephen, with his daft Australian twang. Maybe he wasn't such a clodhopper after all.

Standing in their bare feet on the warm rocks, they had taken off their clothes. Helena had a blue and white striped bikini, Cass a red one. He was used to being around a lot of half-nude females, at the local pool and on the beach at home, but he sensed the girls' curiosity and felt suddenly embarrassed by his Speedos. He'd never given his trunks a thought before now: it was fine when there were loads of boys around, but he was acutely aware of being the only one here.

Cass was the first in. At first Stephen didn't think he'd be able to stay in for any length of time. The water was shockingly cold after the warmth of the day, like a slap. His feet turned a strange yellowy white, but he got more used to it each time they swam, clambering back across the rocks to the rope after a few strokes, to swing themselves again across the brown rippling water.

Glancing downriver, he caught sight of Georgie. She was naked on the bank and the sunlight, filtered by the trees, fell in pools across her skin, catching her throat and her belly. Her breasts in shadow looked heavy, like the carved breasts of a statue. The weight of her hair was like another shadow, falling across her features. Seeing her there, just before she stepped into the water, felt intensely private. It was like a glimpse of a solitary animal, like the sight of a deer through green trees in that moment just before the creature becomes aware of being watched. Georgie seemed somehow to be outside of time; as if she was the first girl ever to have come to this riverbank; the only human in this wild place. It made something in him constrict and ping, like a rubber band snapped against a wrist.

Stephen felt pretty confused. It was already a bit of a situation. To be fair to himself, living in a house with three girls, it was bound to get complicated. Each night, Helena came and got into his bed and they turned to each other, naked and oddly familiar, as if they'd always known each other. Stephen woke earlier than Helena and slipped out of the room, leaving her sleeping. Sometimes they made love two or three times a night, ardent and tender. But during the days there was no alteration in the way they were around each other. Helena was Georgie's friend and spent her days with Georgie; while Stephen didn't really belong to anyone in the house. He did whatever Nick asked him and offered to help more besides. They all dispersed, meeting at lunch and again just before dinner. In their waking hours the most Helena and Stephen would do was grin at each other, sometimes, when the others weren't looking.

He liked Helena very much. Actually he liked her the best of the girls. But the strange thing was that when she was in her clothes, in daylight, he didn't really fancy her. Well, no more than he fancied any half-good-looking female. When he was making love to her he never imagined that she was someone else:

he concentrated on her happily, on her essence. He was totally absorbed in her body. It would have felt wrong to think of someone else. Yet by day he constantly imagined making love to Cass. He pictured her hair falling over his face, or trailing down across his belly. He pictured her knees drawn up. Her face. Everything. When Hamish had turned up it had interrupted these imaginings: for the next few days he had found himself envisaging Hamish with Cass, which was horrible. It had felt as if darts of ice were being constantly thrown at him; an actual, physical sensation of pain. Mercifully, these images had abated.

But this glimpse of Georgie had thrown him. It was like taking off your sunglasses on a bright day: he felt dazzled. He tried to bat it off by thinking of the things he didn't really like about her: the way she teased her sister, the annoying habit she had of calling attention to herself, the trace of a moustache across her upper lip. She was quite bossy. She treated Helena as a sort of glorified handmaiden; not even glorified, in actual fact. And yet her breasts as pale and plump as a seagull, the darkness at her groin; the way she'd lifted her arms and held them out, for balance, so she wouldn't lose her footing on the slippery river-pebbles . . . Even the thought of her toes in the cold water, curling over to keep her grip, made him catch his breath. He didn't want to be thinking about her, but it was like being tugged by a current under the water, a current you couldn't swim against.

On Helena's last evening, at dinner, Celia suddenly challenged him: 'I keep meaning to ask you, how is it that you're related to us?'

Stephen didn't get it. During the conversation he'd had with her about the medals on the top landing she'd known full well how they were related. Why was she saying she'd forgotten, now?

'It's through the medal guy,' he told her. 'Gale. He was my dad's great-grandfather. I'm pretty sure that's what my mum said.'

'But your name's Nolan,' said Celia.

'Well, our name's Clarke and the VC hero wasn't called that, was he? Anyway, Stephen's mother wrote to you ages ago, explaining it all. Remember?' Nick joined in.

'He was called Gale,' said Celia, ignoring Nick.

'Stephen just said that, Mum,' said Georgie. Celia ignored her.

'William Gale. That's why Mummy had it as her middle name. She was going to make it my middle name too, but she said it was such a nuisance that people always got it wrong. You know, filling out forms, passport applications. As in Gail the girl's name.'

'Oh, do regale us with the lost glories of your family tree,' said Nick. 'It must be at least a fortnight since you last told us about them.'

'Well, at least I *had* a family. People who were quelqu'un. Not just civil servants from Solihull, or wherever your people sprang from,' said Celia.

Nick put his head in his hands. 'Shropshire. You know bloody well it's Shropshire.'

'You did all right, thanks to my family,' Celia persisted. 'I didn't see your lot put anything into this house.'

'You should have married a landowner, is that what you mean?' asked Nick.

'Did you have anyone in particular in mind?' asked Celia.

'Guys!' said Georgie. 'It's Helena's last night. We're meant to be having fun.'

Cass stood up abruptly. 'Who wants coffee?' she asked.

Stephen was the only one with a driving licence. Nick said he could take his car to go into Truro for the weekly Friday night disco. It'd be fun to see Helena off with a party. She wore a yellow halter-neck top, which fastened at the neck and back with red binding. Her breasts pointed upward, like the snout of a little terrier. Cass was in a floor-length skirt with a purple crochet top and Georgie wore her velvet trousers and a turquoise shirt with a big collar and wide sleeves. With the front of her hair pinned up and a swoop of eyeliner to match the shirt, she looked exotic, older, as if she'd come from a job as a croupier in Las Vegas. Stephen had one good shirt with him, white with a cowboy-style piping across the chest and cuffs. He'd ironed it that afternoon.

The disco was in an old Baptist hall. Stephen didn't like dancing all that much, but after a couple of beers he could usually be persuaded to at least sway along to the music. Georgie and Cass weren't physically self-conscious; that was one of the things that drew people to them. Within seconds they were on the dance floor, alternately jumping and wiggling their hips from side to side in each other's direction, laughing and joining in at the top of their voices:

Ain't gonna bump no more with no big fat woman

Stephen felt shy with Helena by his side. He felt as if she was expecting something, but he didn't know what it was. Did she want him to ask her to dance? Or was she hoping for some kind of assurance from him, that he'd wait for her; wait until she came back from France and then come to her in London? But he couldn't say that, because he didn't know. He didn't have a clue, really, what would happen. He didn't want to promise anything, because that wouldn't be right. You should never make a promise unless you were sure you'd keep it.

Cass and Georgie came back over. 'Someone's rolling a joint out the back if you want to come,' Cass told Stephen, leaning up and into him to make herself heard above the music. Her breath on his cheek caused him pain and longing: so close to kissing and yet so far from her intention. He and Helena followed them out to a parking area. There were dustbins by the wall, and a couple of girls he'd never seen before.

Helena had told Stephen that she didn't really like to smoke, but it was her last night and she obviously wanted to be part of the group, so she took the joint and inhaled a couple of times before passing it on.

'It's strong shit, quite trippy,' the joint roller assured them all. He was an older boy with a leather jacket.

'Yeah,' said one of the unknown girls, earnestly.

'Come on, let's all go and dance together,' said Georgie, suddenly impatient with the solemnity required of the smoking.

Back in the hall, Georgie took Helena's hand and Helena grabbed Stephen's. Cass skipped alongside. A song they all loved came on and the four of them swirled around and around, their hands linked, singing along:

> . . . *You'd laugh and run away*
> *And I'd chase you through the meadow*
> *Without you I'd die*
> *Let's never say goodbye*
> *Oh, Lori . . .*

It was the perfect summer song, with its carefree image of a boy riding his bicycle while the girl he loved balanced on the handlebars. The falsetto chorus lent it an innocence which would come to haunt them all whenever they heard it, in later life; when their lives grew, stretching like shadows thrown by that one long summer. *Let's never say goodbye.* Already there were one or two boys at the disco who shunned such sugary pop: they were cultivating impressive glowers to sit beneath their peculiar coxcomb hairstyles and refused to dance unless something by the Stranglers came on, or the Sex Pistols. Then they'd make a particular point of moving energetically with their open cans of beer in their hands, welcoming the spewing foam that spilt out, darkening the fronts of their jeans. But for now Cass and Georgie and Helena and Stephen were happy to ignore the new cynicism, to twirl around each other, joyful and a bit giddy.

'You will come and see me, won't you, when I'm back in London?' Helena asked Stephen, when he woke her early the next morning. She'd tried to play it cool with him, not to talk about the future, but lying next to the warm familiarity of his long, pale body she felt a flutter of panic at losing him. The imminent parting made him urgently dear to her, whereas the time of his proximity had been calmly fond.

' 'Course. I'll be heading to London anyways, when I leave here,' he said. He wouldn't go to London and not call on her. 'But you'll be coming back this way to school, won't you, after the summer?'

'I know, but . . . I suppose we don't know how long you're here for?'

'Well, the invitation was to help out on the farm over the summer, so that's until the end of August, is it, I'd guess?'

'I s'pose it is. Around then.'

'There you go then,' he said. 'I'll see you in the city.'

Celia had an early appointment in the town and was taking Helena to the station there. Georgie and Cass – both barefoot in Victorian-looking white nightdresses – and Stephen and Nick came out to the yard to wave her off. Stephen felt himself flush as he bent down to kiss her briefly on the lips. He'd never kissed Helena in front of the Clarkes before and although he knew they knew, it felt suddenly exposing. The prospect of the day ahead felt flat to him, after she'd gone. He hadn't realized the extent to which he'd come to depend upon her, the warmth of her atten-tion that was reserved for her nightly visits to him. It was that, as much as the sex. The feeling of somebody especially liking you. He suddenly felt very far from his family. The Clarkes were great – amazing, really – but they were unpredictable. He found himself, for the first time, missing the quiet routine of his own home.

Routine. That was the thing. Once the car was out of sight down the lane and the girls had padded back into the house, he turned towards the walled garden and the hen-coop. He liked the quiet gurgling of the hens in the mornings, the warmth of the bedding where they'd sat, the satisfying weight of an egg cupped in the palm of your hand, as if it was designed for no other purpose.

He knew there was something wrong as soon as he saw the trail of sticky feathers, leading from the enclosure towards the trees beyond. There was a quality to the silence which wasn't right. Inside the coop there were feathers everywhere, as if someone had emptied a pillow; so many feathers that it took him a few moments to understand that the birds weren't moving. Couldn't move, because their heads had been bitten off and discarded, as carelessly as sweet-wrappers. And then he saw a living eye surveying him. In one corner was a little black and white speckled bantam, still alive.

Perhaps the predator had been disturbed before the orgy of killing was complete, or perhaps it had missed the bird in the frenzy of it.

The living bird upset him more than the dead ones. He felt his throat constrict, tears come to his eyes. The poor little bird must've been so terrified. He approached, moving as slowly and un-jerkily as he could so as not to frighten it more, and managed to pick it up and cradle it under his arm as Celia had taught him to, holding its legs in his hand. He could feel its heart beating against the soft skin of his forearm as he took it away from the carnage and out into the light morning.

Stephen didn't know what to do. He knew this was his fault, totally. In the excitement of getting ready to go to the disco last night he'd forgotten to shut the hens up. It wasn't like he had a whole lot to do, here, but he'd failed even in the small task that he'd been given. He'd let them down.

Still with the bird under his arm, he went to look for Nick, who'd vanished into his studio as soon as Celia had driven off. He felt too sheepish to walk straight in and knocked instead. Nick didn't call out to come in, but appeared at the door and stood in front of him. Seeing the concern on the older man's face made the guilt unbearable. Stephen began to sob as he tried to explain what had happened.

'No, no – you mustn't be upset. It happens at least a couple of times a year. We've all done it,' Nick assured him. 'Fucking foxes! They only ever take one, two at the most. They just kill the rest for the fun of it.'

'Yeah, but I . . . I never shut them up last night,' Stephen wept.

'Honestly, we only asked you to do the hens because we're so hopeless about remembering ourselves. Between you and me, the noise drives me mad in any case, right outside my studio. It's Celia's thing, really: she likes hens because her parents kept them. Why they have to make such a bloody commotion every time they lay an egg! They may as well be serenading the fox to come and get them.'

'Look, I'll get you replacements if you tell me where I can find them. I'll clean up the mess,' said Stephen, calmer now.

'No need, honestly. Our friends Bruce and Carolyn'll give us some more. They've always got a glut. Be great if you would dispose of the evidence, though. You could get one of the girls to help you. Celia will mind, otherwise.' He smiled at the boy. 'She liked that bigger brown one, I suppose it didn't escape? No?'

'Just this little guy. Girl,' said Stephen.

'Lucky she's not here. You've got plenty of time to tidy up the carnage before she gets home.'

Stephen didn't have the heart to ask Georgie to help him,

much less Cass. He felt too ashamed. And he didn't want them to see that he'd been crying. He wondered if the surviving bird felt traumatized by the sight of all the feathers, or by being brought back into the henhouse. She didn't seem too fussed. He couldn't scoop up the mess with just one arm, so he set the bantam down on the ledge where the birds had sat. Gently, gently. He stood still beside her so that she would become used to his presence, but the henhouse was too low for his full height, so he had to stoop. He tried to move smoothly, not to alarm her. He generally liked the smell in there, a peaty smell of straw and warmth, but now it began to cloy. He deliberately looked the other way as he gathered up the feathers, afraid to see entrails, or severed heads. He imagined finding a disembodied hen's claw, yellow and scaly and somehow prehistoric. He prayed he wouldn't, but the image of a bird's talons curling upwards to scratch for air – like the hand of a man buried alive – lodged itself in his mind. The picture was so vivid that it felt like presentiment.

Suddenly he was burning, his mouth full of saliva. He was going to chunder. He was too doubled over to run, so he propelled himself – it was almost like diving – out of the coop and on to the morning-cool grass outside. He lay on his front, the grass tickling his face. He could smell the earth. It was lonely, to be in this place. He thought he might never move again, but stay there until the grass grew up around him. He remembered that Cass had shown him a spot at the bottom of the snowdrop field, where a deer had lain. It had left an impression in the shape of a bicycle seat and a neat, shiny pile of droppings, like chocolate raisins. He wondered if his body would leave a shape in the rough grass. Sometimes he had a floaty sensation, as if he wasn't tethered correctly; as if he was not a real person but just an assembly of sensations and feelings, lighter than air. He almost felt that if someone came to find him they'd see no one there.

11

'He'll have to go,' said Celia. The children had gone down to the river to swim and she was alone in the kitchen with Nick.

'Because of the hens? Are you still annoyed about that?'

'Only fairly. But he's getting too attached to the girls, I can just feel it. It'll end in tears, as Nanny used to say. It was better when he was sleeping with Helena. She's more his speed. Kept his mind off Cass and Georgie.'

'Mind, or hands?' Nick teased her.

'Both. I just think it's slightly asking for trouble to have him here, a boy from the back of beyond, with two beautiful girls in the house.'

'I like him. He's no trouble. I was thinking we might've kept him on, for the apple-picking.'

'They get stupid, when they think they're in love.'

'Who, boys?'

'Young people. I don't think it's a very good idea, Hamish sniffing around Cass again. I thought that was just a fling, last summer.'

'Seems pretty harmless to me. Anyway, you're the one who said Stephen could come,' Nick reminded her.

'I don't want anyone to get in a state, that's all.'

'The voice of doom.' Nick went across and hugged his wife.

'The voice of reason, more like,' she said, not hugging him back.

Stephen had been despatched to Bruce and Carolyn's farm to collect new hens as replacements. Cass had gone with him, in theory to show him the way – all those little lanes were impossible to navigate, unless you were a local – but her real motive had been to see Hamish, Stephen supposed. In the event, Hamish hadn't been there. The daughter was out at the stables.

Carolyn had been more animated than she'd seemed at the Clarkes' dinner and invited them to stay for lunch. Bruce had appeared just as they were sitting down to eat. Stephen, ever sensitive to the smallest alterations in Cass, felt something like hostility emanate from her towards the man. If this was so, Bruce himself betrayed no sign of being aware of it.

'What-ho, cobber!' he said in a bad Australian accent. 'It's our friend from down under!'

Stephen smiled politely.

'Are you a cricketing man, yerself?' Bruce continued, still imitating the accent. 'Following the Ashes, at the mo? Bet you didn't take too kindly to that thrashing at Old Trafford.'

'I don't really follow cricket,' Stephen said.

'That man Packer wants shooting,' said Bruce, in his real voice this time.

Stephen thought, not for the first time, how slow English people were to take a hint. Sometimes it was as if they didn't listen at all. Still, he tried to be polite.

'My dad says the same thing, if I recall rightly. But, like I say, I don't follow it myself.'

Bruce looked at Cass, as if to enlist her in the folly of Stephen's position. But she ignored him and turned to Carolyn instead.

'Has Hamish gone to collect Lucy? I thought I'd told him we were coming.'

'No, I think she's there all day today. He's . . . actually I'm not sure where he's got to.'

'Oh.'

'I'd been hoping to say hello to him,' Stephen interjected,

untruthfully. He wanted to cover up Cass's disappointment. 'Was going to ask him if he wanted to come to Friday's disco with us this week.'

'Hamish doesn't like dancing,' said Cass.

'Yeah, well, he could come along for the company,' said Stephen.

'I expect he'll turn up,' said his mother.

'You looking forward to going home, Steve?' Bruce asked Stephen.

'Yeah, we'll see how it goes,' said Stephen.

'When are you off?' Bruce persisted.

'He's with us for the summer,' said Cass. 'Ages yet.'

'Guess I'll head to London when I'm done here,' said Stephen. 'I'm not in any rush to go back.'

Hearing himself say these words surprised him. He missed his family, sometimes acutely, and yet his life at home felt almost like someone else's life, now.

'I did a season on a cattle farm up north when I was about your age,' said Bruce.

'In Australia?' asked Cass.

'Yes. They were old friends of my parents, who'd emigrated. They thought it would teach me some discipline, farm-work. It did, too. Bloody long days. We had to get up at dawn and ride for hours, some mornings.'

'They're pretty big, a lot of those cattle farms,' said Stephen.

'Huge,' said Bruce.

'I don't think Stephen is going to learn much discipline from us,' said Cass.

'No,' said Carolyn. 'I don't expect he is.'

Hamish appeared in the kitchen at Stony Hill Farm a couple of days later.

'Oh good,' said Nick. 'I need some brawn, I want to shift

around a couple of things in my studio. If you're here I might go and find Stephen, then you can both give me a hand.'

'Sure,' said Hamish.

'Dad! He's not your private removal man,' Georgie protested.

Georgie and Cass were out in the yard standing around when they'd finished.

'Shall we go up to the orchard?' Hamish suggested.

'Or for a dip in the river?' Georgie said.

'Orchard,' said Cass, and somehow that decided it.

Right up at the top, just below the summit of the hill, was an old dovecote. It was a round building, with many patches where the plaster had come off. There were holes in the roof and no door, but the walls still had the wooden partitions where the birds would have nested, stacked like so many open shoeboxes. It would have been nicer to sit on the grass beneath the trees, but they trooped in and sat instead on the earth floor of the dovecote, like children making a camp.

'I've got something for us,' said Hamish. He pulled a small leather wallet out of the back pocket of his jeans and from it produced a little fold of paper. Inside were four tiny squares of paper.

'What is it?' asked Georgie.

'Acid,' said Cass.

'But doesn't that make you go crazy and think you can fly and stuff?' asked Georgie.

'You don't have to do it if you don't want,' said Hamish.

'Will it be OK though?' asked Georgie.

'Sure,' said Hamish. 'You've got us to keep you safe. Anyway, if it's too much you can make yourself come down with vitamin C. Eat some oranges.'

'Really?' said Stephen.

'It's quite gradual,' said Cass. 'It comes on fairly slowly, so you're sort of used to it by the time you're fully tripping.'

Hamish was still holding the paper in his upturned hand. Georgie leant forward and took a square, then Cass. Hamish held his arm out towards Stephen. After a moment's hesitation he too took a piece.

They all waited for Hamish to go first and put it in his mouth. Then the tension of the moment somehow evaporated and they all leant back against the cobwebby pigeon boxes and giggled.

Cass told Hamish about his dad putting on an Australian accent to talk to Stephen. She imitated him and for an instant it was as if the spirit of Bruce had come among them: she just had him.

'I didn't know you could do impersonations,' said Stephen.

'I can't really,' she said.

'Yes you can,' said Georgie. 'You're brilliant.'

'You are,' said Hamish. It was the first nice thing Stephen had heard him say to her.

'Who can you do?' asked Stephen.

'Oh, I'm not like Mike Yarwood, I can't do politicians or people on telly. Just people I know, really.'

'She can do you,' said Georgie.

'No I don't! I don't do you,' Cass said.

Stephen felt his smile fix on his face. It felt almost sore, like when the dentist filled your mouth with that pinkish plaster to take an impression and you had to stay still.

'I don't do you, honestly,' Cass told him. 'All I did was imper-sonate a phrase you'd used because we all thought it was funny. I only did it once. It was when you said something was only an ant's dick away.'

'A bee's dick,' said Stephen. The relief made his eyes prick, as if he might cry. So she hadn't been sending him up behind his back, mocking him.

There was a pause, which Georgie broke. 'A woodlouse's vagina,' she said. 'A ladybird's groin.'

They all began to giggle.

'A fly's flies,' said Cass.

'I don't get it,' said Hamish.

'Good one,' said Georgie. 'A beetle's bollocks.'

'A cockroach's crotch,' said Stephen.

'A dung beetle's arsehole,' said Georgie.

They laughed and laughed and laughed.

They did acid once a week or so for the next month, when Hamish would come over, bringing the drugs. Once they took it down by the river. This was Stephen's best time. The late afternoon light was like a liquid, creating eddies across the darkness of the water. Like gravity-defying syrup, it slid up the trees as the sun dipped lower behind the hill. He was transfixed by the bark of the tree-trunks, how it seemed almost to glow from within. If the sun could shine on to things, maybe it could gather in them and shine back out? He couldn't stop moving the flat of his hand over the warm rock where they were sitting, its smoothness against his palm satisfying a kind of skin-thirst. He heard trills in the sound of the river and it seemed to him that this must be where birds found their song. It was fucking amazing! It was like being a part of nature, being right inside it, hearing its secret music.

Sometimes Cass and Hamish would go off alone together and he and Georgie would sit side by side, somewhere out of doors. Time went weird: two hours could feel like brief minutes, or moments could swell into something momentous and grand. They'd sit up in the orchard or down by the river and what felt like a whole afternoon might only have been half an hour; or else dusk would pass unnoticed and they'd be surprised to find themselves out under the stars in the late summer darkness. Luckily Celia and Nick never fussed about whether people turned up to supper, but just left food out on the table.

Occasionally Georgie and Stephen would lie on the two divans in the end room, playing records. You could hear things you didn't normally notice and get very caught up in it; but music could suddenly jar, too. The mood had to fit.

The fourth or fifth time they took acid together, it wasn't fun. Instead of leading them out into the beauty and mystery of the world, seeming to reveal its hidden connections, the acid drove them inwards. It was as if they were being propelled towards an unsuspected darkness. They all felt it. There was a sourness, a creeping sort of unease. Cass and Hamish went up to her room, saying they were going to try and wait it out lying down. Hamish muttered something about a bad batch.

'Shall we do the same?' Stephen asked Georgie.

'Yes,' she said. 'Your room's better than mine, I haven't got associations up there. I don't want to see my old dolls and stuff now, I think they might freak me out.'

In his room the window was shut and the air felt hot and still.

'Oh God, I'm just going to lie on the floor actually,' said Georgie. 'I'd get seasick on the bed I think.'

'You OK?' Stephen asked. He felt frightened, suddenly. He didn't know what he would do if she started panicking, who he'd turn to. Celia and Nick might blame him if she had a bad time, might think he'd supplied the drugs. He lay on the bed on his front and shut his eyes. Shapes danced across his closed eyelids, as they did in the moments when you closed your eyes after looking up at the sun; only now they didn't stop.

'Can you hold my hand?' asked Georgie.

'Of course, here,' he said.

He reached out his hand to her. It felt nice to be touching another person. He appreciated the warmth of it. This sense of the body-heat of another person seemed very intense. He almost fancied he could feel her pulse, hear the warm blood thrumming through her.

'It must be pretty horrible, being a snake or a lizard,' he said. 'Having cold blood, you know? So that you have to go and find a hot rock or something to warm yourself up.'

'I don't think they mind,' said Georgie.

'I guess not. I guess you're right,' he said, but he didn't feel certain of it.

When Stephen woke the next morning he was alone, still dressed in his clothes, although he'd somehow crawled under the covers. The rancid sensation had not gone away and he felt sadness pressing down on his skull like a physical weight. He ran himself a deep bath and lingered in the soft water until he began to feel better. He went out on to the landing, his bath towel around his waist, yesterday's clothes over one arm. On his way back to his room, he stopped next to the trefoil table. He knew there was no one else on this floor and from the silence he judged that none of the Clarkes were on the floor below, either. He'd hear if anyone was making their way upstairs, because of the lack of carpets. Not that anyone could object, anyway; he only wanted to feel the medal, to hold it in his hand. Just for a minute. There was nothing to say he shouldn't, the glass lids of the table didn't seem to be locked or anything, although he saw that there were little brass-edged keyholes cut into the wood of each of the two lids. The man who'd won them was his ancestor too, after all. Celia and Nick had never said he wasn't to touch the medals, or indeed anything in the house.

The medals beneath the glass of the top layer were nice: silver and shiny, with colourful ribbons. If you didn't know, you'd think they were the interesting ones. The ones on the lower layer looked somehow a bit shabby. Maybe no one had ever given them a polish. It was true what Celia had said: the Victoria Cross was the dullest-looking one of all, the least eye-catching. Stephen lifted the lid and picked them up in turn. One had a faded crimson ribbon edged with green, with an enamelled crescent moon encircling a star, and what looked like Arabic lettering in a circle around a mini sunburst. There was a silver one which had a portrait of a young Queen looking left, and above it little scrolls with tiny acorns at either side which bore the words: Alma, Inkermann, Sebastopol. Lastly, he picked up the Cross and closed his fingers around it, so that the points dug into his skin. It was dingy on the landing, so he wandered back to his room and stood by the window, to look at it more closely. He could have fitted another three of them on to the flat palm of his hand. It wasn't as heavy as it looked. The ribbon was a dull colour, like the dregs of red wine in an unwashed glass.

It felt weird to Stephen, to think that his great-great-grandfather had held this medal, had treasured it. It'd probably been his proudest possession. He might have looked at it every day, might have picked it up and held it in his hand, just as Stephen now did. On the front was a lion standing on top of a crown − completely out of scale − and the words *For valour*. It occurred to Stephen that valour was a word he had never spoken, and would probably never have occasion to speak, as old-world and foreign to him as the medal itself. He wondered about the deed that had won it. He picked it up and turned it over. There was a date inscribed there. He thought he might like to find out about it, teach himself some of the history around it. Then he heard Cass calling him from the bottom of the stairs, and he was jolted back into the present. He needed to find a clean T-shirt and socks.

At the kitchen table there was no sign of Celia or Nick, but Cass was already sitting, a mug of tea in her hands. She looked grey and shaky.

'I've made you a boiled egg and some toast,' she said. 'It may've gone a bit hard by now.'

'Aw, thanks. Is Hamish still here?' he asked her.

'No, he went when it got light. We didn't get much sleep. Jesus. That was not fun.'

'Yeah. Pretty rough.'

'Mum suspects. She's not in the best mood.'

'You do look pretty awful,' said Stephen.

'Thanks.'

'I didn't mean . . .'

'I know.'

'What does your mum think you've been doing, anyhow?'

'Hard drugs, probably. They've always said they don't mind if we smoke pot, as they call it, but that anything else is a no-no.'

'My parents would be really disappointed if they knew I'd even smoked,' said Stephen.

'Sometimes I think it'd be easier if mine were like that,' said Cass.

'Nah, you're lucky.'

'She doesn't like me seeing Hamish, I don't think. She's been quite snippy with me.'

'Well, maybe she thinks he's not a very good, you know, influence.'

'Yeah. Maybe,' said Cass. But she looked doubtful.

Celia usually checked on the henhouse morning and evening now, although Stephen still topped up the hens' feeder and water and cleaned out their bedding. He went out into the brightness of the day, to see to the birds. Sadie the guinea-fowl trotted along behind him and he threw her a little corn. The new birds weren't in any case laying yet. When he came back down the post had arrived, bringing a letter from his mother. It was plump and crinkly. Stephen was always amazed that flimsy air mail paper could make it all the way across the world without tearing or falling apart. It was like the outer casing of garlic, so thin that the impress of the biro carried right through it, yet it had come all this way, undamaged. She'd enclosed a photograph of an old painting and a family tree, for Celia. When he saw how neatly she'd written it out, he felt a pang of missing her: her orderliness, her calm. On the back of the photo was a white sticker with 'Portrait miniature of William Gale, later VC. Probably painted during the 1840s.' The sticker, too, touched Stephen: how much thought she'd put into it, not writing directly on the back of the photo because the ink might've shown through the image, or smudged.

Enclosed, too, were notes from each of his sisters. Eight-year-old Karen had drawn lines across the page, so her writing wouldn't dip as it came closer to the paper's edge. 'Dear Stephen, we miss you I went to sleep in your room I told your bear you wood be home soon. Is it nice in England? Send me a letter just for me, love Karen. xx'

He unfolded Hazel's note. Almost thirteen, she had begun to dot her i's with little circles and he saw that she had drawn a couple of smiley faces after her name, in place of kisses. 'Hi Stephen, we waved you goodbye, did you look down and see us? We didn't know which was your plane so we waved at all of them.' He hadn't stopped to consider that they might not have driven straight home. It was touching to picture them craning upwards as one jet after another sailed away into the blue, taking their brother, their son, so far away from home. Hazel went on: 'I baked some brownies, they were pretty good. Dad had three! Lydia in my class is having a pyjama party on Saturday for her birthday, I hope Caroline Mackenzie won't come she was mean to me. When you come back I will let you win at Monopoly! Please write to me, your sis Hazel Nut.' He felt guilty now for not having written to his sisters. He'd been so caught up with the Clarkes and their world that he'd barely thought of his own family.

Celia and Nick appeared with French bread and cheese for lunch and tomatoes in a brown paper bag. Once they'd made sandwiches and were sitting down, Stephen handed her the family tree and the photograph of the painting.

'Well, that's Gale, certainly,' said Celia. 'I wonder how your father came to have this. We've only got a photograph from much later, when he's all whiskers.' There was a trace of indignation in her voice.

'My mum says in the letter, hold on . . . "The portrait miniature was bequeathed to Gale's first wife, Alice, by his sister Caroline, along with various other effects. Her capital and property went to her nephew George, né Gale; who later went under the name George Nolan."'

'Oh yes, I'd forgotten about the first wife. We're descended from the second one, Sarah. They had three daughters and the youngest, Harriet, was my great-grandmother. I looked it up, after we'd talked about it the other day. At least I think that's it, it's so hard to keep track of the different generations.'

'Is this your Boer War man?' asked Nick, glancing at the photograph.

'Crimea, not Boer,' said Celia. 'Although they're all a bore, aren't they? Not the people, but the wars. Nothing drearier than battles and dates.'

Celia handed the papers back to Stephen.

'Mum says you can keep the picture and the family tree.'

'Oh. How kind,' said Celia. 'I wonder why your fellow George changed his name, does your mother know?'

'I've never asked her. I could enquire in my next letter if you like?'

'Perhaps he was a criminal of some kind,' said Celia.

'I don't see why he would be,' said Nick, glancing in Stephen's direction. Tact was not chief among his wife's virtues.

'Lots of the first English settlers were criminals,' said Celia, undeterred.

As the day wore on Stephen's headache abated, but the sadness persisted, like a growing hollow inside him. He didn't think he'd take acid again, after this. He never felt very good afterwards, but this was much worse than the other times had been. It wasn't just physical – the head, the heavy limbs, the slight edge of queasiness – but he felt weepy and alone. When he glanced in the mirror after having a pee, his face looked swollen, as ugly to him as a hatful of arseholes. He felt bad in his own skin.

Nick and Celia were going out to friends for dinner and Cass disappeared to her room early in the evening.

'Shall I make you my treat supper?' Georgie asked him.

'Sounds good,' he replied.

'You won't think so when you see what it is,' she said.

'Try me.'

He sat at the table while she put a pan of water on the stove and fished around in the larder for a packet of spaghetti. The Clarkes had real spaghetti in a long dark blue packet with Italian writing on it, not like the short-cut macaroni they had at home.

'Do you know what I miss?' he asked Georgie.

She raised her eyebrows in answer.

'I miss Icy Poles. Oh and Sunny Boys, they're good too.'

'What on earth are you on about?' Georgie smiled.

'Lollies. The ices we have at home. Sunny Boys, they're orange-flavoured. They're in the shape of a triangle, there's a pointy bit of cardboard at the top that you tear off with your teeth. And Paddle Pops. Banana Paddle Pops. And caramel ones! They're the best.'

'Oh, I wish you hadn't mentioned lollies – now I want one. A strawberry Mivvi.'

'You don't keep any in your freezer?'

'No, we only get them when we're out. At the garage, or sometimes if we go down to the seaside. You haven't been to the beach, have you, since you got here? We should go. Next time it's a hot day.'

The water had come to the boil and Georgie stood over it, concentrating as she spooled the gradually softening spaghetti and folded it into the water. She found the colander and stood it ready in the sink.

'OK, now I'm going to add masses of butter and then – this is what makes it so delicious – ketchup.' She shook great dollops of tomato from the glass bottle.

'That's it?' he asked. It never ceased to tickle her, his way of saying 'it', so it sounded like 'eet'. She grinned at him.

'Yup. My ultimate supper. Spaghetti à la ketchup.'

'It's a lot better than it looks,' he conceded.

After they'd eaten they sat at the table for a while. It was warm in the kitchen and although neither of them said so, the other rooms downstairs felt too cavernous for them. The starchy food made them both feel a bit better, but they still felt bruised, fragile. When Stephen stood and stretched his arms and said he was going up to his room, Georgie padded after him.

'Are you going to lie on the floor, like you did last night?' he asked, smiling.

'I thought I might get into bed with you actually,' Georgie said.

'Oh. Right.'

He took off his jeans, but kept his T-shirt and pants on. Georgie followed suit. Stephen got into bed first and Georgie slipped in beside him before turning on to her side, so that her back lay along his front.

'I love spooning,' she said. 'Sometimes I go into Cass's room and make her spoon me. When it's cold.'

Stephen didn't answer. He was too concerned that he might get a stiffie and was trying to think of other things, to stop that happening. He tried to picture the remains of the spaghetti in the pan downstairs, the chickens, the smell of plaster – or was it clay? – in Nick's studio. But the memory of Georgie, naked on the riverbank in the dappled sunlight, kept inserting itself. And now here she was, in a bed with him, his bed. He felt a tell-tale warmth begin to gather around his groin.

'Look, I'm not sure this is a very good idea,' he said.

She wriggled herself around to face him.

'Because of Helena?'

Stephen felt a flash of guilt. Helena hadn't even entered his mind.

'Well, no. More because . . . I don't know. Just because.'

'We don't have to do anything. It's just nice to have the company.'

'Yeah, but . . .' he trailed off, too embarrassed to explain himself.

'We don't have to do anything,' she said again; but even as the words were coming out of her mouth she was pressing herself up against him, her face now so close to his that he could feel her breath enter his mouth.

Georgie clearly didn't know about his feelings for Cass and maybe didn't care about either of their feelings for Helena. That's what he reasoned now. Otherwise she wouldn't be doing what she was doing, unbuttoning her shirt and twining her legs around his. Maybe he could just go with the moment too, relax into this new and unexpected thing, not worry about the consequences. Maybe it would all be fine.

12.

Hamish's parents had gone off on holiday, to stay with friends in a rented house in the Dordogne, taking his sister with them. He had the house to himself. He didn't arrange the party until they'd been gone for three days, just to be on the safe side. Last year they'd left their passports and traveller's cheques in the kitchen and had had to turn around and come back for them. Luckily he'd only had a couple of friends over that time, but he didn't want to risk his family appearing this year, when he'd invited loads of people.

Stephen had driven Cass and Georgie over in Nick's car. Cass had been in her sunniest mood, her feet up on the dashboard. Georgie sat directly behind him, occasionally snaking her right arm around the outside of the driver's seat so her sister wouldn't see, to stroke his shoulder. Since the night she'd come to his room, they'd been sleeping together in his narrow bed. After the second time, she had confided that she'd thought she was going to be one of those people who don't really like sex. But now she did.

'I was going to experiment on you,' she said.

'So I was just a guinea pig?'

'Yes. Pretty much. I thought if it went badly at least I wouldn't have to see you every day afterwards, at school.'

'Oh. Thanks for that,' he said, stung.

But she didn't notice. 'It's my pleasure,' she said, smiling.

Being so delighted to learn that she wasn't condemned after all to a life of celibacy made her adventurous: she did things that no girl Stephen had been with had done before. Not that there'd been so very many: two girls back home and one New Zealander in a youth hostel in London, before Helena. But this was different, freer. There wasn't an inch of him that Georgie hadn't tasted; the back of his neck, his underarms, even his bum. She'd giggle as she manoeuvred their limbs into new positions, as if they were giant dolls. 'Let's try it like this,' she'd say.

It made him fancy her more than he'd ever fancied anyone. Every minute that they weren't entwined he now imagined her, imagined them together. But he still held a torch to Cass, he just couldn't help it. Georgie was more alive than her sister, more daring: he guessed that Cass would be much more passive in bed. But he couldn't stop himself loving her, reserved as she was and slightly serious and to him infinitely tender. He felt protective of her in a way that he'd only experienced towards his kid sisters. He knew it was hopeless, he wasn't stupid. But still he couldn't switch off the tap of his heart.

Almost as soon as they arrived at Hamish's house, Cass disappeared into the crowd. Georgie stayed by his side as they went to find drinking glasses to fill with the cider they'd brought. On the kitchen table there were big glass jugs topped with fresh mint and slices of fruit. On the side, by the glasses, were several empty bottles of the Pimm's and lemonade which had gone into the pitchers.

'Ooh, I love Pimm's, let's ditch the cider and have that instead,' said Georgie.

'What is it?' said Stephen.

'It's a kind of summer fruity drink. Made with gin, I think. It's not very strong.'

She poured long glasses for them both and they wandered through the rooms. There seemed to be quite a crowd. Hamish went to a different school from Cass and Georgie, and many of the guests were his schoolfriends; a crowd that no one knew but him. The dining-room table had been moved back along the wall and the room thronged. Some people Georgie knew were in the sitting room, playing records and chatting.

Stephen realized something wasn't right when the drums seemed to be louder and more insistent than the guitars or the singing. It wouldn't have seemed off to him, except that this was Led Zep, and weren't they all intricate, winding guitar arrangements and plaintive, wailing vocals? It was the song about the Vikings, with dark-sounding lyrics about Valhalla and Norse Gods and bringing ships to new lands. He'd never noticed the drums on it before. He'd never known drums be so . . . well, so interesting. They seemed to keep coming in at the last possible split second, so that the guitars were nearly bolting away beforehand, only reined in at the very precipice of chaos by the drums. The drums were like the cavalry, rescuing desperate troops on the hill of battle. He wished he could play the song again. He wished he could fall into the drums like falling into a pool.

He couldn't remember how long they'd been sitting there. Had they played both sides of the Led Zeppelin? What had they been listening to before that? But now the music had stopped while someone flicked through a box of albums; and without the jumble of sounds to attend to, the feeling lost its auditory magic and became unmistakable. It was acid.

'Georgie?' he said. His voice sounded as if it was coming from somewhere other than his own head. 'Are you OK?'

'I feel weird, actually,' she said.

'I think that punch must've had something in it,' said Stephen.

Georgie didn't respond. He could see her as if through a magnifying glass, folding in upon herself.

Her whole being seemed like one of those time-lapse films of a flower opening, only she was doing it in reverse.

They sat side by side on a low sofa, comforted by the sensation of each other's legs and arms against their own. Someone put on an Emerson, Lake & Palmer record, but it didn't reveal its secrets, if it had any, to Stephen; it just sounded like noise. Noisy noise.

'I feel sick,' Georgie said.

'Let's go outside for some air,' said Stephen, taking her hand.

They went out through the kitchen door and around to the quieter side of the house, where they sat on the grass outside the window of Bruce's study.

'Any better?' Stephen asked her, after a few minutes.

'Yes, much,' she said. 'That's awful of Hamish, to spike the drink. If anyone freaks out it'll be his fault. I wish we could just go.'

'We'll have to stay here now until after we've peaked,' said Stephen. He felt frightened at the thought of navigating the narrow lanes in the dark while he was tripping. 'And anyway, we couldn't leave Cass.'

'Let's just lie here,' said Georgie.

Stephen lay on his front, Georgie on her back. They didn't talk much. Words didn't feel of much utility to them. The sounds of the party floated out across the late summer air.

The ground cooled and dampened beneath them as the noise coming from the house grew more raucous. After a time there was a thrum, like the buzzing of flies. Stephen rolled over and sat up. The sound grew louder, becoming a roar. He saw a number of lights flickering towards them from the lane. All at once a group of eight or more motorcycles drew up and their riders dismounted, two from each bike, removing their helmets and shaking out their long stringy hair. They were older than the people at the party, young men of perhaps twenty-two or -three. Several of them carried bottles. There were a few girls with them, barely distinguishable from the men in their leather jackets and jeans.

'Oh shit. There was a rumour they were going to show up,' said Georgie.

'They're not Hell's Angels, are they?' said Stephen, scared.

'No, no. They're just St Austell Greasers. Hamish buys dope off one of them, that's how they'll have heard about the party. They won't hurt us. They're fine, just a bit boisterous.'

But it didn't feel fine, even from out here. Something had shifted and darkened and didn't feel right.

'We could go back in and look for Cass?' Georgie suggested.

Inside, the temperature of the party had risen. All the rooms felt pressing and over-warm. The bursts of laughter jarred, as if the sound sprang not from merriment but from the desire to defuse threat. Stephen had a metallic taste in his mouth and he felt afraid, of what he did not know. A sense of unease pressed down on him; a physical sensation, as if someone was attempting to push him underwater. All of a sudden Cass appeared at his side.

'Let's go,' she said.

'Really?'

'I've had enough of it here,' she said.

Hamish disappoints you all the time, Stephen thought, but I wouldn't. If I was in his shoes, I wouldn't let you down.

'Did you drink the punch? It's definitely spiked, I feel kind of poisoned,' he said.

Cass looked closely into his face, tilting her own as she considered him.

'You do look a bit green around the gills. Shall I make you a cup of tea before we go?'

'That'd be great.'

She disappeared and Georgie came and stood where her sister had just been.

'I can't find her,' she said.

'She was just here. She's gone to get some tea.'

Georgie leant against him. Cass came back with a mug of tea.

'Oh good, there you are,' she said to Georgie. 'Once he's drunk this we can go.'

'I thought you'd stay over,' said Georgie.

'No. Hamish doesn't . . . I'd sooner go home.'

Stephen drank the tea and the heat of it cleared his head somewhat. But still he couldn't shake off the feeling of apprehension. He didn't know whether to tell the girls this, whether to say he wasn't ready to leave yet, that he needed a little longer to get back to rights. But Cass was impatient to go, he could see that, so he followed her out of the house and to the car.

'I'll go in the back,' she announced.

Georgie got into the passenger seat.

It was funny how you could do mechanical things almost in your sleep, however you were feeling. As soon as he took the key out of his pocket, the sequence became automatic. He had to back a couple of times to turn the car around in the cramped yard, but it was no problem. Maybe he'd feel better once they got out of there. Hamish's place was down in a dip: maybe that was why it'd brought him down, being there. The doomy feeling he'd experienced was horrible.

Now the warm night air came in through the open window, denser somehow than daytime air, as if soft dry brushes were caressing his face. They climbed the track, up and up. The roots of trees twisted in the high banks which lined the lane. Lit up by the headlights they looked like something from a fairy tale, gnarled places where goblins or fairies might gather. They processed through a series of inky glades where branches met above the lane and made the night darker. Stephen drove very slowly.

When they came to Tregony it was as if a spell had broken. Everything felt normal again, or almost. The small quiet streets were orderly. The feeling of dread Stephen had been carrying began to ebb. Once they got back to Stony Hill Farm, he thought, they could have bowls of cereal at the kitchen table and laugh off the evening as just one of those nights when nothing quite falls into place. It was funny: you could have the perfect place and the perfect setting – a whole farmhouse to yourselves, far down a track where no neighbours would tell you off if the music got too loud – and yet a party just didn't come together. He wondered now if Cass would tell them why she'd wanted to go home, whether something had happened. Probably not. She tended to keep things to herself.

Emerging from the western edge of town, Stephen turned on to the big road. Not long to go now. There was very little traffic at this time of the night; or morning, as it now was. He accelerated as Georgie put her hand on his thigh, feeling lighter than he had all evening. And then out of nowhere there was a sound like a bomb going off.

He was lying on a wide grass verge by the side of the road. Someone must've lifted him out of the driver's seat, or had he climbed out himself? But where was the car? Where were Georgie and Cass?

Someone was saying his name.

'Stephen,' he heard. 'Stephen. We're going to put you in the ambulance now, OK?'

'I can walk. You don't have to carry me,' he said.

'We're going to pop you on to the trolley, my love, just to be on the safe side. We don't know if you've broken anything.'

'I'm OK. Really, I'm OK,' he said. But he didn't know if he was. He felt sore and exhausted. Tears began to roll down his cheeks. He wished with all his heart that he was at home. He wished his mum would come out of the night and hold his hand.

As they lifted him he saw the other ambulance, its doors closing. There was a police car with its light flashing and beyond it, the car he'd been driving, its side buckled, windscreen shattered. There was another car beyond it, at a strange angle. He could taste blood inside his mouth.

'Are my friends OK?' he asked.

'You're a very lucky young man,' the male paramedic told

him. 'You've had quite a nasty bump, but you're going to be fine. One of the girls has been in the wars, but she'll be all right. If it had happened during the daytime it might have been a different story. If you'd hit other vehicles when your car spun round.'

He didn't feel lucky. He felt like the unluckiest person in the world. He'd broken Nick's trust in lending him the car; he'd broken both Nick and Celia's trust by not being careful enough, driving their daughters. The girls had accepted him into their home, their family. Georgie had welcomed him even into her own body. And he'd hurt them, done them harm. He wanted to be a good person, kind and reliable and considerate of others, as his parents had brought him up to be. But he wasn't. He wasn't a good person. And now he'd ruined everything.

'Can you tell me any more about my friends? Are they all right? Is Cass all right, the girl who was in the back?' he asked the woman paramedic, who was sitting in a small flip-up seat beside the trolley.

'We won't know till we get to the hospital and the doctor sees them, my darling. A few fractures, I'd say. Bruising, certainly. I don't think it's anything worse, but like I say, we don't know yet.'

Stephen felt his face become hot. The shame was scalding. What if the paramedic wrote down what he said? What if there was a police report and it got read out in court, somehow? Then they'd know that he'd asked about Cass first. Georgie would know. Cass would too. What kind of a person wouldn't ask about the girl he was sleeping with first? A bad person, that's who.

'You don't sound as if you're a local man, are you, my love?' coaxed the paramedic, seeing the frantic look on Stephen's face. Sometimes they got frightened, these young ones.

'Australia. Melbourne. Well, just outside. But people have mostly heard of Melbourne so it's easier to just say that.'

'Hot is it, over there?'

'Yeah. It gets pretty warm,' said Stephen.

'Lucky you came to this part of the world then. We get the best of the British weather, in the summers. Should have been here last year: it was boiling then. Beaches were packed out.'

'People have their Christmas on the beach, at home.'

'Hear that, Tony?' she called to her colleague. 'They eat their Christmas dinner on the beach!'

'Well, we maybes have our dinner at teatime. You don't want a roast on the beach.'

'Be nice though, to celebrate outside.'

'Yeah, it is,' said Stephen.

As much as he didn't feel he was deserving of her kindness, it was a balm. She was a nice lady. Nice, like his mum. Not like all the complicated people he'd been with this summer.

At the hospital he was wheeled in across a waiting area, where a handful of people were sitting on orange plastic chairs. One of them was moaning. He hoped he might catch a glimpse of Cass and Georgie, but they were nowhere to be seen. He was taken straight to a cubicle.

'Perk of coming in with us lot, you get seen first.'

His friend patted him gently on the shoulder.

'Right, well, they'll look after you from here. Remember us when you get home and you're in your paper hats, pulling crackers by the sea,' she said.

Stephen felt his eyes fill with tears again. He didn't want her to go.

'There'll be a nurse along to see to you shortly,' she said.

'My mum's a nurse,' he said.

'Well, there you are then. You're one of us.'

Once she had left him, Stephen could no longer keep down the sobs which had been banking at the top of his chest. He didn't have a hanky with him, so he wiped his nose on his sleeve, then rolled the fabric over so no one would see.

Someone came to take his blood pressure and shine a torch into each eye. Someone else took his pulse and asked if he'd been drinking. His limbs were checked over, his neck and back too. It all seemed to take a very long time. He wasn't sure if this was really so, or whether it merely felt slow because he was very tired. At least the acid had worn off and the crying had made him feel less tainted, as if the tears were a sort of moral rinsing. Whatever came next was going to be worse than waiting around in a cubicle, of that he was certain. The police hadn't asked him to breathe into a bag or anything; he wondered if that meant that they thought the accident hadn't been his fault. But what had happened? Would he be prosecuted? Could he get deported? He wished he could picture what had occurred, but there was just the noise it had made, as loud as a jet engine; as loud as any sound he'd ever heard. Louder. In the split second before he blacked out it had sounded as if something the size of a small building had exploded on the roof of the car. Or someone had fired a gun. He hadn't had a clue what it was, the sound had been so overwhelming and sudden that he hadn't had time to think.

He felt hungry. He wished he could see Cass and Georgie, ask them what had happened. Eventually a nurse put her head around the curtain and said, 'Someone's come to pick you up.'

Stephen stood and walked back along the corridor towards the entrance. The linoleum on the floor made the soles of his shoes squeak. He remembered this later, he wasn't sure why. The waiting area seemed different in daylight, less like a dingy last-chance saloon, more brisk; like a departure hall at a coach station. Nick was standing near the doorway.

'Hi Stephen,' he said.

'Nick, look, I'm really, really sorry. You know I'd never want to hurt the girls, right?'

'Let's get out of here,' said Nick.

Stephen followed him out across the car park to Celia's car.

'Celia's put your stuff together, so we can go straight to the station. I think that's the easiest way to do this.'

'Pardon me?' Stephen said.

'Your things. Celia went up to your room and packed for you. She doesn't want to have to see you; doesn't want you coming back to the farm. She's too upset.'

Stephen couldn't take in what he was hearing. 'Are they all right? Are the girls OK?'

'Georgie's broken her collarbone, she's in a lot of pain. Cass's wrist is broken. She's got a really nasty bruise under her chin from the impact. It's absolutely awful, frankly.'

Nick, who had a lit cigarette in his right hand, now inhaled fiercely. But Stephen felt a surge of relief so intense that he had to fight to stop himself from laughing.

'Nothing else? I mean, they're going to be OK?'

'What do you mean, nothing else? Isn't that enough? You've broken the bones of our daughters, left them encased in bloody plaster of Paris like a pair of mummies. They won't be able to write or paint for weeks. Cass won't be able to play her flute. We're going to have to cut up her food for her. Christ!'

Through force of habit, Stephen was at once intrigued to learn a new fact about Cass. He hadn't known she even owned a flute, much less played one. He hadn't noticed either of the sisters doing much painting or writing, either; but he didn't say so. He just felt overwhelmed with relief that neither of them was seriously hurt. Young bones would mend, he knew that.

The consolation of understanding that Cass and Georgie were going to be all right was so great that the fact he was being removed from them hardly registered. He could maybe spend a week or two in London, he reasoned inwardly; come back after that, once Celia had calmed down.

'I don't know what happened back there. The road was empty, I . . .'

'It's pointless trying to justify it now. Celia wanted you to go after the henhouse fiasco. She said you'd make trouble and you have. I should've bloody listened.'

Stephen didn't know what to say. 'Oh mate, I'm just so sorry.'

Nick seemed to deflate a little, at this. He looked less puffed up with fury, more rumpled and tired.

'We've been up all night, you can imagine. When the call came from the hospital we were absolutely shattered. Then we had hours of waiting before we could get them home. Celia's completely done in.'

'Do the girls know that I'm not coming back with you?'

'No. They're both asleep.'

'Oh. Right.'

'We didn't see any point in prolonging the agony. Celia wasn't in the best of tempers when she went to collect up your things, so it was rather rushed. But I don't think she missed anything; you can always write if she has.'

'Yeah, well, I only had the stuff that was already in my case, and some T-shirts on the chair.'

Stephen looked out of the window. He could see the green hills rising behind the sloping streets of bungalows. Neither of them spoke for a while.

The station's name was displayed on a number of brown enamel signs, as well as the more modern-looking red ones. They came to a standstill and Nick made a point of pulling hard on the hand-brake, as if demonstrating that he, at least, was a responsible driver.

'I don't know if you've got any money?' said Nick.

'Oh, no. No, I wouldn't want you to.'

'Here. It'll tide you over, just for a bit.'

Despite himself, Stephen took the cash. Some of the notes were the same brown as the railway signs.

'I'll pay you back,' he said, although he didn't know how he'd be able to. Maybe he could get some bar work, till they let him come back to the farm.

'Well,' said Nick. He had his hand on the door handle, as if he intended to step out, but didn't make to open his door.

Stephen said he was sorry once again. But Nick appeared to have run out of steam and of words and only stared ahead through the windscreen. Stephen got out of the car and went around to the back for his case. His duffel bag was beside it on the carpet which lined the floor of the boot. He lifted them both out and went around to the driver's door to make his goodbye, but Nick had started the engine and, not so much as glancing in the boy's direction, he pulled away and did not look back.

13.

There were a few Australians at the hostel and it was comforting to hear the familiar accents around him. On the Earls Court Road nearby, too, he heard snatches of voices with the cadence of home.

But as glad as he was of their proximity, he didn't feel that he was quite like them, any more. These types seemed pretty basic now; the things they wanted were predictable and straightforward. London to them was Madame Tussauds and pubs and a chance of getting laid. Beer, burgers, backpacking. Whereas Stephen felt he was no longer the same person he'd been before the time with the Clarkes. For instance, Cass had told him that when she was in London she always went about on the top floor of the bus — at the front for preference — so she could see the architectural details high up on the buildings. He'd never have thought of that, before. There were scrolls carved out of stone up there, and curling leaves; even statues. And Nick had told him about the little painted sketches of clouds that you could see for free in the V & A, Constable's record of the weather and the skies. The museum could be full of visitors downstairs, but you could nip up the back stairs and have all those pictures to yourself. And afterwards you could go to the little Polish café by South Kensington Tube station and drink hot chocolate out of a tall glass and be scowled at by the fierce waitresses. And while you were in the mood for being insulted, there was a pub in Soho where the landlord specialized in being brutal. The Coach and Horses. People went there, just for the guy — Norman, did Nick say his name was? — to be rude to them. And around the corner from there was the French pub, a legendary drinking spot. Stephen had memorized all these things they'd told him. It was as if he had a different map of London now.

But he was lonely in the city and wished he had some company. The Clarkes were totally different from his family, but it was a structure he was used to: mother, father, two sisters. He fitted, being the fifth, as he did back home. He didn't know what to do about Helena. She'd wanted him to ring her when he got to town, but that was before the thing had happened between him and Georgie. He didn't know if she knew. He guessed not. If he saw her she'd expect them to go on like they had before, but he wouldn't be able to, not now. On the other hand, crashing at her place would be an improvement on the hostel. And it'd be nice to see her. Also, she was close to Georgie and Cass and the family: she was someone he'd be able to talk about them with.

There was a pay-phone in the hallway at the hostel, but someone was always using it. The Spanish-speakers were especially voluble, talking for what seemed like hours at a time. They seemed to always be repeating the same few words and Stephen wondered if all languages sounded like that, if you weren't familiar with them; or whether they really did say nothing but *claro* and *es muy difícil*. His third day in town, he rang her from a phone-box outside the underground station. A woman answered, Helena's mother he supposed.

'I'll just see if she's here,' she said.

He was happy to hear Helena's voice, when she came on the line. He could feel himself smiling into the receiver and realized he hadn't used those muscles for days, not since before the party. She said she'd meet him outside the Tube near her house, otherwise he'd never find the way.

She looked very clean. Her skin was browner and her hair fairer. She was still wearing her cut-off jeans.

'Your hair's so long!' she said.

'Yours too. And you're blonder.'

He felt shy, being looked at. Helena stared at him as if he was a newspaper she was studying, with a frank interest that had been absent from his time with the Clarkes. In his studio, Nick had observed him closely when he was drawing, but it hadn't felt personal at all. He'd have regarded a tree in the same way, if he was sketching it. Celia only ever glanced in his direction and Georgie and Cass were like their mother. They didn't meet your eye much. Helena was more direct.

'Georgie told me what happened. Jesus! That's terrible, that your drinks were spiked and then her parents chucked you out so she couldn't even say goodbye. Apparently the accident was completely the other driver's fault. The police told Nick the man was paralytic.'

Stephen felt fear and hope at this, and a sliver of indignation. Maybe he didn't need to've been so ashamed of himself.

'Can we talk about it in a while? It's all a bit mind-blowing. I didn't know that, about the other driver. Maybe once we're sitting down?'

'Sure. Sorry, didn't mean to deluge you.'

They walked up the hill and along a street until they came to a tall wooden gate set into the wall.

Stephen was surprised to find himself in a large, tangly garden. It didn't feel as if they were in a city any more: the path up to the house went through an arch covered with jasmine, flanked by a jumble of flowers and bushes. On one side was an area of long grass with a striped hammock slung low between two old apple trees.

'Nice place,' he said.

'The house looks bigger than it really is. It's only one room deep. It's basically a lean-to with a giant garden. You've come at just the right moment, Mum's out.'

She grinned at him.

In the sitting room, Helena lay on her back across one sofa, Stephen on the other. His legs hung over the end, his feet almost touching the floor. There were a couple of round tables with tall lamps, patterned rugs and plants dotted about the place. There seemed to be an awful lot of cushions.

'So, what are you going to do?' she asked him.

'I'm kind of hoping Nick'll have me back for the apple-picking. So I guess I'll do a few day-trips, maybe go up to Oxford on the coach, have a look around. Be great if you came along? And my mum's friend told me Bath is worth a visit.'

Helena sat up.

'Stephen, I don't want to be the bearer of bad news, but there's no way Celia is going to let you go back to the farm. Once she goes on the turn, that's it.'

'Yeah, but I thought you said it was definite that the crash was the other guy's fault?'

'I think it is. But if she decides something, that's what happens in that family. You must've noticed? She's got the purse, she's got the power.'

'Really? She doesn't look as if she's even noticing anything. The way she drifts around the place.'

Helena sighed. 'I've known them longer than you and I can tell you it's not actually quite like that. She comes across all vague and airy-fairy, but she's bloody wilful. The iron whim, Nick calls it. Georgie's the only one who's not scared of her.'

'Yeah, but if the accident wasn't even my fault?'

'Georgie said her mum thought it was "all getting a bit incestuous". She said the same thing last summer, when Cass started getting serious about Hamish. She managed to break that up by sending Cass off to Italy, supposedly on holiday. By the time she got back Hamish had gone back to school. She does stuff like that. Works behind the scenes to get things how she wants them.'

Stephen knew that Helena was trying to be helpful, but she didn't know how well he fitted in with the Clarkes, how easily they all got along together. If he could just speak to Georgie, he was sure she'd cajole his way back to them. But he didn't dare telephone, in case Celia answered. He figured he would have to write to Georgie – and maybe to her parents as well – before he rang the house. But it was surely just a waiting game and then he'd be back.

'Stephen?'

'Yeah?'

'Did anything happen between you and Georgie, after I'd gone? Is that what she meant by incestuous? I want you to tell me if it did. I won't mind. Only why would Celia have said that?'

Now it was his turn to sit up.

'Look, Helena, it wasn't anything premeditated. Nothing against you, I want you to know that. It was that Hamish kept bringing drugs over to the farm and then he and Cass would go off and one night we just . . . it just kind of happened. It wasn't against you.'

'It wasn't exactly for me either, was it? How long had I been gone for? A week?'

'I know it doesn't sound great, but it wasn't something that got planned or anything like that.'

Helena had begun to cry. 'I really liked you. I thought you'd wait for me. It wasn't as if I was away for long.'

Stephen stood and came over to her and crouched beside her. Her face was hidden in her hands.

'I'm sorry. I'm really sorry,' he said.

'You'd better go. Please. Just go now,' she said from behind her hands.

'Helena,' he said.

'Please,' she said.

'Can I at least phone you again? In a day or two.'

'I don't know,' she said. Her voice had gone squeaky.

Stephen felt furious with himself. How could he have fucked this up? Helena was a fantastic girl who'd shown him nothing but kindness and generosity and how had he rewarded her? By sleeping with her best friend as soon as her back was turned. They weren't really going out, it was true; nothing had ever been fixed between them. But still. He'd behaved like a total bastard. He could see that, from her point of view, it made things worse that it had happened without premeditation, because that meant he hadn't even had a thought for her. He was careless. And it was true that from the moment Georgie came into his bed, he had all but forgotten Helena.

Stephen couldn't remember the way back to the Tube station, only that he needed to go down the hill. In any case he thought he might walk for a while, try and get his head clear. The other driver had been drinking, he knew that now; knew that it hadn't been his fault. Yet everything was complicated by the fact that he'd known there was going to be an accident: he'd just felt it in his bones. He hadn't pictured the car crashing, it wasn't a visual thing at all, more like a sensation in the back of his head, a tingly kind of pushing. He kept getting flashbacks to the party, to lying out on the grass with Georgie, listening to the sounds of music and people's disembodied voices. Out there on the grass the feeling had weighed down on him, a sense that something bad was going to happen. That's why he'd been driving so slowly. Well, you couldn't really drive fast, not on the banked, narrow lanes. But he'd been planning to take it gently, still, once he got on to the Truro road.

Was it possible, though, that the bad feeling hadn't been specifically about the car accident? Could it be that the sense of foreboding had actually been because Celia was going to throw him out, bringing the summer to such a cruel and abrupt end? Or was it both? Did the feeling foretell the accident and then the accident bring about his expulsion? In which case, was more horrible stuff going to happen; going to keep on happening? Was it like a chain of bad luck?

He could feel his heart beating faster as this idea took root. First there was the feeling. Then the accident had happened. Then Nick and Celia had decided to make him leave. And now Helena – sweet, sunny Helena – had thrown him out too. Oh shit. Was it going to stop there, or was it just going to keep coming, the bad stuff? How could he make it stop?

Stephen felt a terrible kind of restlessness, as if columns of insects were skittering through his bloodstream. He hadn't felt this too much, in England. At home he'd found that there were two ways of quieting it: by lying completely still and waiting for the disembodied feeling to come; or by walking. He couldn't just lie down, now, in the street; even if he went back to the hostel there'd be people milling around and it was necessary to be alone in a room if lying down was to work. He'd just keep walking. He'd looked at the underground map at Earls Court station, on his way to meet Helena. The Tube near her house was called St John's Wood. If he kept going downhill he'd get to the big road and then he could ask someone the way. But what way? He didn't want to get on a train, he wanted to keep moving, keep putting one leg in front of the other. Abruptly he turned around. He didn't want to be heading back towards the hostel, he wanted to go in the other direction, up the hill. That would be better, he was sure of it.

All the streets looked the same. There were white houses with big windows and he could see in through some of them, to rooms where people lived. He saw a piano in one, a tall vase of flowers on a polished table in another. Long bookcases and gilt mirrors above mantelpieces. He guessed it was a rich neighbourhood, here. Some of the houses had overgrown hedges, so he couldn't see in, but others were separated from the pavement by only a low wall. He could see straight through some of them, through the street-facing window to the far side of a room, where there were windows which looked over the gardens at the back. It was strange to him, to imagine that people's whole lives went on in these rectangles. Kids came in from school with their bags, men and women kissed or argued or had friends over. But the rooms were quite bare, mostly. They didn't seem very homey.

Stephen decided that if he turned right and then left, that would be a good system: that would get him somewhere where he needed to be. After a handful of turns, he came to a bigger road. There were shops and buses and people with little kids in buggies. He turned left here. He kept going until there was a right-hand turn and then crossed the busy street to get to it. He walked for an hour or so, not thinking of time. The buildings were different now, tall and solid and made of red brick; they looked more like apartment buildings. It seemed as if he had been walking uphill all the way.

It was a relief when he came to a path which seemed to lead up to a park and trees.

The anxiety was coming under control now. He began to breathe more slowly. It was as if he'd left London behind him, as if he'd walked out of the city and was back in the countryside, now. He strolled on and up, through a meadow of long grass, towards a wood. He'd just get to those trees and then he'd sit down for a little while, see where his imagination took him. Because that's all it was, imagination. He wasn't really cursed with some sort of black prophecy. He hadn't brought forth a chain of ill-luck, just by feeling strange when someone spiked his drink at a spoilt teenager's party. He remembered that he'd been listening to Led Zeppelin when the sensation first started to creep up on him. Those guys were into all sorts, weren't they? The occult and stuff. Pentagrams and black capes and the Tarot.

That was probably what had brought on the sense of doom he'd had at the party.

There was bare earth under the trees and it felt cool in the shade, substantially less warm than in the open, as if it was a different day altogether. He felt the coolness on his skin, the relief of it. Maybe he'd just got too hot walking around and that was why his heart had started racing, earlier. Sitting with his back to a tree, he felt almost normal again.

What he needed to do was to write to them all, as a family. That was it. Not separate letters, one to Georgie, one to Cass and one to Nick and Celia, but just a single letter. This way, the girls would tell their mum that they wanted him to come back, because they'd all read the letter together. He pictured them in the kitchen, Georgie reading out loud. He'd keep it really straightforward: he'd fucked up by attempting to drive back from the party, he should've made them all sit it out longer, drink some more tea, maybe have a bite of something to eat to help them sober up. But it wasn't his fault that someone had spiked the drink and the accident wasn't his fault either, he knew that now. It was just that: an accident. He wasn't to blame. Having said that, he was really, really sorry that the girls had been injured, but also he was thankful that their injuries hadn't been more serious. He missed them, he couldn't wait to get back to them. He appreciated that they needed some time as a family, so he was going to suggest that he come back in a week or two, in good time to help with the apple-picking. And once he'd written to the Clarkes, he'd take the opportunity to send a note to Helena, too.

Now that he had a plan, Stephen was calm. He felt the agitation melting away. He sat under the trees for a little while, then got to his feet. There was a branch of W. H. Smith on the Earls Court Road, just around the corner from the hostel: time to get back there, get himself kitted out with notepaper and a biro. He could get some airmail paper, while he was about it, to write home. He'd never answered his sisters' letters, he realized. He felt ashamed, to picture their expectant little faces, waiting for the post.

There was a communal room at the hostel, with a couple of tables where people could eat, as well as some soft seating. Stephen installed himself at one of the tables and set about his task. Within an hour he'd composed his letters and addressed the envelopes. Feeling he was taking control of his situation gave him a boost of energy. There was a launderette down the road: he'd take his things in for a wash, get a load of laundry on, then nip to the post office.

Up in the bunk room where he was sleeping, he pulled his case out from under the bed. He could almost smell Celia's fury, as she'd shoved his T-shirts and socks and pants in, any old how. He grabbed at them and stuffed them into his duffel bag. There were already a couple of T-shirts rumpled up in there, along with a paperback book he'd been half-reading at the farm.

It was hot in the launderette and the smell of cheap washing powder and heated air from the dryers was comforting. He figured it would be quite nice to come back here after he'd been to the post and just sit on one of those slatted wooden seats. He selected a machine, fumbled for the right coins, filled one of the paper cups that were provided for the purpose with detergent. He squatted down and opened the thick glass door of the machine and began to pull out his clothes from the bag. When he put the final T-shirt from the bottom of the bag into the wash, he heard a clink. Something metal against the perforated metal drum of the machine. A ten pence piece, probably. He put his hand in and under the clothes, feeling for the loose coin.

As soon as he touched it, felt its sharp little points, he knew what it was. He didn't even need to look at it. When he stood up he could feel his face and neck flushing as the blood rushed to his head. He was acutely aware of the soft thickness and weave of the ribbon, its tiny ridges against his fingertips. All the calm, the sense of purpose and resolve which had come to him up on the Heath deserted him now. It was as if he'd been given an electric shock. He opened his hand and glanced at what it held. He couldn't bring himself to put it in a pocket, to have it so closely about his person. He didn't want to be holding it, didn't want to have to think about it. Instead, he dropped it back into the duffel bag, where it had come from.

14.

One of his roommates at the hostel was going into town to sight-see and asked Stephen if he wanted to come along. National Gallery, Trafalgar Square, then down to have a look at Number 10 Downing Street and finish up in Parliament Square, maybe grab a sandwich from somewhere: make a day of it.

Stephen had spent the last couple of days alone, walking. He'd barely eaten. He had walked through the Brompton Cemetery and on, along the Fulham Road; past the football ground, farther and farther past streets of identical rows of squat brick houses until he reached the Fulham Palace Road. He didn't know that the river was only a minute or two away, that there was a park he could have visited, with an avenue of tall plane trees whose branches skimmed the water at high tide. There was an *A–Z* at the hostel, kept behind the desk so no one went off with it, but Stephen wasn't aiming to visit anything in particular. He walked to try and burn off the terrible anxiety he was experiencing, not as a way of getting to know the city. The second day after he'd found the medal in his bag he walked north, crossing the Cromwell Road, into the sober streets of Kensington, uphill to a shabby area where paint peeled off the high flat fronts of buildings and music thudded from open windows.

He didn't know what to do. He'd thought of not sending the letter to the Clarkes at all; of writing a new letter, in which he told them that the medal had somehow found its way into his bag. But he couldn't face it. Celia was the only one who gave a shit about the medal – even she didn't care that much, it seemed to him – and she was already furious with him. All he wanted was to get back to the farm, but now Celia would be able to say he'd stolen from them, as well as killing all their chickens and practically killing their daughters. He didn't want to hand her any more ammunition.

So he'd sent the original letter and also posted the notes to Helena and to his parents and sisters. He hadn't told his mum and dad about the car accident, just that he was having a week in London before going back for the apple harvest. He didn't want them worrying. He was waiting for a reply from the Clarkes. Something told him that Nick would be the one to write. Once he'd heard from him and knew when he could go back, he'd simply bring the medal with him. When he got there he'd just put it back in its place on the faded velvet: no one would ever know it had been missing. No one really went up to the third floor anyway, let alone studied the contents of the trefoil table. Even if someone did glance in its direction, they'd never notice that anything was absent from the lower shelf.

He couldn't get his head around the Cross being in his bag at all. How had it got there? He remembered getting the medals out one morning, just to feel what it was like to hold them; but he could have sworn – would have sworn, if he'd been asked to, in a court of law – that he'd put them all back. Could it be that it had been Georgie who'd been asked to pack his things, and that she'd slipped the medal into the bottom of the duffel bag, knowing it would give him a reason to return? Or Cass: might she have done it? And yet Nick had given him the impression that the girls hadn't known he was being sent away. It had still been fairly early in the morning when Nick came to collect him from the hospital and take him to the station: surely the girls would still have been sleeping, exhausted by the ordeal? He couldn't recall what Nick had told him on the way to the station. It had all been such a shock. Nor could he imagine either Nick or Celia deliberately inserting the Cross into his bag – why would they do that? Which left the possibility that he had not, in fact, put the medal back, but had somehow forgotten it, left it on the bedroom chair with his clothes. And that whoever had packed his bag had simply caught it up, unseen, with his T-shirts and socks. It didn't weigh much and it didn't glint in the light or anything. It could've been bundled into a piece of clothing without anyone noticing it was there.

Stephen didn't feel too good. He felt light-headed and kind of disembodied: floaty, but not in a pleasant way. The sense of dread had come back. He was hoping that spending time with another person might jolt him out of it. This guy Glen from the hostel didn't seem to notice anything amiss, but then he barely knew him. He chatted as the Tube carried them from Earls Court to Embankment. Glen'd been to Italy, Rome and Florence, looking at the art. What they had in these European museums, it was mind-blowing. A girl carved out of marble who was turning into a tree, right there in front of your eyes, as if it was a special effect in a film. Women looking straight at you, holding on to their own nipples; or coming up out of the sea in a huge shell. He'd seen one painting of a woman getting raped by a sodding great bull. Glen didn't know the stories behind them, but the images were amazing, violent and sexy and strange. You didn't get a lot of that sort of thing back home in Brisbane.

'Where you from, mate? Melbourne, is it?' he asked.

'Yeah,' said Stephen.

'Caught a lot of the museums here?'

'No, not yet. Just the V & A actually.'

'British Museum is pretty amazing. They've got Egyptian mummies. Fucking weird, I tell you. You can still see what they looked like, as people. Their faces, you know? Load of carved stuff in there, too. Stone.'

'I like paintings better,' said Stephen, just for something to say.

'Reckon we'll see some good ones in the National Gallery. Van Gogh and what have you. I'm getting really into the older stuff, though, now I've been to Italy. It's cool that they're free to get into, here. The museums cost a fortune, over there.'

They arrived at the entrance. Stephen felt faint. He hadn't had any breakfast; come to think of it, he hadn't had supper last night either. Had he in fact eaten anything, over the past couple of days? He couldn't remember. The feeling of dread was so overwhelming that it left no room for appetite nor thirst. He let Glen lead the way, grateful not to have to take responsibility for anything, just to trudge after someone else. There was an enormous portrait of a man with a pointed beard on a horse. The horse's head looked too small. There was a woman with a lot of very pale skin, her torso twisted, clinging to a pillar as if a tornado was about to blow her away. They came to a large picture by Leonardo da Vinci, and stood in front of it, dutifully.

'It's pretty dark, isn't it? Looks like it's been dipped in cold seawater,' said Stephen.

Glen laughed. 'I'm glad you said it. I was trying to figure out why he's meant to be so incredible.'

They traipsed through the rooms. The Virgin Mary never looked too pleased to find herself with the infant Jesus on her lap; less still when the angel came to tell her she was expecting a child, who was going to be the son of God. Some of the angels were beautiful, though. Their wings were mostly white tipped with gold and they had wise, solemn faces.

Glen wandered over towards a shadowy painting of some people sitting at a table. A bearded man on the right of the picture had his arms outstretched, as if he'd just received terrible news. Stephen followed and they stood, looking.

'Caravaggio. Fucking incredible,' Glen whispered.

The bearded man's hand came towards you, so realistic that you could almost take it in your own. He had a red nose – the kind of old-man nose that is always dripping – and some sort of clam shell pinned to his clothing. On the left, another man was leaning forward, pushing down on the arm of his chair, as if he was just about to stand up. You could imagine that this chair might be about to fall backwards and the table topple over, bringing that teetering bowl of fruit at the very front of the canvas tumbling to the ground. It was really dramatic, almost like a scene out of a film. It looked as if the people around the table were in the middle of a serious argument. A sorrowful-looking person with long hair – was it a man or a woman, Stephen wasn't sure – sat in the middle at the back, eyes cast down. If this character hadn't been wearing a kind of robe, you could have mistaken the picture for a scene in a Western: stranger rides into town, brings some calamitous news, a fight breaks out. Even the way it was lit was like the lighting in a film; menacing, with long shadows. *The Supper at Emmaus*, it was called.

There was a lot to take in. The white tablecloth was painted so perfectly and a glass jug too, the liquid in it catching the light, the glass itself gleaming softly. Stephen was fascinated. He didn't want to look at any more paintings, but just stand and drink this one in. It was the most lifelike picture he had ever looked at and he felt drawn into it, inquisitive about what was going on within its frame. But then he saw it. There on the table was some kind of a roasted bird. The way it was arranged on the plate, its legs were sticking up: black legs with yellow talon-like claws reaching upwards. Claws. Dead claws. Stephen felt the foreboding rush into his whole body. It was like a tidal wave, choking him, coming over his head. He felt as if his skeleton was an empty cave and the dread and fear was like a tide, slapping and sucking its way into him. Of course. He'd known this was going to happen. This was what he'd envisioned after the henhouse had been ransacked by the fox. Claws. Upside-down claws, dead claws. But what did it mean? Obviously it was a sign; but a sign of what? How was he to interpret this by himself? Was the answer in the painting? Was that what had brought him here, in front of it? Claws. They were waiting for him. Waiting to bring him bad news. He turned to Glen and started to talk, but the talk didn't come out right. It didn't seem to sound like words. It was too loud. He grabbed at Glen's shirt, at his shoulder. He needed to explain what was going on. It was urgent. The other people in the gallery were coming towards him. But they mustn't. They needed to keep away. He was too powerful for them, they could get hurt if they got too close. But Glen, Glen would be all right: Glen was part of it. But he didn't seem to be understanding what Stephen was saying. He looked terrified. Stephen heard screaming, but he didn't comprehend that it was coming out of him. He felt so hot now he thought he might explode or combust. Spontaneous combustion: that was a thing, wasn't it? A thing that happened. An unexplained phenomenon. Was that what was going to happen to him? Was it to do with hell, with flames? Was he actually evil?

Afterwards, he couldn't remember all this with any coherence. There'd been a room he'd been taken to, a small side room; and then an ambulance. He'd been OK about going to the room, but when he saw the uniformed paramedics he tried to fight them off. Because they were going to bring him back to the hospital where he'd been taken after the car accident: it was all going to happen again, just like before. Waiting for hours in a curtained cubicle, not able to reach Cass or Georgie; the loneliness, the shame. Then Nick would come to collect him and take him to the station, and send him away. It was going to keep happening. He knew that as soon as he saw the ambulance crew.

It didn't look the same as the Cornwall hospital. But that could be a trick, to lull him. He shouted as loud as he could for someone to help him. If he called their names, Cass and Georgie would hear him and come to get him out, wouldn't they? But they didn't appear. His mouth was dry and there was a ringing feeling in his ears; the kind of underwater, deaf sensation you got after you'd been to a gig. Maybe he'd damaged his hearing with the volume of his own cries. He was trying to escape, trying to get up out of the chair they were wheeling him in, but then a doctor came and gave him an injection and there was a feeling as of a great pressure being released, like a valve being undone, and everything went black.

When he woke up he was in a bed with a tube in his arm. There wasn't anyone else in the room.

He tried to piece together the sequence of events that had brought him here, but his head was sore, as if he'd stood up suddenly and hit it on a beam. Maybe it'd be better to just lie still. He lay back and closed his eyes. For the first time since before Hamish's party he didn't feel anxious or full of fear. He just felt tired now.

He didn't know how long he'd been there when someone brought a trolley round. He wasn't sure if it was lunch or supper. Stephen was given a sandwich and an orange drink.

'We're going to spoil you. You can choose: ice-cream or jelly?'

Stephen couldn't decide. He loved ice-cream and he loved jelly as well.

'I don't know,' he said. 'Is it red jelly?'

'More like yellow. Pineapple, I'd say.'

'Can I have the ice-cream, then?'

Once he was alone in the room, Stephen ate the ice-cream. It was vanilla; custard-coloured, with little splinters of ice-crystal. Ice-cream was incredible! Vanilla was actually pretty terrific, too, if you stopped to think about it. Stephen thought it was maybe the best thing he'd ever eaten in his whole life. He put just a little on the tip of the spoon each time, to make it last longer. But lifting his arm repeatedly made him feel exhausted.

He left the sandwich and the drink to have later on. Before long the orderly came back to collect the spoon and to bring him a hot drink.

He slept for a while. A woman came into the room. She wasn't wearing a white coat, or a uniform or anything. He guessed she was some sort of a therapist, but she introduced herself as Dr Capple. She sat on the end of his bed. She told him the tube in his arm was just saline, because he'd been very dehydrated when they brought him in. They were going to keep him in for a few days, see how he got on. Was there anyone he'd like them to get in touch with, any family over here? He thought of the Clarkes. They were family, kind of. But he shook his head and said no. He certainly didn't want his mum and dad to find out that he was here, he wanted them to think he was benefiting from his travels, enjoying himself. He didn't want to be a disappointment to them.

The second day, Dr Capple came back. She sat on the chair this time. She had very clean shoes and her feet looked long and narrow inside them. This time she asked him questions and made notes on A4 paper, cradling a clipboard in her left elbow. The first thing she asked was whether he'd ever received psychiatric help before: he told her he hadn't. He felt inclined to like her: she seemed gentle. He explained it all to her: the henhouse and how that had been his fault; the haunting feeling he'd experienced, afterwards, and the recurring picture he'd had in his head, of the dead claws of the birds. How that same image had been staring him in the face, straight in front of him, in the gallery: that must mean something, mustn't it? Because it was just too much of a coincidence, otherwise. Then he told her about the car accident and how he'd known something bad was going to happen, beforehand. How he thought he might bring bad luck around with him. How he loved Cass but had been sleeping with Georgie. How much he was counting on getting back there, to the farm, to be with them. How much he loved it there: the tussocky green snowdrop field, the smooth rocks by the tumbling river, the ancient orchard.

'That's the thing though, isn't it, with every paradise?' she said, quietly. 'It always ends with expulsion. With a fall from Grace.'

He wasn't too sure what she meant, but he nodded anyhow.

'And what about before now? Have you experienced any of these feelings before, over the past year or two?'

Stephen said that he'd been quite sad and isolated, back at home. That was why he'd come away, travelling. But the clairvoyance was new. The growing sense that there were patterns of meaning underlying the visible world, if you looked hard enough for them. He hadn't felt as if he was a messenger, before, but now he was pretty sure of it. The problem was interpreting the message. And trying to work out if carrying it made him dangerous.

'So it makes you feel powerful, does it?' asked Dr Capple.

Stephen said that it did, kind of.

'More powerful than you usually feel?'

He laughed at this, the first time he'd done so for days and days. 'I don't usually feel very powerful at all. I'm not really that kind of a person. It's just now I've got this feeling, like it's an emergency, you know? 'Cause whenever I've had the bad feeling, something bad has actually happened. And now I've got to work out what the message is that they're trying to send me; and who I've got to take it to. It feels pretty big.'

'Who is sending you the messages, do you think?'

'I don't really know,' Stephen admitted.

'Do you ever consider injuring yourself, or others?'

This question threw him. Injury was an odd word. Was she saying he ought to be considering these things? Was there an oblique suggestion in there, or was it a straight enquiry?

'I'd never hurt anyone. I don't even kill spiders. I shot a cane toad, once, when I was around eleven or twelve. It was up at my uncle's farm. He had an air-gun, but it was horrible. I'd never do anything like that again,' he answered.

'And have you used any drugs at all, since you came to England?'

He didn't know whether to admit to this or not. Maybe it'd be better not to own up about the drugs. He didn't want to get anyone into trouble. Could she get him arrested? Deported, even? Would he get a criminal record? Would his parents find out?

She noticed his slight hesitation and spoke again: 'It's OK. What you tell me is confidential. I'm just trying to work out what would be the best course of action for you, meds-wise.'

So he told her about the acid – the times it had been great, and also the one time it had felt so wrong, at the farm; and then the spiked drink at the party – and she wrote it all down in her notes.

'OK, well, thank you for being so open with me about what you're experiencing. The more we communicate, the more we can help you. We can certainly get you feeling better, but a lot of it will be up to you, ultimately. It's good that we've got some beds available, so you can stabilize. I'll see you again in a day or two.'

A nurse came round before lunch and took out the saline drip and handed him an egg-cup-sized plastic pot. There were three tablets in it: two capsules and a small, pale blue pill. She handed him a paper cup with an inch or two of water in the bottom and stood over him while he gulped them down. A little while later, the same person who'd offered him the ice-cream the day before appeared, bringing soup. There was a white bread roll and a little gold-topped pack of butter to go with it. It reminded Stephen of aeroplane food and this was somehow comforting. There wasn't any ice-cream, this time, just tinned fruit salad, with or without Instant Whip.

He dozed. He felt slightly groggy and didn't seem to need to listen to music, or read; it was enough just to take it easy. It felt like an exertion to walk down to the bathrooms along the corridor, past the nurses' station. He noticed that the toilets didn't have locks on the doors. There were a couple of shower stalls, uncurtained, and the hot water felt calming, falling on to his shoulders and down his front. He'd had to ask a nurse if there was any shampoo he could use and she'd found him a bottle from somewhere. Having clean hair felt great; it made him feel more in control of himself, of his body.

The next day – or was it the one after that, he'd lost track of time in there – Glen came to see him, bringing his case and duffel bag. He seemed nervous.

'You don't want to stay too long in here, mate, I'll tell you. They've got some real loons along there, in the TV room.'

'I think they're letting me out soon, maybe after the weekend.'

'Right you are,' said Glen. He stood, shifting from foot to foot as if he was warming up to go out on to a sports field. He seemed to take up too much room.

Stephen couldn't think of anything to say. 'I'm sorry about that . . . what happened.'

Glen shrugged. 'Just one of those things, isn't it. You'll be fine now.'

'Thanks for coming in. For bringing my stuff.'

'Letter came for you, I've brought that too,' said Glen, fishing into the pocket of his windcheater. 'Here you go.'

Stephen's heart skipped. But when he looked at the envelope, something about the writing told him it wasn't from Georgie or Cass; it looked like an adult's writing. And if it wasn't from one of them, maybe it wasn't good news. He half wanted Glen to leave, so he could read the letter in peace; but on the other hand, when Glen had gone he'd have no one, no one from before he got here, no one to link him back to the outside world.

He could just not open it. He could pretend it'd never arrived. It wouldn't even be pretending, not really, because he wasn't staying at the address on the envelope now, was he? The Clarkes didn't know he was in hospital. If Glen hadn't brought his mail, he'd never have received it. He could use the medal as a pretext to go back: just tell them straight that it must've got scooped up in his clothes and that he wanted to bring it back himself. He could get on a train and go to Cornwall, walk or take a taxi up to the farm. He still had the money from Nick. If they saw him, if they saw him in person, they wouldn't make him leave. Georgie and Cass definitely wouldn't let their mum chuck him out, not if he was flesh and blood in front of them. They'd be glad to have him back.

Once Glen had gone, Stephen sat with the letter. He felt agitated. He could feel the fizzing sensation in the back of his head that had been in abeyance over the past couple of days. He hadn't had to make any important decisions since he'd been here, but now there were lots of different courses of action that presented themselves. There were suddenly too many things to think through. It felt as if he needed to accelerate to keep up with the thoughts that were racing in his head, but he couldn't speed up. It was as if he was driving a car stuck in second and the gears were grinding, resisting the impetus, the pull of the thoughts.

Outside. It'd be better to open the letter out of doors, then if he needed to walk around to help him think through its contents he'd be able to. There was nowhere to pace in the room: the bed and the chair took up all the available space. Stephen went to the door and along the corridor. The bathrooms were to the left of his room, so he turned right; this must be the way to the stairs and lifts. His room was on the second floor. He came to the television room that Glen had mentioned. There were flamingo-coloured plastic armchairs with pale wooden arms arranged in a semi-circle. The television squatted in front of the chairs, the sound too low to catch, the picture flickering like a fish-tank. A couple of people sat slumped. By the window a woman was rocking back and forth, muttering. Stephen suddenly felt frightened. Who were these people? They were nothing like him.

Seeing them made him feel more alone than being by himself in his room. Beyond the TV room was a door, with a thick glass panel reinforced with wire. There was another identical door only a few feet further along, as if the two functioned as a kind of air-lock, like the kind you saw in prison films. He went to push the aluminium handle down, but it wouldn't give. He tried the door again, yanking, pulling at the handle.

He hadn't thought he was shouting, not out loud. But a male nurse appeared as if responding to a commotion, and took him gently by the elbow. The softness of his touch was so surprising to Stephen that he allowed himself to be led back to his room without resisting.

'I need to get out, I need to just walk a little while,' he told the nurse.

'Someone will take you out in the morning, if you want a walk. There aren't enough of us on duty at the mo, I'm afraid.'

'I don't need someone with me, I'm fine. Just got some think-ing to do.'

'Someone will take you in the morning, once rounds are over. I'll make a note of it so it doesn't get forgotten.'

'But I'm free to go, right? I don't have to stay here?'

'You're free to go, but if you do you won't be able to come back without being formally readmitted. Otherwise we wouldn't be able to keep track of everyone, keep you all safe.'

This sounded reasonable. It wasn't as if he had any place else to go, not until he went back to Cornwall. Stephen felt calmer now. 'OK,' he said.

'They'll be round with the trolley soon, for your tea,' said the nurse.

He thought he'd wait to open the letter. There was no hurry. He could leave it till the morning, which would actually be better because that was when mail ordinarily got delivered, in the morning time; so clearly that was when post was meant to be read. Yes. He felt a little less shaky, having reached this conclusion.

He sat on the bed and waited for the trolley. His suitcase and duffel bag were in his room, behind the chair in the corner where Glen had left them. He thought of opening them up, looking through his things, but it seemed like too much of an effort. After a time the supper trolley appeared and a little while later the male nurse came round with the three tablets for him. Once again they were presented to him in a little plastic pot; once again he was handed a small paper cup of water with which to gulp them down.

He lay down on his back and slept for a while. He woke with a start some time later. It wasn't morning, because it was still dark; but he thought the darkness was maybe thinning. There was a greyness behind it that might be the approaching dawn. All at once he felt very wide awake, as if he was an electrical appliance newly plugged in to the energy supply. He didn't feel happy, he didn't feel sad: he just felt super-alert.

He could look at the letter. Not read it, not even take it out, but just open the envelope and peep at it like that; get the gist of it. You could tell a lot from the words people selected. Then he'd know roughly what to expect in the morning, when it would be time to remove it, unfold it and read. It wasn't very thick, he judged it would contain two pieces of notepaper. As he ripped through the envelope he saw that this was so. He looked down and saw the word *destructive*. He saw the phrase: *wish we'd never. How you can think that we'd ever want to see you.* He

183

felt himself flushing. It was hot in the room, suddenly. He took the letter from its torn casing now, and read it through.

He didn't need to read it a second time. He put it down on the bed in front of him and then he stood and went to his suitcase and took out his other pair of jeans. He noticed that they could do with a wash. He must have been wearing them when he'd been to the launderette. That felt as if it had happened years ago, now. Another lifetime. Because there were other lifetimes, where different outcomes could occur. Different planes of being. He thought so. He unthreaded the belt from around the waist of them and wound it up tightly so that it fit into the palm of his hand, then quietly he left his room and walked along the corridor, past the empty nurses' station, towards the bathrooms.

PART 3

15.

Cornwall, 2015

There had been a certain amount of bitterness between the Clarke sisters, concerning the farm. Obviously they couldn't both live there. It was too big for a single person, in any case, even Georgie would have had to admit that. Cass and Adam seemed to assume they would continue their tenure, after Celia died: they'd already been living there for three years by then, looking after her. Georgie didn't envy her sister that, at least. Dementia was no joke. Although at the outset it had sometimes seemed to her, visiting from London, that their mother was faking it, as if she was playing at dementia, just to spite them all. Georgie fancied that she had caught a malevolent glint in her mother's eye, occasionally, as she sent them all scurrying about the house in search of her keys, her purse, her pen. Celia was still a commanding presence, as determined and as futile as a King Canute, bidding back the waves. *But you don't use money, nor keys: you never go anywhere! And you can't write any more!* Georgie had wanted to shout at her. Celia hid things, endlessly and – considering how doolally she was – with surprising resourcefulness and cunning. There were flashes of vituperation.

'What do you bloody want?' she'd asked Georgie one day, in the final months.

The district nurse was there, to help them with what was euphemistically called Celia's personal care.

'Mother doesn't mean anything by it,' the nurse had said. 'She's disinhibited, you see. She can't help it.'

'Disinhibited!' Georgie had retorted. 'She's always been like this.'

But then Celia would look utterly lost and forlorn and Georgie would feel guilty for questioning the course of her mother's decline. Her ebbing memory seemed to take her body away with it: she shrank. Her mouth looked too small, like a child whose grown-up front teeth had just grown in. Georgie would have liked to talk about what she felt about Celia, the loss of Celia, but Cass and Adam didn't seem to want to. It was hard to know what Cass felt about their mother's deterioration. In fact, it wasn't easy to know what Cass felt about anything. She had always been the more reserved of the sisters.

At least Celia had forgotten that she liked a drink. That had been a blessing. Demented was one thing, but demented and drunk with it would have been too great a burden for anyone, even Adam, who had been totally brilliant with her. She'd always preferred men, if the truth be told. Georgie wondered if she might have been a different sort of mother, if she'd had sons. Of her grandchildren, she'd certainly favoured Georgie's son Jake over Cass's daughter Skye; whereas with her own offspring Cass, her firstborn, had been the favourite. The distribution of good looks had been reversed in the next generation: Jake was the beautiful one, the child of the less beautiful sister; while Skye was ordinary-looking, unlike her mother. Skye had beetly brows which somehow exaggerated the fact that her eyes were just a little too close together. Looks had mattered to Celia. She'd never made any secret of it.

Cass was still remarkable to look at. She had a natural grace and elegance; her gestures were economical and neat, like the smoothly retracting drawers in one of her ergonomically designed kitchens. Her hair was always freshly cut, steel grey now, in a long, even bob. She could appear stern: laughter was further away from her than it had been when she was young, her humour more buried. She dressed in the sort of sharp-angled, asymmetric linen clothes that were the international uniform of architects; as if membership of RIBA opened the door to a special outfitters, known only to the trade. Adam was scruffier. He always looked as if he'd just come in from planting a row of something in the vegetable patch.

They'd agreed not to talk about the farm until after the funeral. Everyone was on their best behaviour for the occasion, but it was a long day. By the time the last of the mourners — although how many would actually mourn Celia was open to question — had left, there were empty glasses everywhere. No one could be bothered to make supper. They flopped in the kitchen and agreed that they'd just finish up the sausage rolls and fruit cake they'd served at the wake, along with any remaining sandwiches.

'Funeral baked meats, they're called, aren't they?' asked Georgie. She was a bit tipsy.

'Eh?' said Adam.

'The food after a funeral. That's what you call it,' said Georgie.

'I've never heard that,' said Cass.

'I think it might be Shakespeare. It's ringing a bell from my acting days.'

'Nice of Hamish to've come,' said Adam.

'I hadn't seen him for donkey's years,' said Georgie.

'I saw him at his father's funeral last year,' said Cass. 'You'd never know, now, how nice-looking he was.'

'It's typical of Mum to've died in the winter. We could've had a really nice wake out on the snowdrop field, if she'd gone in the summer. Wouldn't have been left with all this mess to clear up,' said Georgie.

'People don't *choose* when they die,' said Cass.

'Well, duh,' said Georgie. 'I just meant, she'd never make things easy for us if she could find a way to make them difficult. Same thing with this place.'

'That's a bit unfair! She left everything to us both, jointly,' said Cass.

'Exactly,' said Georgie, as if this proved her point.

Cass sighed.

'Let's not talk about this stuff now,' said Adam. 'Everyone's exhausted. Let's discuss things in the morning, when we're all feeling a bit more rested.'

Cass and Adam had already agreed that it made sense for them to buy out Georgie's share. Their daughter Skye was currently living in the lower half of their house in Penzance, while the top half was rented out. They would have to wait until the tenant's shorthold lease came up before putting the place on the market. They had no mortgage, having profited from selling their old London house.

If they also sold off the three fields at the bottom of the farm, alongside the river, they could just about afford to keep the rest. Skye could move into Nick's old studio, at a pinch. Georgie was never going to move out of London now, was she? And she'd be well-off, with the money. She could even get herself a cottage somewhere. She could take more holidays, help Jake out if she wanted to. Not that he needed the cash, the way his business had taken off. And yet it wasn't a conversation they looked forward to. It was never just about the money, with Georgie.

The following morning they put their proposal to her. They'd pay her in two instalments: one now, the second once their house had sold.

'I was thinking it'd be a fresh start for all of us if we just put the whole place on the market,' Georgie said.

'But that doesn't make any sense. It'd be silly to sell, when one of you wants to live here and the other really doesn't,' said Adam.

'Does he have to be here for this?' Georgie asked her sister, gesturing in Adam's direction. Cass looked pained. 'Anyway, who said I don't want to live here myself?'

'Well, do you?' asked Cass.

'No, actually. What would I do down here? No one needs a voice coach around here.'

'Precisely,' said Adam.

'So you don't want us to have it even though you don't want it yourself,' said Cass.

The fact that Cass was able to summarize her sister's position so neatly rankled with Georgie. All her old feelings of injustice and rivalry were dangerously close to the surface. Cass always seemed to win. The temptation of saying something so dreadful as to cause an unbridgeable breach rose up in her. Cruel words threatened to spill over and stick, like boiling milk. It was the only ammunition she had. But it was the weapon her mother had used, and Georgie did not want to be like Celia.

'OK. Can you give me a few days to think it over? I'd like to talk about it on my own with Jake, see what he feels. He's very attached to this place too, you know.'

'I think we should try and resolve things as soon as we can. We don't want to drag this out,' said Adam.

'I agree,' said Cass.

'Fine,' said Georgie. She had a splitting headache suddenly. It'd be a relief not to go on with this discussion.

As soon as she and Jake stepped on to the Paddington train at Truro, Georgie felt better. She was disappointed and angry with how she had behaved at the farm. She had hoped it would stop, when Celia died, this childish petulance. No wonder her husband had never wanted to come to Cornwall with her. The sense of injured competition she felt towards her niece was especially shaming. Always, in the back of her mind, the words *What about me?* were going round and around, on repeat.

There had been a time – years in fact – when Georgie's star had seemed fated to shine brighter than her sister's. She'd sailed straight into a major TV serial, fresh out of drama school. It was an ingénue part, inevitably, but with a twist: her character had risen up out of the fake Victorian mist to plunge a dagger into the heart of her faithless lover. The words she'd uttered as the knife found its mark had become something of a catch-phrase, with the viewing public: 'If I can't have you, Francis Fitzgibbon, then I'll make damn sure no one else ever will!' Georgina Clarke had been on the cover of the *Radio Times,* widely tipped as an actress to watch out for. For a time, afterwards, people smirked at her in the street, in shops, sure they'd seen that face. Another television part followed, as the gaslighted younger sister of a secretly psychopathic doctor. And then she'd met Duncan.

Duncan Newhouse was already well known in the advertising world by the time she met him. He had a table of his own in Langan's Brasserie, where he lunched most days; a Patrick Procktor drawing of him, cigarette in hand, was on the wall, alongside portraits of leading film stars and directors. He wore a pale, expensive trenchcoat, like a European film director's. He took slightly longer to respond to a question than was comfortable, which made him seem important, as if people were hanging on his every word. Georgie was introduced to him at her agent's summer party.

'Georgina Clarke. No relation of Nick Clarke, the sculptor?'

And she'd laughed, surprised, and said that yes, that was her father.

'I've got a head he did of me, must be getting on for fifteen years ago. Nick Clarke! Haven't thought of him for yonks.'

It turned out that the head had been commissioned by the mother of Duncan's former wife, as a wedding gift to her daughter.

'Of course she couldn't stand the sight of me, by the time she left, so I hung on to it. You should come and have a look.'

Georgie wasn't really interested in seeing her father's work, but it was as good a way as any of getting to know Duncan. She didn't fancy him, not at first: he was already in his late thirties and she'd only ever gone out with guys her own age. But she was intrigued.

In fact her working life came to an end within months of meeting Duncan. He didn't want her to be out six nights a week, treading the boards, or off on a film set. He was used to getting his own way. It was his special area of expertise, he told her.

'I haven't waited thirty-seven years to meet the woman of my dreams so that I can sit at home by myself while you're on location in Huddersfield or somewhere, miles away,' he told her. To prove it, he gave her things: a topaz ring the size of a throat lozenge, an open-topped car.

'But I can't drive!' she laughed, when he took her outside and showed her.

'You can take lessons, now that you're going to be living with me.'

This was his way of inducing her to move in with him. It was irresistible, the force of his personality. Or the force of his will, which only later did Georgie come to understand was essentially the same thing. She'd moved into his Kensington mews house within weeks of meeting him. She became pregnant before they'd been together for six months and they were married three weeks before Jake was born. Georgie had looked incredible at the registry office, where a jumble of hair-pieces and a heavy hand with the mascara wand had lent her a close resemblance to the singer Bobbie Gentry. And had the desired effect of taking people's eyes off her tummy. Celia had got drunk and insulted the other guests.

'Who are all these ghastly people?' she'd demanded, before Nick took her back to the hotel room their new son-in-law had paid for.

Celia did not approve. Advertising wasn't art, it was commerce; and coercive commerce at that. It was no accident that people like Duncan were doing well under the frightful Mrs Thatcher. The fact that it called upon the techniques of real art – photography, film – made it all the more shoddy. Celia had been brought up to believe that to call someone 'ambitious' was scathing, but Georgie only laughed when her mother applied it to her husband. Yes, Duncan was ambitious and she celebrated this in him.

Incurring her mother's distaste made Georgie feel powerful. She discovered that money was a fortress that protected you from what other people thought. And it had been fabulous, in the early years. They'd travelled and, because Duncan was extravagant and considered himself a gourmet, they'd eaten in all the best restaurants. Their picture had appeared occasionally in Nigel Dempster's column. They had glamorous people over to dinner, actors and designers. And then all at once Duncan started to say he had to be away for work. Sometimes he didn't appear for days at a time. Georgie wasn't stupid, she could read the signs. There had been many nights of tears, recriminations. After they got the Wiltshire house for weekends he might announce over breakfast on a Saturday that something had come up at work and he had to go back to London. Georgie would be left alone with Jake. When she looked back on that time, she didn't remember being a family. Her abiding image was of her by herself, constantly changing Jake's footwear: stuffing his plump little feet into their shiny blue gumboots, doing up

Start-Rite sandals or jelly shoes while the child looked on, solemnly, as if his own feet had nothing to do with him.

Duncan was never unkind to her. He didn't say nasty things or shout or throw plates. She'd have preferred all that, in a way. What he did was simply withdraw his attention from her. To begin with it had been as if he'd been a spotlight and she the only player on the stage. She had felt so vital, so attractive, while she existed in the beam of his desire. But then he'd switched the light out; or more accurately, fixed it on other things: his work, women. Duncan had always been impulsive and restless and at first Georgie had taken these qualities as a sign that he was somehow more than other people: more alive, more intense, more exciting. Later she came to change her mind. To always want new things, new shiny things: wasn't that really just the behaviour of someone very spoilt?

She said nothing to her family. She couldn't face the humiliation, her mother crowing to have been right about him all along. Once Jake started at school she began training as a voice coach. She didn't have the appetite to go back into acting: in any case, she wanted work that could be fitted in around her son. It had been her desire to keep up with Cass that had originally got Georgie into doing accents. Cass was only an occasional mimic, but she could just get someone, their voice, their mannerisms. Seeing her sister gather approval and laughter had made Georgie want to emulate this talent. It was ridiculous, really, to want to impersonate the impersonator. But at drama school she'd found that she loved voice sessions the most. The way you could alter the set of your jaw to get at a voice; by the smallest adjustment of the palate the words came out so differently. The way you put your lips together, flat, like a carp, to enunciate a final consonant. Controlling the breath. How one word could be the key into a character's way of speaking. Now she discovered that she had a gift for helping others to capture patterns of speech. And from the speech came the character. Once someone had the voice, they were able to access everything else that they needed to inhabit another person: the movements, the motivation.

Duncan left her when Jake was in his teens. At least the girl in question was a completely different type from herself: she was spared the cliché of being thrown over for an identikit younger version. Unlike her predecessor, Georgie took away the sculpted head of Duncan which her father had made: Nick had died suddenly, of an unsuspected heart condition, and she was glad to have work of his. The head reminded her of her father more than it did her husband. She didn't mind seeing it every day. Her pride was injured, there was humiliation, but she wasn't heartbroken to find herself alone. The hurt had happened long before, when she first became aware of his infidelities. He'd left without leaving long before the real split took place. He'd wanted to keep on the London mews and the house near Tisbury and she hadn't put up a fight. It was always easier to let him have his own way. He'd given her a cash sum and she'd bought herself the place in Fulham and had some money to spare. You could say what you liked about Duncan, but he'd never been stingy.

By that time Celia had been tipping towards dementia for some months. There were odd transpositions: a yoghurt pot was put into the oven, a hairbrush into the washing machine. Anyone who came into her path was blamed. Someone has taken my watch, she'd accuse. Someone has stolen my cup. Everything which went missing was someone else's fault.

But her ability to spot a weakness or a wound was undimmed.

'Where's that husband of yours?' she'd challenge Georgie.

'In London. He's working in London,' Georgie would answer. This was not untrue.

'I always knew he was a weaselly one,' said Celia, with some satisfaction.

During the early years of Georgie's marriage Cass had gone through her architect training and met Adam. Two years after they qualified they'd been married from Stony Hill Farm, the guests – as brightly dressed as parrots – spilling out on to the snowdrop field with their glasses of fizz. Nick had made a speech all about building: building a marriage, building a family, building together. The family part had proved difficult. Cass had had two miscarriages before Skye, and although they'd tried for more children it hadn't happened. Perhaps this was partly why she'd always spent time at the farm: if she couldn't produce brothers or sisters for her little daughter, then she could at least reproduce the idyllic conditions of her own childhood. And Adam had got on especially well with both Nick and Celia.

Cass and Adam had settled in Penzance after they each quit the London firms they'd been employed by. Skye had been a toddler then and Cass wanted her daughter to have a childhood like hers, with nearby streams and creeks and woods to scamper in, and the coast. They'd set up their own architectural practice, which consisted mostly of extensions for second home owners. The incomers all wanted big kitchens with islands and bi-fold glass doors and utility rooms for their wetsuits. They'd also worked on a number of boutique hotels in the south-west, which brought in new clients. They made a decent living. When Celia became too unwell to live alone at the farm, they'd carried on their practice from there.

Back in London after her mother's funeral, Georgie had raised the subject of the farm with her son.

'What would you feel about Cass taking over Granny and Grandpa's house?'

'She's already taken it over, hasn't she?'

'Well, yes. But I mean, it's been left to us both jointly.'

'Do you want to share it with her?'

'God, no. I wouldn't want to have to have coffee with Adam and Skye every morning.'

'Well then.'

'Yes, but what about you? I know you've always loved it there.'

'I do love it, but I'd never want to live there. It's miles from anywhere.' He'd paused. 'You could always have the barns and Grandpa's studio, I guess? We could even get Aunt Cass to convert the buildings and have one each, for holidays and stuff?'

This had not occurred to Georgie. They could actually share the place. It didn't have to be all or nothing.

'Do you know, that's not a bad idea. We could rent them out as holiday accommodation when we're not using them.'

'If Aunt Cass didn't mind,' Jake said.

'If Cass didn't mind,' echoed his mother.

But Cass did mind. Georgie rang her when she got home, excited by the new idea.

'The thing is, we were planning to convert those buildings ourselves. Skye is going to be using Daddy's studio for her classes. It makes sense for her to come up here, there're loads of people in Truro who are keen on yoga and body work. We were thinking she could live in the old milking parlour, once it's done. Then we might rent out the top barn for holiday lets, to try and recoup some of the costs.'

'Goodness. Well, you've certainly thought it all out,' said Georgie. It was like a punch in the solar plexus, to discover that they'd planned all this without mentioning anything to her.

'And to be honest, I'm just not sure it would work, us both trying to be here. You'd always feel weird, being shut out of the house. It'd be awkward, potentially. And anyway, we'd like you to stay with us when you come. I'd like that. Then we can see you properly, spend time together.'

Stung, Georgie decided she'd leave it for some weeks before she went to Cornwall again to start sorting through their mother's things. Cass had won, again.

When she and Jake next went down to Cornwall, it was in a rented van. Jake had asked if he could have the round, marble-topped table in the top room he had always slept in, as a child. He'd loved that room, being up so high, level with the tree-tops. He'd imagined he was perched in the rigging of a pirate ship, the green fields below transformed into blue waves. The carved wooden bed had seemed like a cabin bed, containing and safe. When it rained in the night it sounded as if the sea was just outside the open window.

Georgie had made a mental list of things she wanted: a series of prints illustrating the Song of Songs by Lettice Sandford, the portrait of Celia's mother that some friend of Augustus John's had painted in the 1930s. The little armchair from her childhood bedroom. She felt she ought to want something that her mother had made: one of the bits of crude appliqué Celia had experimented with in the 1980s, or a blanket she'd crocheted. The childishness of her endeavours was at such odds with the acerbic, demanding woman who had crafted them. For someone who'd set such store by art, she had had no talent of her own, and only occasional enthusiasm; but perhaps that had been one source of her anger. Georgie certainly wanted a share of her father's drawings and sculpted heads. His studio had remained untouched after his death, all his materials still there, as if he might return at any minute. Now it would have to be emptied, for Skye to convert it into a space for what Georgie privately thought of as her pseudo-mystical PE classes.

Cass seemed to be giving her first dibs, which was reasonable, given that she was going to take ownership of the actual house. Jake hadn't had grandparents on his father's side, so Georgie was especially set on the idea that he should choose a few things to remember Nick and Celia by. He'd enjoyed going to the farm, being doted on by Celia. Georgie had felt fonder of her mother then than at any other time, watching her with Jake.

It was curious how denuded the place felt without the presiding force of Celia. The sparseness of the downstairs rooms now looked threadbare rather than daringly artistic, as it had seemed when the sisters were younger. The rugs were stained with ancient dog pee or wine, the rush seats of the chairs and settles darkened and split. Georgie saw that what was lovely about the house was the rooms themselves, their high ceilings and tall windows, rather than the stuff in them. Only the kitchen felt as it always had, cosy and welcoming and dishevelled.

Cass still used the bedroom which had been hers in childhood, and Georgie too slept in her old room when she visited. Celia and Nick's felt very different from how it had when both their parents were alive. The accoutrements of decrepitude — a walking frame, a clunky invalid's tray, the plastic commode — gave it the impersonal atmosphere of a care home. It was a lovely room, with windows on two sides, the only one in the house to have been wallpapered. The blue Chinese paper had faded in places but was still grand, with its pattern of twisting branches and elaborate, long-tailed birds. The bureau that Celia had inherited from her mother was still in place, dotted with envelopes and papers and silver-topped pin boxes. Celia had used it as her dressing table and to write letters at: it had always been covered with bits and pieces. As children the girls had loved being allowed to open the little drawers with their tiny ivory knobs. Each was lined with brown velvet, spotted with age. Here was treasure: Celia's jewellery, antique letters tied with ancient ribbon, a contemporary photograph of Alfred, Lord Tennyson. They weren't supposed to look in these drawers unless their mother was close by, hovering. Their contents were the only things in the house that she guarded.

'Do you want to go through Mummy's desk with me, later?' Cass had asked Georgie. 'It's all pretty good rubbish, I should think.'

'God, yes! You never know what we might stumble across in there.'

'I took most of the jewellery out when she was ill. After Adam found her trying to hide Granny's diamond bracelet in the loo cistern.'

'I didn't know Granny had had a diamond bracelet. Mum never wore it, did she? What's it like?'

'Not as nice as it sounds, actually. I'll show you.'

'What happened to that locket, the one with the human hair in it? Do you remember? It always gave me a sort of thrill, a bit, to think that the hair must've belonged to someone who was dead.'

'You were always quite morbid. Do you remember, we used to do elaborate funerals for dead birds and stuff?'

'Yes, and I always wanted to be the vicar. And we tried to mummify a pigeon once.'

'I'd forgotten that! I suppose the person whose hair it was was dead when the locket was made. I mean, it's mourning jewellery, isn't it? That's why it's got the little edging of black enamel and the forget-me-not on the front. It's in the box with the other stuff.'

'Weird. I wonder who the dead person was?'

'Some ancestor. Take your pick,' said Cass.

'Maybe it was from a child who died at birth. Maybe their mother wore it, to remember her baby by,' said Georgie. As soon as the words came out of her mouth she wished she could unsay them.

'Yes, perhaps that was it,' said Cass.

While his mum and aunt were busy in Granny's old room, Jake took himself up to the top floor. He put his head around the bathroom door, to make sure that nothing had changed. The bath still bore the greeny-brown stain where the tap dripped; the loo was still flushed by a long chain, weighted down with a dense rubber ball. He could recall the scratchy surface of that bath against his skin, when he was a child, unlike the slippy-smoothness of the bath at home in London. He went into the room he only ever thought of as his, and sat down on the bed. He liked the things in here best of everything in the house. It was a pity he didn't have any use for the carved wooden bed. Actually, now that he came to think of it, that little table out on the landing, that was a nice thing too. Bit spindly, but he liked the shape, like a clover leaf. And the two glass-topped shelves would be a good place to keep some of the small treasures he'd accumulated: the ancient worked-flint arrowheads he'd found on walks at his dad's place in Wiltshire; the cufflinks and studs that Granny had given him for his twenty-first, gold, set with little sparkling sapphires; some photos he and his girlfriend had had done of themselves in a passport photo booth, pulling faces and, in one, kissing. The table had had a bunch of old medals on the two shelves. When he was a child, Granny had let him use them for dressing up, when the pirate craze abated and he'd had a new-found fascination for soldiers. He stood up and wandered out on to the landing. Both shelves were empty now. He'd ask his mum if he could have it.

Georgie found it emotionally draining, looking through her mother's things. One drawer had been full of old lipsticks, so anti-quated that their casings were almost like jewellery themselves: torpedoes of fluted gold, some of them studded with bright stones. The lipsticks still twisted up out of them, cracked and dried out, but with their ancient colour preserved, like cheap jam.

'Do you think they're worth anything?' Georgie had asked, doubtfully. 'They feel very solid.'

'Shouldn't think so. They're not real, just fake gold and

coloured glass. Rolled gold, maybe,' said Cass. 'Speaking of which, shall we go through the jewellery box, see what we'd both like?'

Cass had put the good jewellery, the things that were in their original old leather boxes, into one shoebox; the costume jewellery, beads and odds and ends into a second. There were a number of medals, some Greek or Roman coins, two old pocket-watches, one with an inscription on the back. Most of the jewellery in the first box had come from Celia's own mother: only her engagement ring, wedding ring and a pair of pearl earrings dated from after her marriage.

'Skye should have Mum's engagement ring,' said Georgie, somehow hoping to make up for her tactlessness about the locket and to gain points for good behaviour.

'I thought you might have wanted it,' said Cass.

'I'm OK. I've still got the Rock of Gibraltar from Duncan.' She smiled. 'I don't really wear much jewellery anyway.'

'Same,' said Cass. 'I suppose we could flog anything we don't want?'

'Shall we see what there is, first?'

Cass took the lid off the shoebox and they began to open each leather case. In one they found a diamond lizard brooch with little ruby eyes; in the next a necklace with matching earrings, prettily set with amethysts and seed pearls. One box, tantalizingly, was empty. Neither of them could recall the piece that it must once have housed. The placid velvet was raised in a circle, where the necklet should have been. There was a tiny gold mesh purse with a gold half-sovereign inside, which they both remembered from childhood as a particularly delightful thing. The clasp was set with tiny turquoises.

'Granny's mother got given this, the day she got engaged,' said Cass.

'How do you know?' said Georgie. She realized how childish she sounded.

'Mum told me.'

Another box contained the mourning locket, still suspended from its thick gold chain.

'I can't help sort of loving it, even though it is a bit macabre,' said Georgie.

'You have it, then,' said Cass. 'I'd sooner keep the purse anyway.'

'Oh, but I love the purse!' said Georgie. She felt crestfallen, outplayed; as if her toy had been snatched from her hand, mid-game. 'I was going to say I'd like the purse. It reminds me of when we were little.'

Cass sighed. 'Well,' she said, levelly, 'you have the purse, then. You have the purse and the locket.'

'But is that fair? I want it to be fair. If Skye has the engagement ring and you have the amethyst things and the lizard . . . what do you think?'

'I think that's fine. Why don't you take the earrings, then, and we'll call it quits?'

Georgie felt aware that her hoard was likely of considerably lower value than Cass's. Her pieces were made of gold, while Cass would get the precious stones. But she had sounded querulous already and could not think how to mention the discrepancy without appearing more so.

'We didn't find the diamond bracelet that you mentioned,' she said.

'I've already got that, remember?' said Cass. ' 'Cause Adam salvaged it from Mum's squirrelling.'

She did not now repeat her earlier offer to show it to her sister.

'I'll leave them back to Skye in my will, if Jake doesn't have a daughter,' said Georgie.

'Oh God, let's not think about that now,' said Cass. 'Do you want to go through the other box, or shall we leave it for today?'

Georgie felt too flat and defeated for any further division of spoils. 'Shall we do it tomorrow?' she said. 'I feel too tired to do it now.'

'Let's go down and have a drink,' said Cass.

'Let's,' said Georgie.

But the next day Cass did not bring up the subject of the second box and Georgie had not had the heart to prod her.

16.

Melbourne, Australia

Owen hadn't been looking to meet anyone, not so soon after he'd had his heart almost broken, but there was just something about Hazel. She wasn't the young woman everyone would have fallen in love with, he could see that. It was sometimes puzzling to him that he had. She was so different from the girl he'd been with before. That first time he met her, he didn't think he'd seen her smile more than once or twice all day. She was a solemn little thing, compact and watchful. She wasn't heavy, but there was a suggestion of sturdiness, as if she'd be the sort of person who'd insist on carrying their own luggage.

A bunch of them had been going down to Mount Martha. It was the beginning of October, early in the season for a day on the beach, but it'd been warm all week and the roads wouldn't be chock full of caravans just yet. They went in two cars, seven of them. Owen's sister Dawn was doing her teacher training, which is how she'd met Hazel. She'd invited her along, together with a couple of friends from her schooldays.

They'd set up a net for volleyball on the sand and brought the cool-boxes out of the boot of one of the cars. They all stripped off their tops, keeping just their shorts on. Hazel was the only girl who wasn't wearing a skimpy bikini, and wore a navy blue one-piece. She and Dawn and the other two girls had gone down to the water's edge in their bare feet. The wet sand there had formed small ridges, like the half-buried ribcage of some vast whale. It felt nice to walk on. After their paddle they'd come back up to join the others.

'I don't know about you lot, but I'm starving,' Owen had said.

'Yeah, it's like when you used to go on a school trip. You'd have eaten your packed lunch before the bus even pulled out,' said one of the other boys.

'Then you'd be begging your mates to share theirs, when it actually came to lunch-time,' said Dawn.

There was an elderly couple sitting just along from them, in fold-up aluminium chairs. The woman was glancing through a copy of *Woman's Day*, while her husband looked at the sea. After a time he stood and advanced towards the water. When he came back a little while later, his wife started shouting. The young people looked across to see what was making her so agitated and saw that there was blood all over one of the old man's feet. With no hesitation, Hazel went across and knelt beside him. Owen followed her, to see if he could help out.

It was a nasty gash. Probably he'd trodden on a piece of broken glass. Hazel asked the woman if she had anything with her that could be used as a bandage, but she nodded no. The wife looked more shaken up than the injured husband. Hazel darted back and grabbed her T-shirt. The man's foot was like a root vegetable left too long in the ground, misshapen and with prominent veins in thick strands. It wasn't a foot most people would have been in a hurry to take hold of, but Owen looked down and saw that Hazel had it in both her hands. He saw that she had freckles on the back of her hands and sprinkled along her arms. Mulling it over later, he thought that maybe that was the moment he'd started to like her. It seemed to him that there was something honest about freckles. She'd bound the wound tight, tucking the fabric under itself neatly, and then Owen helped the old guy back up the sand to his car. Likely he'd need a few stitches. Hazel followed, carrying the chairs, chatting calmly to the woman.

'How come you knew what to do there?' Owen asked her, after they'd driven off.

'My mum's a nurse,' she said.

'I hope that wasn't your favourite T-shirt?' he'd smiled.

'It's fine.'

They'd gone in the water a few times, over the course of the afternoon. He'd noticed that Hazel was a strong swimmer and he liked that about her, too.

When he'd turned up at her parents' house the weekend after, to take her out for the first time, he'd brought her a new T-shirt.

'What's it got written on it?' she'd asked.

'The name of an American university, I reckon,' he'd said.

'Oh. Is Yale somewhere you've been?'

He'd laughed. 'No, I just thought it looked, you know, quite cool.'

'Oh. Right.'

He liked it that she didn't say thank you. She didn't waste words. That was one of the things which drew him to her, that she was careful. He had the apprehension that she would be careful with people's feelings as well.

They never forgot the old man on the beach with the cut foot. Owen even mentioned it in his speech at the wedding, how the first thing he'd seen her do was a kindness. It'd come up in conversation now and again, over the years. And when he got sick and they were told the diagnosis, Owen had said, 'You're not going to be able to just sort this out with an old T-shirt, Haze.'

It wasn't often that Hazel cried, but the tears came then. She didn't know how they were going to find the strength to break it to the children.

★

Since she'd been widowed Hazel had found herself staring at women of her own age or older, in cafés, at the library or in the shops. Had some of them lost their husbands too? And if so, how did they manage? How did they go about the streets, post letters, cook their evening meal for one, answer the telephone and sound normal? How did they do everything, alone? She wanted to ask someone how it was possible not to just lie on the floor, for the rest of their lives. It always surprised her, that she too seemed capable of mimicking ordinary life, that she kept putting one foot in front of the other: getting dressed in the mornings, making a cup of coffee, glancing at the news. So much of what you did was automatic. All the time she felt the tug of grief, pulling and pulling at her, as visceral as indigestion. I can lie on the floor and weep after I've done this, she'd think as she performed each little task. But somehow she managed to stay upright.

People said a happy marriage didn't leave the one who was left behind as devastated as an unhappy one, but that didn't seem to be true. They said that time made it better, but that was a lie as well. What they didn't tell you was that it was the same as when someone was away travelling, or the children went off to uni: the longer they'd been gone, the more you missed them. The first few weeks hadn't been so bad, apart from the silence in the house. The quiet had a thickness and a weight to it, like wet wool. But there'd been a sense of relief, to begin with, that Owen wasn't sick any longer, wasn't in any more pain. And the kids had been around a lot, in that early period. Her maternal feelings had trumped her own grief, then, so that she felt it was her job to comfort Anna and David for their sorrow at losing their dad. Then arranging the funeral had kept her busy, and responding to the nice cards and letters people had written. Everyone had liked Owen. More than they liked her: she knew that. He'd been more outgoing than her, sunnier. She knew she was stubborn and could come across as dry.

She often thought of her mother now, and wished that she could talk to her. She found herself missing her more than she had in years. This fresh loss seemed to open a door to the losses that had gone before. Her mother had known all about grief. Hazel wished that she'd thought to ask her about it, how you got through mourning. Did you in fact get through it? Did it ever go away, or did it – as she now suspected – stay with you like an aching knee, an impediment, a constant pain, that you just learned to live with? Lately, when people asked her how she was, she could see the wary look in their eyes that said: be OK. It wasn't that people didn't have sympathy, she got that: it was more that grief was embarrassing to them. It was too raw, too messy. Grief wasn't just a glassy single tear rolling down a dignified cheek. It was snot and spit and choking sobs and it went on and on and on. In the first months, crying at night, she practically embarrassed herself with the noises that came out of her, more animal than human.

Researching family history had been something to take her mind off the loss of Owen and keep her occupied, now that she'd taken early retirement. She volunteered at a primary school, listening to the youngest kids reading, two afternoons a week. But still, time seemed to hang around her in dusty drapes and folds, like curtains from a big house rehung in a bungalow.

Her mother had been keen on genealogy and Hazel had inherited all her papers. Her sister Karen didn't see a lot of point in looking backwards. Too much retrospection could get you down, she said. She only wanted to look ahead. After their mother died, it had been Hazel who had sorted through everything, with Owen as her helper. That had been eight years before. The task of clearing the house had fallen to her, Karen having been too busy with her shop to stay on after the funeral and help. In any case, she hadn't wanted anything from the house, not even photographs. Owen had been fantastic. There was so much stuff: ancient Christmas cards and receipts, stacks of magazines, every single one of the three children's school reports.

There had been suitcases full of old clothes, blankets, linens. One had contained her deceased brother's clothes. There was something terrible about the fact that the things Stephen had worn so long ago were now back in fashion. The young were all for 1970s style now: the flared jeans, the cheesecloth shirts, the tank tops. A vintage store would've given good money for these old clothes, but Hazel knew she could not allow his T-shirts and jeans and the rest of his clobber to go out into the world and have a life without him. She'd either have to keep them, as her mother had, or destroy them. Her mother had not been able to take the latter course, and neither could she. But Owen, Lord rest him, had taken care of it. He'd quietly put the things back into the case and taken it out to the car. The next time she went to put some groceries in the boot, it had been empty. She never asked him what he'd done with the case and he never told her.

The other case had been more difficult to whittle down. It contained the drawings her brother had done in primary school, his art-school portfolio. There were school photographs, in an envelope, all together. Something about them – their simulation of the formal tradition of portrait photography, the pathos of that little boy in school uniform – had made them almost unbearable to look at. When Hazel had pulled them out to see what was what, she had recoiled like someone burnt. To see his six-year-old or nine-year-old face was brutal. He looked so innocent, so full of hope, a little embarrassed smirk playing around his mouth. Her mother had kept two or three framed pictures of Stephen out on display, maybe so as to avoid being ambushed like this by the unexpected sight of him. But Hazel only had photographs of her own children on show in her house. She hadn't seen Stephen's face for a long time. She could not look through the school pictures, she could not throw them away: she could only replace them in the envelope they had ended up in. There were letters. Notebooks, abandoned after only a handful of pages, in which he'd started writing a diary or jotting thoughts down.

A long time before, Hazel's feelings about her brother had settled into an anger that was dull enough not to cause her trouble, as long as she didn't poke at it.

The initial childhood grieving had been sharp and short. The fury which came later had come as a shock: hot and sticky, destroying everything it spilled over, like lava. It was murderous: it made her want to kill him. The trouble was, he was dead already. More than she loved him, more even than she missed him, she began to hate him for the suffering he'd wrought on the family. Their mother, most of all. Dad, too. And Karen. And herself, too, if she was honest. They'd been destroyed, almost. But, again like lava, that anger had hardened over as the decades went by. It could bear a little weight without cracking. And yet the sight of Stephen in his school photographs was like a chemical reaction, corroding it in an instant. And when the stiff layer of rage disappeared, the pain, the sadness were still there underneath. They hadn't gone away after all.

Under her mother's bed had been a smaller suitcase. Hazel knew what was in it: the duffel bag Mum and Dad had brought back from England after he died. They'd brought his body home, too, so that his grave would be close. Repatriation, was the word. The duffel bag was plastic, the colour of butterscotch, with greyish rope around the top. The rope must once have been white. Owen had seen her flinch at the sight of the duffel bag.

'I'll just have a quick look through this lot, shall I?' he'd asked, and unceremoniously he emptied it out on the neat counterpane.

Hazel had only nodded. There were a couple of T-shirts, none too clean, a pair of jeans, a paperback book. There was a pair of plimsolls, stiff now and misshapen, like dried-out banana skins. There was a little dented handful of letters and cards that had been pressed together at the bottom of the bag. The medal was pressed against the papers, in a little envelope made of what looked like tracing paper. Owen had taken it out and examined it.

'Reckon this belongs with your old family material, the little painting and the documents and what-not,' he said, handing it to her.

'Mum always kept it in with Stephen's stuff. Well, as you can see. She felt it ought to stay in with his things.'

'I'm going to get one of the document boxes and put all the papers in there. No need to throw any of them away. The duffel bag and these clothes, though, they're going to go. Do you want the suitcase?'

She shook her head, no. Hazel felt almost faint with relief. The duffel bag had been like a land mine, something that had to be stepped around with the greatest caution. She'd been afraid of what was in there for her whole adult life. She didn't know which would be worse: if the things in the bag offered some clue as to why Stephen had done what he did, or if they didn't. Her husband had defused the bomb, simply by tipping its contents out.

Owen had come back into the room with an empty box, into which he had put the school photographs and the rest of the papers. The few letters and cards, the paperback and a notepad from the duffel bag he placed on the top. Now was not the time to take them out and read. Now was the time, he knew, to just get this stuff shifted. Hazel watched him, then stepped over and placed the envelope with the medal on the top, before putting the lid on the box. Let it stay with Stephen's things. It had belonged to Stephen, after all.

Now she was on her own, Hazel decided to use the dining

room table to spread out all the papers from her mother, so she'd be able to see where there were gaps. The family tree had been compiled before the advent of the internet; she'd be able to access all sorts of new information now. It made sense to start with Alice Gale. It was Alice after all who'd started the family off here in Australia. Over the weeks which followed, Hazel read through all the papers concerning her ancestor. There were a surprising quantity of them: William's letters from the Crimea, tied with papery old ribbon; his later letters, so different in their tone, harsh and inflexible. No wonder his wife had looked elsewhere for affection. There were a handful of letters from Edward Nolan, who was to become her husband; correspondence from the friends and relations in England she had left behind. Hazel found that she looked forward to the evenings, now that she was absorbed in the lives of these people. She understood why her mother had become so absorbed by family history: it was like being a detective, unearthing clues, joining the dots, following a trail. After she'd prepared her evening meal, eaten and cleared the things away, she would make herself a cup of tea and settle down in the dining room. She'd pulled the chairs out so that papers relating to each individual could be put into separate piles on their empty seats.

She began to augment her mother's records with research of her own. She tracked down a copy of the marriage certificate from William's second wedding, to a woman whose name was given as Mrs Sarah Lockwood, née Gregory. A widow, she'd been. She found, too, the birth certificate of their daughter, Harriet. Neither of these were strictly a part of her research into her ancestry, but still: Harriet's descendants were her and Karen's cousins, albeit distantly. But the dates on these documents caught her interest. This second marriage had taken place in the same year that Alice had set sail for Australia. Gale had clearly been in a hurry. Turning to Harriet's birth certificate revealed why. The infant had been born only two months after her parents were married.

Had Mrs Lockwood's pregnancy already been known to him, when he divorced Alice? Was Harriet in fact his own daughter, or had this Mrs Lockwood been expecting at the time she was widowed? Here was a little riddle. Each possible answer showed Gale in a very different light: he could be a scoundrel who had begun an affair while still married to Alice, or a cuckold who had gallantly given his name to a poor widow's child. If she could track down the date of Mr Lockwood's death, she'd have more to go on.

Hazel did some further digging among the papers already in her possession, to find the date of the divorce. William Gale had cited Alice's adultery as the cause of their rift and yet his marriage to this Mrs Lockwood had taken place only weeks later. It seemed a bit too neat, that both William and Alice should have been involved with new loves at exactly the same moment. Hazel wondered if Alice had been framed, in order for William to obtain the freedom to legitimize his unborn child. She knew enough history to be aware that to be born a bastard in Victorian society was to live for ever under the cloud of disgrace. And yet, Alice had travelled to Australia with the same Dr Nolan whose name was mentioned in the report of the divorce proceedings. And then she had married him: he couldn't have been only a pretext of William Gale's.

You could never find out everything, she realized. A family consisted of elders long buried, as well as the living: stories were the bridges that connected the generations. But not everyone had a story. Looking through the papers and researching online, Hazel saw that you could look all you liked at birth certificates and marriage certificates and death certificates and census and baptismal records, but you couldn't always fill in the gaps that made the fabric of a life. Nor could you know the things that really mattered, what someone's voice was like, their movements. Their motives and desires. Until cameras became an item owned by most families – and when was that, the 1960s? – you couldn't even see someone's smile. Hazel thought that would've been a beautiful thing, to have your ancestors smile at you across the centuries. But the photographic studio portraits of Alice's time required that the sitter be still, maintain a certain gravitas. Probably in those days they all had terrible teeth, too, another reason the antique sitters had kept their mouths clamped shut. Even in old wedding photographs there was no sign of joy or of affection. Brides and their grooms were grim-faced, as if facing a prison sentence. There were no snapshots of people laughing at a shared joke, their eyes shaded by a tree; no casual, carefree holiday pictures.

Among the older papers there was a large padded envelope with *William Gale* written on the outside in her mother's writing. How many birthday cards and Christmas cards, how many gift labels and postcards had Hazel received, in that same writing? The sight of it made her feel at once hollow with sadness. Her poor, broken mother.

At the bottom of the envelope was the painted miniature portrait of Gale as a young man. Her mother had always said it was too precious to expose to the Australian sun. It was painted in watercolour; the light would have faded it. Hazel held the little frame in her hand. It must have been strange for Alice, older and on the other side of the globe, to have looked from time to time at this memento of a young man she had once loved. Hazel wondered if she had been glad to see him as he had been in the days of their courtship. Had she kept the portrait for herself, or for her son, so that he would have some idea of the distant man who was his father?

At least he had not removed the boy from his mother. That was something to be said in his favour. Reading around the social history of the time, Hazel realized that Alice had been comparatively lucky. Some unwanted wives were consigned to lunatic asylums. Most were obliged to relocate to an area distant enough that they could at least attempt to evade the whiff of scandal which would have attended them. Divorced mothers were generally separated from their children, forbidden to write or visit them. A woman could never hope to regain her good name, her place in society. Alice had had the opportunity of a new life and she had seized it.

She and Dr Nolan had had a child together, a daughter. Hazel was glad about that: a daughter would have been company for her mother. There was a photograph of the child, perhaps on her christening day, lying on a satiny cushion dressed in cascading frills. Hazel went to the family tree that someone – her paternal grandfather, perhaps – had written out and saw the entry for the girl: Augusta Caroline Nolan, b 1862 d osp 1911. She went to her computer to find out what that meant. When the stark words *Died childless* came up on the screen she felt disappointed. No long-lost cousins, there, to be unearthed and befriended. Invisible pathways connected you to the generations who'd gone before, snaking on and on, forking innumerably, each leading farther and farther back in time to the people you came from. But a path could end too, as Augusta Nolan's did, in a cul-de-sac.

She thought of Stephen. Who would remember you, if you lived only half your life? Some amateur genealogist like herself, beavering away at family history, might chance upon your name, but that was all. Unless you were famous, there was no memorial for just an ordinary person. It seemed to Hazel that this was the trouble, with the dead. You either thought about them all the time, as she did now with her husband; or there was the risk that they were forgotten. Stephen was just a lanky red-haired kid who'd dropped out of art college. Once the people who had known him were gone, there would be no one and nothing to remember him by. Her mother had made her promise that she and Karen would tend to his grave after she was gone, but with Karen living so far off, the task had always fallen to her. She visited once or twice a year, on his birthday and latterly on their mother's. But what would happen, when she died? Her kids had never met their uncle, she couldn't expect them to traipse off to the cemetery for the rest of their lives. Hazel wished she could think of a way to keep his memory alive.

Hazel felt some apprehension about getting the box full of Stephen's photographs and papers out, now that she no longer had Owen as an emotional bomb disposal operative. But somewhat to her surprise she found that there'd been a further shift in her feelings about her brother, in the years that had elapsed since her mother's death. She appeared to have come to some kind of accommodation with him. This time she knew she would be strong enough to look through the photographs. She wasn't getting any younger: if any pictures needed labelling, if the people in them wanted identifying, now was the moment.

She began to sift through the pictures of her brother. To her delight she found that, this time, she was pleased to see him. Yes, there was always the tinge of sadness, but now even the school photographs made her smile. A memory flashed into her mind, of sitting beside him at a table, drawing a little hand-made comic book together. Lord knew what had happened to it. She was intrigued to see a look of her own kids in some of her brother's expressions, something she hadn't remarked before. Strange to think that her two were older, now, than Stephen had ever become. Hazel thought that maybe it was time to discard the school reports; likely no one would ever want to look at them again. Her daughter Anna and son David might just about glance at their own parents' old school stuff, but it was doubtful they'd be interested in these. His drawings and notebooks, though, those she would keep. She glanced through one or two of them.

The flattened letters that had once been in the duffel bag she opened out. Some of them were from their mum, addressed to *Stephen Nolan, Stony Hill Farm, Nr Truro, Cornwall, UK*. She began to read through them, her heart in her mouth. But the familiarity of the things their mother wrote about brought a warm glow of memory, for all the nostalgia they evoked. She found herself recalling some of the prosaic details of their home: the colour of the kitchen Formica, the bathroom tiles. They'd had a little fishtank, for a time, with a tiny stone grotto; she and Karen had fought to feed the fish. She hadn't thought of this for years. Among the letters was an envelope that was fatter than the rest and this she kept until last, thinking it would contain a longer letter. Instead there were two pieces of paper folded within their mother's usual breezy summary of family news. She opened them out and saw that they were notes from her and her sister. 'Hi Stephen, we waved you goodbye, did you look down and see us?' Hazel had no memory of writing this, yet here it was. She felt tears gather, to be reminded how much she'd loved her big brother and missed him, even then. It sometimes seemed as if she'd spent her whole life missing him, or trying not to.

Hazel wished that Owen was here so that she would have someone to show it to. She put the letter and her little sister's back into their envelope and picked up the notepad. She flicked it open, expecting to find only blank pages. But there was handwriting on the first page. Stephen's handwriting.

Dear Nut,

Sorry this is so tardy (as Mum would say), I keep meaning to sit down and write to you, but a lot has been going on. I was with our cousins down on their farm in Cornwall, it is an amazing place. They swim in the river (no snakes!), it's icy cold. Maybe I'll take you there one day when you're older. At the moment I'm in London, going to see some sights for a few days before heading back to the Clarkes I hope. They have

horrible soup here in England if you go into a pub for a bite of lunch, it's
a bit like gravy, but with bits in, you would HATE it. The lollies are
nice though, especially one called a Mivvi, which is strawberry on the
outside. Tell Mum I

She lifted the page, but the next was blank. The letter was still fixed to the pad. For a moment her heart sank, to think there might have been more, but then she realized how lucky she was, to've got the letter at all. He had never sent it, but after all it had found its way to her. If he'd posted the letter it would likely have ended up in the bin, whereas now it was fresh, as if Stephen was writing to her across the decades. He'd been the only person who'd called her 'Nut'. At the time she'd protested against the nickname, but now the sight of it in his handwriting felt like a precious gift. He had been thinking of her, all the way over there in England. He hadn't forgotten her.

There were still a few other odds and ends to sort through, in the box containing Stephen's things, but they could wait. It wasn't every day that a letter reached you, forty-odd years on. Hazel felt quite overwhelmed, both from the sight of her own childish letter to her brother and from the unexpected appearance of his reply to her. Once again, she wished Owen was there. But instead, she went through to the kitchen to make herself a cup of tea and then lifted the telephone to call her sister.

'You know what we ought to do?' said Karen, after Hazel had told her about the letters.

'No, what?'

'We ought to plan a trip over there. Now you've done all this family research. We could visit the ancestral home, or whatever you'd call it. Do a bit of a tour.'

'That's a fantastic idea! Would you be able to take the time off, from the shop?'

'Why not? Ginny could hold the fort for a couple of weeks. Three.'

Ginny was Karen's adult daughter. She'd been raised without a father, her dad having disappeared to the other side of the country when she was still a toddler.

'We could look up the cousins Stephen was friendly with, when he was there.'

'Have you got addresses for them?'

'No, but I could find them online, I'm pretty sure. Mind you, Clarke's not exactly a rare name.'

'Well, I could go pretty much any time, if I have a few weeks' notice.'

'Shall we aim for next year? What about April, after your birthday?'

'Sure. Then we can have two springs in one year. That'd be pretty nice.'

After she'd replaced the receiver, Hazel sat still holding her empty cup. It had been a long while since she felt like this and it took her a moment to recognize the sensation. Then it dawned on her. For the first time since Owen died, Hazel found she was looking forward to something.

17.

2016

Cass's husband Adam had been half-watching the evening news when a story about a Victoria Cross came on. A school somewhere up north had been planning to sell a VC. The medal had been entrusted to them in the 1920s by a grieving mother or widow whose son, or husband, had been killed in action during the First World War. The school now wanted to use the money raised from the sale to build a sports pavilion. A sum of money – a large sum of money – was mentioned. It was this which made Adam's ears prick up. He hadn't known medals could be so valuable.

The words 'Victoria Cross' sounded a sort of mental klaxon. It reverberated, like the afterthrum of a bell. Hang on a minute. He sprang up and went through to the kitchen.

'Didn't someone of yours win a Victoria Cross?' he asked Cass, who was cutting up leeks with her Japanese cleaver.

'Mmn. Yes. I can't remember what his name was, someone on Mum's side. It's here, somewhere. There was a collection of them.'

'Here? Where?'

'I'm not sure. They used to be in that glass table on the top floor, do you remember?'

'When you say they, how many are you talking about?'

'Well, there was only one VC, obviously. But there were always a few other medals with it, a collection: probably about seven? Something like that.'

'Well, apparently they're worth a couple of hundred grand.'
She put the cleaver down. 'You're joking.'
'I'm not. You might want to start thinking where it's got to.'
'Are you sure?'
'They just said so, on the news.'
'Jesus,' said Cass.
'Exactly,' said Adam.

Cass couldn't think when she'd last seen the medal. After supper she'd gone to look through the little drawers in the old desk her mother had used as a dressing table. It wasn't there. Then she and Adam together had gone through every drawer they could think of: the three shallow drawers in the sideboard in the dining room; the tallboy on the half-landing where most of Nick's drawings had ended up; the dresser in the kitchen. Next they went up to the first floor and started through the chest of drawers in Georgie's old room. The mirrored cabinet and the shelves under the basin in the guest bathroom. The blanket chest on the landing. At last they had moved up to the third floor and gone through every nook and cranny where the medals might have ended up: the old wooden wardrobe in the back room, the bedside cupboard in the little room Jake had slept in as a child. Nothing.

The following morning Cass rang Georgie.

'I know this is going to sound odd, but have you got any idea where those old medals we used to have up on the top floor could've got to? Only Adam saw something on telly about a VC last night and he thinks it might be very valuable.'

'Oh what larks!' said Georgie. 'A treasure hunt.'

'Any ideas?'

'How valuable, anyway?' asked Georgie.

'Possibly very. He mentioned two hundred thousand.'

'No way! Shit.'

'I know.'

'Didn't you have all that sort of stuff in a shoebox in the cupboard in Mum's room?'

'Genius! I'd completely forgotten. I'll go and look now.'

'Keep me posted. Let me know when you find them, so I can start planning my holiday of a lifetime.'

'I will,' said Cass.

Cass could feel her heart thudding as she went up to Celia's old room. She didn't consider herself to be an especially acquisitive person, but the prospect of unearthing something of such value was a bit like a fairy story. It was hard not to feel excited. The cupboard had long been emptied of her parents' clothes and shoes, but on the shelf above were four or five boxes. She hadn't opened any of them since sorting out her mother's stuff after she died. She took the chair from in front of the dressing table and stood up on it. The boxes were heavy. She lifted them down and one by one took them over to the bed. Adam came in with two cups of coffee.

'Oh, there you are,' she said. 'I could've done with a hand getting these down.'

'I told you I'd be up in a couple of minutes,' he said. 'Anyway, I'm here now. What do you want me to do?'

'Nothing, I've done it now.' Sometimes Cass sounded sharper than she meant to. She worried that she was slowly turning into her mother and wondered if Adam shared the same concern. If he did, he was too kind to say so.

They began to sift through the contents of the boxes. The first was full of old letters, the second of photographs. In the third were a couple of old pocket watches. And there they were: several medals. There was one with a red and white striped ribbon, another with a ribbon of palest blue edged with yellow. Several more had stripey ribbons, but mostly the ribbons were various shades of red.

'Which one is it?' asked Adam.

'I don't know!' said Cass. The sight of them made her feel strangely agitated.

'It's got to be one of these,' said Adam, pointing at two crosses, each with white enamel decoration.

'Let's take them all down to the office, look them up online,' said Cass.

Neither of them liked the look of computers with their endless wires, nor of filing cabinets. After Celia died, when it was established that they would be staying on at the farm, Adam had created an office from the old lean-to by the kitchen, where the deep freeze had been in Cass's childhood. All the admin stuff was confined here, so that the house would retain its period feel.

'What did he win it for, anyhow?' asked Adam as they made their way downstairs with the shoebox.

'Do you know, I don't think I've ever been told. It was in the Crimea, that's all I know really. I had to do a school essay once, at primary school, about a woman from history that I admired. Well, I didn't really know of any: we'd done Queen Elizabeth the First and I'd heard of Cleopatra, but that was about it. So I cribbed the whole thing out of the Ladybird book about Florence Nightingale. The writer was called L. Du Garde Peach. That's literally the only thing I can remember. I thought it was a variant of the name Hildegarde, but actually I think the writer was a man. Anyway.'

'Someone must know, though,' said Adam. 'About the medal.'

'I suppose,' said Cass. But she sounded doubtful.

Skye was already in the office, using the photocopier.

'What are you two up to?' she asked.

'Dad's just found out that one of the old medals we've got is very valuable,' said Cass.

'We're just trying to work out which one it is,' said Adam.

'What? How come?' asked Skye.

'Well, it's a VC,' said Cass.

'From the Crimea,' said Adam.

'I did the Crimea in Year 5,' said Skye.

'Did you?' said Cass. 'I don't remember that.'

'Yes. We did Mary Seacole. Mrs Seacole.'

'Who's that?' asked Cass.

'She was a nurse. Jamaica, she'd come from, originally. Pretty amazing woman, actually. She had a restaurant and a shop and she looked after the soldiers. Bandaged them up and gave them tea and stuff.'

'We were just talking about Florence Nightingale. I suppose your one worked for her?'

Skye rolled her eyes. 'No, Mum! That's the whole point. Mrs Seacole had learned all about herbal medicine and stuff, from when she was in Jamaica. She was more like a traditional medicine practitioner. Closer to a doctor, actually, than a nursey type of nurse. And, like, a businesswoman. She was this really cool woman of colour. Ahead of her time.'

'Oh. Well, that's good.'

Adam was getting pictures of medals up on to the computer screen.

Skye took her photocopies and wandered off.

They drew a blank. None of the medals in the box was the Victoria Cross. Adam got up a couple of images of VCs, one from the front, the other from the back. At least now they'd know what they were looking for.

'You don't think your mother would've put it in the bank or something, for safe keeping?' Adam suggested.

'God, no. She didn't even lock the house, she'd never have put anything in a strong room.'

'Did she know it was valuable?'

'I don't think so. She never said so to me. She hated things like the *Antiques Roadshow*: well, she didn't watch any television, did she? I don't think she'd have known what it was worth. Although, having said that, she always assumed everything to do with her side of the family was important and unique. Do you remember? She'd say things like: "That tallboy is frightfully valuable." When brown furniture is literally worthless.'

'Might she've sold it, that's what I'm getting at?'

'I doubt it. She kept all the things she got from her parents, anyway. Remnants of their glorious past and all that. I don't know of her ever selling anything. Or buying anything much, now I come to think of it. We don't know if it was even worth anything when she had it. They could have just recently shot up in value.'

Over lunch, Adam and Cass made a list of all the people they could think of who'd been in the house since they first arrived there themselves. There'd been three cleaners: Celia's old daily had died and had been replaced by a girl who kept breaking things; since then they'd employed a woman from the other side of Truro. They couldn't remember the name of the accident-prone girl, but they agreed it was unlikely she'd have stolen it: unlikely that she'd have even known what it was. There'd been the electrician who'd had to rewire, he'd had a lad with him; the decorators who'd repaired the ceiling in the dining room, where the bath above had overflowed. Adam said he would ring around, ask everyone about it. The trouble was, with a thing like that, it would've been so easy to pocket. Adam went through to the office to make the calls. He and Cass agreed that they wouldn't mention what the medal actually was: they'd just say it was an old family one, that they wanted to find it for sentimental reasons. No need to broadcast the fact that they had – or, rather, had mislaid – something so valuable in the house.

'How's it going?' asked Georgie, when she rang that evening.

'We still haven't found it,' said Cass.

'Jakey used to play with those medals, when he had the craze for dressing up as a soldier, do you remember? He used to wear that old red dressing gown of Dad's and . . .' said Georgie.

'Fuck! Why didn't you say that yesterday?' said Cass.

'Well, because it's got nothing to do with anything,' said Georgie.

'Yes it has! He might know where it's got to. He might even have it himself.'

'I think I'd have seen it in his room if he'd nabbed it when he was seven,' said Georgie.

'Well, I'm going to ring him,' said Cass.

'Be my guest,' said Georgie, cross now. Cass was the one who'd grabbed everything. She should have taken care of it.

Cass suddenly felt suspicious about Jake having wanted the trefoil table which the medals had been housed in. Maybe he'd asked for the table because he already had the medal? But she found it maddeningly difficult to get hold of Jake. He had an assistant and his assistant had an assistant, too.

They weren't even all that polite, these people. She'd rung more than once. Mr Newhouse would call her back, they said. When at last he did ring – they were in the middle of supper, by then – Cass came straight to the point: had he got the medal? And if not, did he recall where it had been when he last saw it? But he hadn't and he couldn't.

'But you've got the table, haven't you? The display table they used to be kept in?' said Cass.

'Yes, I have. It looks really nice, actually. I've got it in the hallway at my flat. Emma put some of her crystals in there.' Emma was his girlfriend.

'Can you look and just make sure it didn't somehow get underneath the velvet?'

'Sure,' said Jake. 'Hold on, I'll go and look now. But I really doubt it.'

And he was right, it wasn't there.

The next day Adam telephoned the insurance people. No, Celia had not claimed against it; nor would Cass and Adam be eligible to do so, since an item of that value would've had to have been listed separately. It wouldn't be insured under their general household contents policy.

'It was always just kept up on the third floor in a sort of case they had,' Adam said, pointlessly.

'Well, nowadays, with an item of that value, we'd have insisted that it be kept securely. In a safe or bank vault. These days we usually ask clients to install home safes, somewhere discreet. In some of our older houses there was a safe in plain view, but we don't like to make it that easy for potential burglars. The difficulty always is, with something like a medal or a coin – even a piece of jewellery – it's all too easy to remove undetected. When did you say you'd seen it last?'

'My wife is fairly sure it was there at the time of her mother's death,' said Adam, even though Cass had never said anything of the sort.

'So it could have been taken at any time, really.'

'Yes, but that doesn't help us much,' said Adam.

'If there's anything else that you feel should be itemized on your policy, it might be an idea. Strictly speaking, jewellery and so on should be revalued every five years or so, for insurance purposes. And it makes sense to have photographs of small items.'

The call over, Adam groaned with frustration. Now what were they supposed to do?

'Look,' said Cass, without preamble, as soon as her sister picked up her phone, 'are you busy this weekend? Is there any chance you could come down, help me and Adam go over everything with a fine-toothed comb? We think Mum must've hidden the medal when she was going batty. It must be here, somewhere. You know what she was like, squirrelling. We could do with a fresh pair of eyes. There might be some very obvious place we haven't thought of.'

'OK,' said Georgie, at once. It was nice to be needed.

Cass came to collect her from the station. Even before Georgie had done up her seatbelt, Cass asked her, 'Did you know that Mum had had an affair with Hamish's dad?' She had come alone, in order to have this conversation in private.

'Bruce?' said Georgie, astonished.

'Yep,' said Cass. 'I wonder if that's why she was always so tight-lipped about me and Hamish, do you remember? She was always trying to stop me seeing him.'

'Are you sure?' said Georgie.

'Absolutely. I found some letters he'd written her, while I was hunting for the medal. You can read them, if you want.'

'Where?' asked Georgie.

'Where what?' asked Cass. 'Where did I find the letters or where did they have their trysts?'

Georgie laughed. The idea was so implausible. Celia and Bruce had always seemed to dislike each other. And Bruce was so coarse, compared to her father.

'Both, I s'pose.'

'The letters were in the end room, where the telly used to be. In a box behind some books. God knows when she stashed them there. I don't know where it went on. It was when we'd already started at big school, though. I mean, they would have been quite old by then.'

'I wonder if Dad knew,' said Georgie.

'I hope not. I don't think so, actually, do you? He and Bruce were always so pally. The letters were written over a period of about eighteen months, so it was more than just a roll in the hay.'

'Eugh,' said Georgie.

'Sorry,' said Cass. 'I think it got quite serious. She was talking about leaving Dad.'

'Oh my God. That's really awful. Do you think Dad cheated on her as well? He was always quite flirty around women.'

'I don't think so,' said Cass. 'It was all just chat with Dad. It didn't mean anything.'

'What do you think they saw in her? I mean, she could be such a bitch, to be honest.'

Cass sighed. 'Well, she was very beautiful. And spirited.'

'I suppose so,' said Georgie.

'So, what are we going to do with it, when we do find it? If we do, I should say,' asked Georgie.

They were having supper in the kitchen, well into a second bottle of red wine.

'We will find it,' said Adam.

'We may not,' said Cass.

'Yes, but if we do?' said Georgie.

'We were thinking it'd pay for the converting of the old buildings.'

'Oh. But I thought you were going to go ahead with all that anyway,' said Georgie.

'Well, yes. But we'd have had to take out a loan and this way we could do it without the bank. Plus we don't want to go on working for ever, you know,' said Adam.

'How much were you budgeting, to do the building work? I thought you said the medal was worth about two hundred grand?' said Georgie.

Neither Cass nor Adam answered right away and Georgie detected a shiftiness in her sister.

'I think it might be worth a bit more than we'd thought originally. Because it's one of the first actions that a military VC was awarded for. I've been looking into the history of it,' said Adam.

'How much more?' Georgie asked.

'Maybe as much as four hundred thousand,' said Adam.

'Cass?' Georgie pressed.

'Well, look, we talked it over and we came to the view that really we'd be entitled to the lion's share of whatever the medal fetched. Because it was here, presumably, when you agreed to sell out your half to us; so effectively we paid you for your share of everything then. I mean, I offered you pretty much anything you wanted out of the house and you never mentioned the medal at the time.'

'You didn't offer me things! I was left half this house and half its contents by Mum, just as you were. It wasn't up to you to offer me stuff that already belonged to me. And you didn't mention it then, either.' Georgie could hear her voice rising.

'But you had plenty of opportunity at the time we bought you out. If you'd been interested in the medal then, you could easily have said so,' said Adam. 'There has to be some limit, time-wise, otherwise you could start taking the teaspoons or whatever every time you visit.'

'Hang on, let me get this straight,' said Georgie. 'You get me to come down here to help you rifle through every inch of this house, every drawer and cupboard, to search for this medal. And then, even if I find it, you keep it. And when you sell it, you don't split the money with me? Fucking unbelievable.' Georgie could not help looking around the room for supporters, even though there were only the three of them at the table.

'Look, of course we'd give you something from the sale,' Cass said. 'But the fact is that you're really well set up. You own your house outright, you've got no mortgage; and you've got savings. You've presumably still got cash from when you made your share of this place over to us? And money that Duncan gave you. And even if you got through all of that, Jake is loaded. He'd bail you out, if all else failed.'

'What, and Skye is a pauper? We're all supposed to feel sorry for Skye because the only thing she stands to inherit is the whole of this place?'

'Skye's business is less lucrative than Jake's, that's all. Therapists make less money than entrepreneurs. That's just a fact.'

'She's not a therapist, she's a gym teacher with pretensions,' Georgie snapped. 'In any case, I'd never go to Jake for a handout. Yes, he's doing really well, but that's because he's bright and hard-working. He spotted a gap in the market and he went all-out to build his business. He's put in eighteen-hour days to get to where he's got. In any case, money ought to be like water: it ought to go down the generations, not up.'

'Yes, and that's all very admirable,' said Adam. His voice had flattened with an exaggerated kind of patience.

'Oh, fuck off, Adam,' said Georgie.

'OK, look: let's just step back, shall we? We don't even know where the bloody VC is at this moment. We don't need to be squabbling about it now. Let's get to bed, and tomorrow hopefully we'll find it and once it's been found we can get it properly valued and then we can weigh up outcomes,' said Cass.

Adam wasn't around in the morning, when Georgie came down for breakfast.

'I'm really sorry about what I said last night,' Georgie said to Cass.

'Telling my husband to fuck off, do you mean?'

'God, no. Not that. If anything I ought to tell him to fuck off more often.'

They grinned at each other.

'I meant when I was unkind about Skye's work. I'm sorry. Of course that's not really what I think, I was just cross.'

Cass sighed.

'No wonder they say money is the root of all evil. Look at us, bickering. It's dreadful.'

'I don't know that it's money that's the trouble. I think maybe unfairness is the root of all evil, when it comes down to it.'

Cass didn't reply.

'If I find it first I'm going to snaffle it without telling you,' said Georgie.

Neither of them were entirely sure if she was joking.

After lunch they went for a stroll, just the two of them. Adam was very visibly keeping out of Georgie's way.

'Oh, by the way, I've been meaning to tell you: I've had a letter from Stephen's sister.'

'Stephen who?' said Georgie.

'You know, Stephen. Stephen Nolan. Australian Stephen.'

'Oh God,' said Georgie. She wasn't sure if it was because feelings had already been running high, but hearing his name brought her a pang of almost liquid sadness.

'Yes. She's coming to England in April, going to various places with a connection to family, a sort of mini heritage trail, you can imagine. Anyway, she wants to meet us. I was going to ask if you'd come down for a night or two when the time comes, so we could tackle her together. You may remember things I don't. I expect she'd like to hear about him, when he was young.'

'He was only ever young,' Georgie said quietly.

'What? Oh yes, I see what you mean. God, that was awful, when he died. Awful. It's surprising how often I think of him, even now. He just comes into my mind. Does he you?'

'Yes. Well actually, no and yes. Sometimes I'll go for a year or two and hardly think of him at all; and then the thought of him will come up out of nowhere and he'll be on my mind a lot.'

'I wonder if we were more traumatized by it than we knew at the time?'

'Probably,' said Georgie. 'Before that it had never even

entered my mind as a thing that was possible, suicide. Let alone someone of our own age.'

Cass sighed. 'I know. It was as if we lived in a house that didn't have that room in it. And then it did, after all.'

'Yes, and once the door to that room had been opened, you could never quite close it again. Never forget that it was there.'

'Poor Stephen,' said Cass.

'Poor all of us,' said Georgie.

18.

England, 2017

Hazel was planning to visit the place in Cornwall where Stephen had stayed that summer, which was still in the family after all this time. The night before she left for England, she got out the box of her brother's papers. It occurred to her that there might be information about the Clarkes she hadn't previously paid attention to. There was a thick white envelope, addressed to Stephen in London, with handwriting she did not recognize. She must have missed it, before. She took out the letter, glanced at the signature. Celia. That was the mother of the woman she was going to meet, Cass. Thanks to her family history research, Hazel now knew that this branch of the family were descended from William Gale's second wife, Sarah. Celia was the one who had given him the medal, her mother had told Hazel.

It was a terrible letter. The woman seemed to be blaming Stephen for a lot of things. Hazel had forgotten that he'd been in a car accident before he got sick, and Celia mentioned some other incidents she seemed to be irate about. It didn't make a lot of sense. There was something about chickens. *I don't want you to try to contact Cass or Georgie again. I think you are very destructive, even though you may not mean to be.* What a horrible person, Hazel thought. She crumpled up the letter into a ball and carried it through to the kitchen, where she stuffed it into the bin. It left a sour taste in her mouth. Stephen had been such a sweet kid, it didn't make sense that anyone could have written such nasty things to him. She had been looking forward to meeting Cass, seeing the place that her brother had loved. But now a flicker of doubt crept in.

Her sister Karen had thought up the idea of the trip, but had broken her ankle the week before they were meant to set off. Owen's sister Dawn had stepped in at the eleventh hour. The trip was meant to take Hazel's mind off things, give her something to plan and think about. Dawn wasn't going to let all that preparation and anticipation go to waste. She knew how much it meant to Hazel, especially the part of the trip she'd arranged in memory of her brother. Her husband Pete would be fine without her, it was only for a few weeks. In some ways Hazel was closer to Dawn than she was to Karen. The two of them had always stayed chummy and they had shared values. You didn't have the friction, with someone who wasn't a blood relative. Dawn was like Owen, easygoing. You could put her down anywhere and come back an hour later and she'd have made three new friends and got a recommendation for a great little spot for lunch. Hazel was more reserved. It wasn't that she didn't like people, she just needed to get to know them at her own pace.

Hazel had written to the current owners of The Grange, a Mr and Mrs Eyres, explaining that her ancestors had lived there in the 1800s and asking if she might, when she came to England, walk around the garden. She was secretly hoping the Eyres would let them have a look inside the house, once they got there. She would be travelling with a friend, she wrote, and they planned to visit the Cotswolds for a long weekend: any of the four days would suit, if it was convenient. Ian Eyres thought it was an awful bore. Of course the Eyres couldn't let these people come all the way from bloody Australia, just to look at the garden. What if it was raining on the day? They'd have to offer them tea. Tea was better than drinks, because it had a natural conclusion, when the food ran out and the teapot had been refilled and emptied for the second time. If the worst came to the worst, you could start stacking the cups and sandwich plates so that they got the message. In his letter Ian Eyres added the word 'afternoon', so as to be extra clear that by tea they meant cake – i.e. an hour, tops – and not supper. They didn't want to be landed with them all evening.

Dawn had selected their lodgings, for this part of the trip. She'd researched places in Broadway, first, but everything was so expensive. Same thing with Chipping Campden. In the end, she'd found a B&B close to Honeybourne which looked nice. The owners, a Mr and Mrs Powell, had a small plant nursery, specializing in ferns. It wasn't far from the places they'd earmarked to visit: Snowshill Manor, the garden at Hidcote, Stratford-on-Avon. Cheltenham they'd do later, on their way to Bath. Hazel had some sort of family connection with Cheltenham, too: Dawn couldn't keep track. During their time in London they'd shared a room, to economize, and they planned to do the same in Bath. City hotels were expensive. Bath was astronomical: that's why they were only stopping there for the one night. But out in the rural areas, where the rates were more reasonable, they booked a room each. Not that either of them was short of money. They were both comfortably off, with their pensions and savings, but neither of them liked to be wasteful.

Dawn loved sleeping in a room on her own. Pete was a snorer, bless him; she got a better night by herself. It was different for Hazel. To her the unshared bedrooms felt desolate, yet another reminder of her solitude. As soon as she shut the door she busied herself on her tablet, emailing David and Anna with news of the trip, looking up things for her and Dawn to see over the coming days. If they were staying more than one night she hand-washed her socks and pants in the basin, using the little bottle of liquid detergent she'd bought for the purpose, then putting her things to dry on the towel-rail. She was grateful when there was a television in the room, so she didn't have to sit with the silence.

Dawn was Owen's sister, the same flesh and blood; sleeping in a twin bed alongside her gave a connection to him which made her feel less lonely. Otherwise the absence of him felt too enormous. A person missed took up so much more space than a person who was there.

It was silly, but Hazel felt apprehensive about visiting The Grange. The people who lived there weren't even her own relatives, but something in the tone of Ian Eyres' letter had made her feel as if she was an impoverished distant cousin, coming to ask for charity from the big house, like someone in a nineteenth-century novel. The Eyres would probably have made changes to the house; it wouldn't be the same as it had been when Alice lived there. Well obviously. That was more than a hundred and fifty years ago. But it would be amazing, just to see the place. The people at the B&B had laughed when she said they were going to Weston-sub-Edge and told her that locals all pronounced it Weston Subidge. She wondered if that was how her ancestors would have said the name. She rolled it around in her mouth a couple of times, like a toffee.

It was a fine day and Ian Eyres suggested they walk around the garden first, before coming in for tea. He had a high forehead with just a smudge of remaining hair brushed back from it.

'Who was it you said had lived here?' he asked Dawn.

People tended to address their comments and questions to Dawn, rightly surmising that she was the more forthcoming of the two, although in this case Ian Eyres had not troubled to distinguish between the visitors, both of whom were short, grey-haired Australians in the sort of brightly coloured anoraks which made the noise of crumpling paper as they walked. It was only the fact that Dawn stood a little closer to him that singled her out for his query.

'It's not my relations actually,' she said. 'Hazel, you're the expert?'

'It was the Gales,' she said. 'Around the early 1850s, I think they were here. Late 1840s, it could have been.'

'Ah, the Gales!' he said. 'Of course. They originally owned the Park, a much bigger house two or three miles away. At least, the parents did. Burnt down after the war. But I believe a son came here, after he'd fought in one of those wars somewhere; brought up a family in this house. His widow stayed on until her death in I think the early part of the century. The last century, I mean.'

'That's right,' said Hazel.

'We think it was Gale who put in some of the specimen trees: they're about the right date. Our son-in-law is a bit of an expert on trees; his family have a rather well-known arboretum. My wife's the one who's keen on the actual garden plants.'

He waved an arm, to signal that the woman who had just joined them outside was Mrs Eyres.

'Hello,' she said. 'Would you like to . . . do you need to . . . come in? Before we look round, I mean?'

Dawn understood that she was referring to the toilet. 'No, we're good, thank you,' she said.

Ian Eyres winced. If only people wouldn't say the word good in place of the word fine.

'Was it the Indian Mutiny?' he asked Hazel.

'Excuse me?'

Was the woman slow-witted? 'Was it the Indian Mutiny, that your chap Gale was involved in? Before he came back here?'

'No, the Crimea. He won the Victoria Cross, as a matter of fact, for his actions there. At Alma. It was one of the very first ones.'

'Goodness, how wonderful. I never knew that. Do you hear that, Penelope? Very glad to think we're living under the roof of a war hero.'

Hazel smiled. They set off at a snail's pace. Both Hazel and

Dawn had been struck by how slowly British people walked, once they got into a garden, heads down, as if they were looking for a lost earring. Hidcote had been like Chapel Street on Christmas Eve, everyone shuffling. Penelope was the next to speak.

'Heavens, I wonder if that's where the snowdrops came from! I've always wondered about that.'

She turned to the visitors. 'We have the most wonderful snowdrops here, in the early spring. *Galanthus plicatus*. All across that slope there. We open the garden for them actually, just two or three afternoons; for the Macmillan nurses. The *Yellow Book*? I expect you've heard of it. What a pity you've missed them.'

Hazel nodded politely, although she had no idea what Mrs Eyres was talking about.

'Many of the best collections are said to have originated from soldiers bringing bulbs back from the Crimea. As I'm sure you know. Are you a galanthophile?' she asked Hazel.

'I might be, if I had any idea what that is,' said Hazel, grinning.

Penelope Eyres decided there and then that she liked Hazel. Her smile was really most engaging, with an intelligence – one might almost say a trace of mischief – behind it.

'You mustn't let me go on, I'm afraid I can be a snowdrop bore,' she told her, as they fell into step together, Ian and Dawn lagging a few paces behind them. 'There are so many kinds, you see. *Plicatus* originates from the lands around the Black Sea, whereas the snowdrops that were already planted in England from the early 1600s were *Galanthus nivalis*, from southern Europe. Not nearly so nice as the Crimean ones. Once you get the bug . . . well. Rare ones have been known to change hands for literally thousands.'

They came to the side of the house. 'Ian was saying, I think, that our son-in-law believes that cedar would've been put in in about the 1860s or thereabouts. Does that fit with your Mr Gale?'

Hazel thought of correcting her, telling her that he was in fact a Captain, not a Mister; but she decided it wouldn't be good manners to do so, especially as she'd invited herself.

'Yes, I think that's exactly right. He'd have been home by then. OK if we go over?'

'Of course,' said Penelope.

In truth it wasn't in homage to William Gale that she had come here to The Grange. When she pictured The Grange, it was Alice that she imagined there. Alice as a young bride; Alice alone, reading and writing at a desk framed by a long window; Alice becoming a mother. If she thought of William at all, it was as an old man, obdurate, unsmiling, with heavy moustaches. She had found a photograph of him on a website about the Victoria Cross, which showed him so. Somehow this version of him had stuck, even though it contradicted the little portrait miniature in her possession, of young William, clean-cheeked and bright-eyed. And the early letters she had of his, his letters to Alice from the battlefront, spoke of kindness and wit. Nevertheless the later image had superimposed itself over the younger man's traits. After she'd read all the correspondence and the notebooks, Hazel had felt, like all children of divorce, that she had to choose whose side she was on. And she had chosen Alice.

Reading Alice's account of her passage to Australia had been the highlight of Hazel's delving into the family's history. The pages were stiff and friable as dried flowers, but the hand was fairly easy to decipher. The earliest entry must have been composed on the very first evening of Alice and Edward's voyage, for in it she wrote candidly of her sadness at leaving friends and family behind. '*Oh the pain of parting with dear ones is something past description,*' she said, '*and the knowledge that I shall no more see them in this life made the bell which sounded before we sailed seem almost as if it were the seven celestial trumpets.*' They had boarded the steamer at Plymouth, with Caroline Gale and Alice's Aunt Felicity there to see them off. The bell signalled that it was time for adieuing friends to disembark: Caroline had had the foresight to bring with her two bright yellow dusters, one for herself and one for her little nephew, George. As the ship drew out of harbour, the child waved his vigorously towards land and was answered by the flapping wing of its twin on the quay. It was the only way to distinguish one person from another, the crowd was so dense. Alice stayed on deck looking back until she could no longer see the tiny yellow flag which was her last glimpse of the woman who had been so dear a friend.

Hazel discovered that Alice had liked to stand on deck and watch the moon rise above the deep. She had felt delight, after many days at sea, when the vessel had come level with the island of Madeira and she had seen cattle walking about on the hillside, like little lead toys on baize. The shadows of the clouds had scudded over the grass, darkening it in patches. The fourth mate had taken a particular shine to George and entertained him with tricks: making a coin disappear from behind the boy's ear; magicking a peppermint from thin air. They had been accompanied for a time by porpoises, threading in and out of the swell like great needles through pleats of velvet; the child had almost wriggled out from his mother's grasp, so eager had he been to watch them. Sailing through the tropics, the Captain had told her to '*listen for the hissing sound when the sun sinks into the water, for it will appear so fiery*'. Three weeks afterwards, having been, as she put it, '*on the brink of roasting alive*', she was astonished one morning to see '*coming down thick and fast snowflakes, something I did not imagine I should ever see on this side of the world*'. A huge storm had frightened even the strongest among the passengers and left the iron door down to the cabins and sleeping decks '*bent and broken like a piece of tin*'. On Sundays they had sung hymns on deck: after the great storm they gathered to sing 'Eternal Father, Strong to Save' and many had had tears of gratitude rolling down their cheeks, that Providence had spared them their lives.

At last, after fifty-two days at sea, one of the mates had come and told Alice he could smell green leaves. All the ladies had disappeared below as soon as the rumour spread, to dress in their best clothes and neaten their hair, for arrival. Children who had assumed the appearance of ragamuffins these past weeks had their faces rubbed with their mamas' moistened linen handker-chiefs. Soon a throng gathered at the forerails '*as lively as crickets*', craning for the first sight of the new land. When a pilot from Sandridge Pier came to guide them into port, he was cheered on board. An atmosphere of gaiety and expectation spread through the steamer, as infectious as laughter.

It had come as a surprise to Hazel that a Victorian English lady could have so much sparkle. She'd always imagined the people from that century to be as fusty as they looked in pic-tures. And she must have been intrepid: almost two months in a cramped steamer, with three hundred other passengers, one of them her own child, barely a toddler, to keep amused and safe. That would have taken a lot of mettle. Then there was the mak-ing of a new life in a new land, from scratch. Finding a house and equipping it. Picnics at St Kilda and Brighton; a boat trip up the River Yarra; evening strolls around the Botanical Gardens. These things she described in her diary, but at this point the notebook was filled. Hazel searched through everything in the bundle for the next volume, but there wasn't one. Perhaps Alice was too busy in her new life to keep a journal; or perhaps she had continued to record what happened, but the diary was lost. Among the papers was a clipping from a newspaper, on which the names Dr and Mrs Edward Nolan had been circled. Theirs were among a long list of those present at a wedding in Toorak, beneath a headline: 'Belle of Melbourne weds son of famous English novelist'. Hazel read on. 'On Saturday the marriage took place between Alfred d'Orsay Tennyson Dickens of Wangagong Station and Augusta Cassie Devlin, of Melbourne. Among those in attendance were . . .' This column of yellowing paper had brought a smile to Hazel's face, for it meant that despite Alice's status as a divorced woman, she had not been shunned in Melbourne society. Toorak had always been a fancy neighbourhood.

So it was Alice that Hazel felt close to, and yet, standing here on the other side of the world underneath the tree which William Gale had planted, she felt almost overcome. The emotion took her by surprise, her eyes suddenly stinging. She wasn't a tree hugger – that sort of thing was more Karen's department – but she couldn't help putting her hand out and cupping it around the cedar's trunk. It struck her very forcibly that this was a living thing, like an elephant's leg. There was a touch of pink about the bark. Its branches stretched out high above her, vertical, into the greyish light. She felt as if this tree would shelter her, if she needed shelter; protect her from rain or fierce sun. It was like being a small child, coming to stand under the outstretched arms of a long-lost grandfather. She couldn't help being moved by the thought of William – young, ardent William – coming home from war, planting this tree. A tree was a symbol of hope, wasn't it? The hope that things would last, would continue unbroken into an unseeable future. Endure. Maybe he had needed to plant trees, after seeing all that death. Maybe the trees stood in for some of the men who had fallen in that war.

'Cedars always remind me of waiters, don't they you? As if the boughs were great, flat serving dishes being borne aloft into some grand dining room,' said Penelope.

Her husband, who had come across to the tree, laughed in response. As crazy as it seemed, Hazel wished she could be alone with the cedar, sit under it by herself for a while and reflect. It was with an effort of will that she reminded herself that these people were showing her hospitality. The tree was theirs now.

'Come and see the walled garden. The structure is still as it would have been in Gale's day. Even the water-butts are original, I think.'

They trooped after Penelope, along gravel paths through low box hedges which gave off a fresh, slightly bitter smell as their leaves were brushed by the legs of the passers-by. Hazel tried to picture Alice here, but was unable to. It seemed too formal for Alice's temperament, too stiff.

'We live in dread of box-blight of course,' said Penelope in a low, confiding voice, as if she thought the blight, whatever it was, might hear her.

'Let's go in and have tea,' said Ian. 'I'm sure our visitors haven't got all day.'

Ian took their coats. Penelope made noises, once again, about whether her visitors required what she called a cloakroom. Hazel followed her directions – along the corridor, second door on the left – to a downstairs toilet. Its walls were lined with old school photographs: boys in sporting teams, boys in debating society, boys in boat races wearing straw hats. It seemed a funny place to showcase your mementos. But it was a relief to have a moment. She pulled her comb out of her small, cross-shoulder bag. If you made yourself tidy you tended to feel more on top of things.

'Do tell us how your family came to be all the way in Australia? Not convicts I hope, ha-ha?' said Ian at the tea table. It was a mirthless sort of a laugh.

'No, the convicts got shipped there long before us lot arrived. There's actually a kind of prestige to being descended from them, or there was, when I was growing up. Because they were among the very first immigrants.'

'Oh yes, like the Daughters of the Mayflower, sort of thing,' said Ian.

'Although it's got a lot more complicated, now that we've got a better understanding of the heritage of the Colonial settlers. Most people aren't as proud of it as they used to be. Because of the terrible British treatment of the First Peoples,' said Dawn.

'Yes, and the incomers brought sickness with them, which led to the epidemics that decimated them. The seizure of their lands and water rights. There's been a big shift in the way children are taught about our national history, even since I first went into education in the 80s. And not before time,' said Hazel.

Ian looked blank. Penelope came in with a tray.

'Well, we came here in '71,' said Ian, as if their arrival at The Grange was a historical equivalent. 'Just weekends, to begin with, when I was still in the City.'

'Only the other day, by your standards!' said Penelope.

'My ancestor, she was William Gale's wife,' Hazel told them. 'His first wife. She went overseas to start a new life, after the divorce. She wouldn't have been able to live in polite society if she'd stayed in England. What was called polite society, in any case,' she added.

'Ah,' said Ian.

'Sandwich?' asked Penelope.

Penelope had made tiny triangles of smoked salmon sandwiches, which she served before slices of coffee and walnut cake, bought from the local Co-op. They drank their tea from shallow china cups festooned with roses and edged with gilt. The Eyres made no further enquiries about the Gale family. They asked where else the women intended to visit and Dawn told them.

'Bath's absolutely ruined,' Ian told them. 'The one-way system is impossible. Whole place seething with trippers.'

Penelope shot him a look. After all, their visitors were tourists themselves. She stood up.

'Before you go, I was wondering: would you like to take some snowdrop bulbs? I just thought, you know, that it'd be rather fun if the bulbs had come from your Mr Gale, for you to plant some, when you get home. To think of them coming here all the way from the Black Sea and then taking root on the other side of the world.'

'I don't expect they've got time,' said Ian. 'For you to go digging about now.'

Hazel was touched. 'That'd be great. Thank you,' she said. 'We'll come outside with you, get out of Ian's hair. I'd love to take a couple of photographs of the trees and the outside of the house, if that's all right with you? Just for my own use.'

'No, no, not at all,' said Ian, standing. 'Feel free.' He went to fetch their anoraks.

In the car on their way back to Honeybourne, the two women agreed that Penelope had been much nicer than her husband. She'd gone to trouble on their account, with the tea: that had been kind.

'Those little cups though, they leave you thirsty,' said Dawn.

'It was funny, the way she pronounced his name, did you hear her? Yarn, she called him.'

Dawn giggled. 'Do you think it's a nickname?'

'I think it might just be how they say Ian, in their social class. It'd be funny if I addressed our thank-you note to Mr Yarn Eyres though.'

They both began to laugh and, once started, found that they couldn't stop.

Back at their B&B, Hazel asked Mrs Powell about the snowdrops.

'They like a temperate climate, snowdrops do. I'm not so sure as they'll grow over there. What do you reckon, Frank?'

'Depends how warm it gets. They don't like it too warm, see.'

'It gets pretty hot,' Hazel admitted.

'You could try them in some shade,' said Mrs Powell, doubtfully.

'But are they all right, in my luggage? We're here for three weeks. Do I need to pack them into some earth, or something?'

'Like a vampire, you mean?' teased Mr Powell.

Hazel grinned.

'You could put them in a sock, if you had one spare. Keep them dry and dark. They'll be all right. But you don't want to go telling them, at Customs, that you've got any living thing with you. They don't like you fetching plants in and out, from different countries. Biohazard, see.'

'Oh dear. Do you think I'll get arrested at the airport for smuggling?'

'Might well do,' said Mr Powell, deadpan. 'You could be looking at a custodial sentence.'

'Don't take no notice of him,' said his wife, batting his arm.

Up in her room, Hazel took the bulbs out of her pocket and laid them out on her bedside table. She went to her case and found an unworn pair of socks, maroon, to keep the light off them. She put one inside the other, so its pair wouldn't get lost. There was a little earth adhering to the bulbs and she was anxious not to lose it: even if the flowers didn't grow, she'd still have brought a tiny quantity of soil from The Grange into her own garden, such as it was. The thought made her happy. The bulbs were not much bigger than Caramel Buds, eleven or twelve of them in all. She dropped them, two by two, into the socks, then swept up the crumbs of soil they'd left behind and carefully, cupping her hand, funnelled those in. Maybe she'd make a bit more of a garden for herself, when she got home.

Take up the paving, put some flowering plants in. She could make a place to sit out there, with some shade.

She went to her suitcase and unzipped a small compartment at the side and slipped in the socks, folded over so nothing would spill out, next to the little wad of tissue paper in which William Gale's medal was wrapped.

19.

Cass had offered to have Hazel and her friend to stay. There was plenty of room, she said. She'd been welcoming, suggesting that they come for a couple of nights; longer, if they wanted to use it as a base to explore the area for a few days. But Hazel had felt hesitant about taking this up, given that her brother had clearly left the place in unhappy circumstances. She'd talked it over with Dawn.

'There's been a lot of water under the bridge since then,' said Dawn. 'They were just kids, weren't they?'

'Yeah, but I know Mum felt a lot of bitterness towards that family. The mother, anyways. I just feel kind of conflicted about it.'

'It must have been terrible for your mother. She was such a sweet lady.'

'Yes it was. She never really got over it.'

'Well, of course. You wouldn't. But, you know, if you want to meet them, talk to them about your brother, that's already bringing an olive branch. It's not like you're going to go there to insult them. You may as well take her up on it, the offer I mean.'

But Hazel couldn't bring herself to accept the invitation, not after having read Celia's scalding letter to her big brother. If he wasn't allowed to sleep under that roof, she wasn't going to either.

As they wound up the lane, Hazel tried to imagine what this place would have seemed like to Stephen, all those years ago. It didn't look as if things would have changed much around here since then. Had he liked this landscape, that looked as if it was covered all over in green baize? Had he been apprehensive, arriving here to spend a summer with these strangers? She found that tears had started to her eyes, at the thought of him here, so far from home. He had seemed so grown-up to her, at the time, but with hindsight she pictured him as just a boy. He'd been years younger than her son was, now.

'I've gone into overwhelm,' she told Dawn, when the two of them were alone, driving back to the B&B after an introductory tea with Cass and Adam.

'I noticed you'd lost the power of speech, there,' Dawn said.

'You're right, I had. I think I'd been thinking of my brother so much that I'd forgotten that I'm kin to these people too. Everywhere else we've been, even to the Eyres' house and to Cheltenham, they're places that my family came from. But here, these are actual, living people who share the same ancestry as me. They're my relatives.'

'Do you notice any similarities?'

Hazel smiled at this. 'Not a lot,' she admitted. 'Not yet, anyways.'

Adam cleared up the tea things while Cass went to the station to collect Georgie.

'What's she like?' Georgie asked, as soon as she got into the car.

'Not like you'd expect. I thought she'd be tall, like him. She's quite short actually.'

'But does she look like him?'

'Not remotely. But I suppose we don't know what he'd have looked like, by now. She's got a friend she's travelling with who looks a bit like Judi Dench. That one seems to do most of the talking. They've both got short grey hair and those shoes that are between trainers and walking boots. And lots of zips and Velcro on everything, so it sounds as if something is being torn, when they come in and take their things off. And those ugly sort of bags that tourists wear around their waists.'

'Like marsupial pouches,' said Georgie.

'Exactly,' said Cass.

The visitors returned to the farm for some supper and to meet Georgie. They brought the wine and chocolates they'd picked up on the way, as well as a book about the buildings of Bath, for Cass and Adam. Hazel, having looked them up online, was aware that they were architects. Georgie at once struck Hazel as the more friendly sister, ignoring her proffered hand and drawing her into a close hug instead. She was busty: Hazel could feel the warmth and bulk of her breasts against her own. Georgie wore hoop earrings with her hair badly pinned up and a loose, patterned blouse. She looked like the sort of woman who'd be good at cooking without bothering to use a recipe: Hazel could picture her presiding over a table crowded with friends. She seemed like a hospitable type of person. But it was Cass who prepared their supper while Georgie sat, a glass of wine in her hand.

They were quizzed about their trip. Where they had been; where they were going next; how long they planned to spend in England; whether they meant to make trips to anywhere else in Europe.

'Not that we're even going to be in Europe any longer,' said Adam gloomily.

'So who did you say it was, who'd lived in the Cotswolds?' asked Cass, keen to steer her husband off the subject of Brexit.

The Grange wasn't actually in the Cotswold hills, but Hazel didn't like to contradict.

'That was William Gale. My great-great-grandfather, and I believe he's your great-great-great. I think you slotted in another generation. Someone in there must have had children earlier in life.'

'And how come you ended up Australian and we didn't?' asked Georgie.

'Because we come from William's first wife, Alice, and your people come from the second wife, Sarah. Alice was the mother of George and your Sarah had Harriet. I don't know how much you know about the family history?'

'Not much,' Georgie admitted. 'Our mother used to tell us about the family sometimes, but you know what it's like. You never want to listen to your mother.'

'Well, after he came back from the Crimean war William seems to have changed quite a bit. I've got some of his letters and the tone is completely different, afterwards. I wondered if he had some PTSD. Must have been pretty traumatic, that first winter. A lot of people lost their lives. His brother was one of them. We'll never know.'

'Did they even have PTSD, then?' Adam wondered.

'I suppose they always had it, they just didn't know what it was. What was the matter with them, I mean,' said Georgie.

'I don't think I've ever heard of a brother,' said Cass.

'Yes. Algernon. He was younger. I haven't been able to find out much about him, except dates.'

'Oh my God,' said Georgie. 'I wonder if that's whose hair it is, in the locket?' She turned to Hazel.

'My mother had a locket, Victorian, with this piece of hair inside. We've never known whose it was. I've got it now, in London I mean.'

'Likely it could be,' said Hazel. She smiled at Dawn a little ruefully, aware that she wasn't a part of this conversation.

'Wasn't it rather unusual, then, to have two wives? I mean, unless one of them died in childbirth or something?' Cass asked.

'Yes. It would've been impossible for Alice to continue her life as it had been. She'd been divorced for adultery, you see. Probably would have made life quite hard for the second wife as well. Did you read *The Reason Why*, by Cecil Woodham-Smith?'

'No, I've never heard of him,' said Cass.

The author was a woman, but Hazel did not correct her.

'Well, it's mostly about the Charge of the Light Brigade, but it goes into the social context a fair amount. Lord Cardigan, he married a second time and even for a grandee like him, doors were closed. Queen Victoria herself wouldn't receive them, because he'd divorced the first wife.' Hazel grinned. 'Adeline Horsey de Horsey. That was the name of the new wife. She was a character.'

'She'd have had to be, with a name like that,' said Dawn.

'You couldn't make it up,' agreed Georgie.

'OK, let's eat,' said Cass.

None of them could face talking about Stephen, that first night. Instead they spoke about their work, their children. Hazel was struck by the apparent similarities between Cass's daughter Skye and her own niece, Ginny. Cut from the same cloth, by the sound of it. Hazel thought she caught Georgie's eye at one point and discerned a look of slight impatience, when Skye's work was mentioned. Then another coincidence emerged: Georgie's son Jake had done well for himself in a similar field to Hazel's son, David. By the time the visitors stood up to go, all present felt less wary.

'I rather like them, don't you? They've got more of a sense of humour than one thought to begin with,' said Georgie. 'She's not stupid, Hazel. Bit pedantic though.'

'Well, she was a teacher, wasn't she?' said Cass. 'Do you think they're . . . you know. A couple?'

'What, dykes, d'you mean?' said Georgie.

'Well, yes.'

'No! They're sisters-in-law, for goodness' sake. Just because they've got short hair. Honestly.'

'She's nothing like Stephen, is she? You wouldn't even guess they were related,' said Cass.

'I wonder what the other sister looks like? Maybe she's more like him.'

'We could ask to see a photo. I bet she's got pictures of everybody, she's just the type.'

'We're all the type, now that everyone has cameras on their phones,' said Georgie.

'True. I'd be interested to see what the son's like, as well. He might have a look of Stephen.'

'He was so lovely-looking, wasn't he?' said Georgie wistfully, but her sister had turned to load plates into the dishwasher and didn't seem to have heard her.

Hazel had agreed to come over to the house for coffee at 11 a.m. Georgie was going to take her for a stroll around the farm and down to the river before lunch. Dawn wanted to catch up with her emails, so she asked if there was a place she could install herself, out of everyone's way.

'Shall we start at the top, work our way down?' Georgie asked.

She took Hazel up to the orchard. The circular dovecote was crumbling, now. It was another restoration project that Cass and Adam meant to get around to, when they had the spare cash.

'We all used to come up here and hide out, when we were teenagers,' said Georgie. 'I think Stephen was with us, during some of the time. It's so long ago, I struggle to remember.'

They strolled down through the apple trees, to the back gate of the walled garden.

'My mother used to grow vegetables here. Lots of things. She was good at gardening. It's one of the few gifts I got from her. I've got a nice little garden in London. It's a shame, they've let it get very run-down.'

'How come your sister gets to live here?' asked Hazel.

Georgie was taken aback at her directness: she seemed rather a shy woman.

'She bought me out, after Mum died. I've lived in London for so long, I think I'd have struggled here on my own, especially in the winter. But the garden would have looked better than this, if I'd taken it on.' She smiled.

'Up at The Grange, the house where the Gales used to live, they've got a lot of snowdrops that they reckon William brought back with him, from the Crimea. They open it to the public. It's quite a display, apparently.'

'That's funny, because we've always called the field in front of the house the snowdrop field. I'll take you down there now. I don't know whether they were here when we came. Perhaps Mum dug them up from her parents' house and transplanted them.'

'Maybe they're the descendants of William Gale's flowers, too,' said Hazel.

'Could be. Keen gardeners are always taking cuttings and dividing plants. I took some bulbs from the field and planted them in my garden in Fulham actually.'

Hazel wondered whether Georgie would offer her some of the bulbs, as Penelope Eyres had, but the thought didn't seem to cross her mind.

The river was flowing fast from the recent downpours, its surface silvered from the pace of the water. If you shut your eyes, it sounded like the swish of an unseen motorway. The path was muddy, the rocks at the water's edge stained dark with the rain.

'We don't actually own these fields any more, but we're still allowed to walk here. We used to bring Stephen down here to swim, the summer he was here. There was a rope we all used to swing on, over that pool there.' Georgie pointed. 'The branch came down a few years ago.'

'Yeah, I was hoping you'd tell me about him. How he was when he was here.'

Georgie felt acutely aware that whatever she said, it wouldn't be enough. The few memories she'd be able to summon would just be tiny flakes of gold, when what this woman wanted was ingots, bullion, bars. For Hazel, Stephen's absence must represent something enormous: a disappearance that had shaped her whole life. Whereas, to Georgie, his loss was a little sharp splinter of regret. It glinted sometimes in the light of memory, but nothing more.

The apprehension of this made her feel somehow ashamed. Georgie wanted to be kind, wanted to supply anything which might make things easier for this woman. Wasn't there someone in a Greek myth, who'd been able to spin gold out of her stories? Or was it in a fairy tale? If she willed herself, perhaps she could call up enough fragments from that summer to construct something like a charm bracelet. The two women walked along the riverbank, and she tried.

Cass had made soup and a salad for lunch. Hazel was looking forward to some time on her own, to digest what Georgie had told her. She thought she'd write down some of the things she'd heard, while they were still fresh in her mind. She and Dawn were going to drive down to look at the shops in Falmouth, get a breath of sea air and have a Cornish cream tea. Find some little gifts to take back for family.

Hazel had offered to take them all out on the second night, but Cass insisted that she would cook. When the two of them appeared at the farm for supper, Georgie offered to take Hazel up to see the room where Stephen had stayed.

'You don't mind, do you Cass?' she'd asked.

'Of course not. Actually, I'll come up with you.'

'It's the same room my son used, when he was little. The bed is French, I think. Is it walnut, Cass?'

'I think so, yes. Or is it pear? Nice wood, in any case, not too dark. It would've been here when Stephen was staying. And the blue curtains are the same, I'm ashamed to say. Look at them, completely threadbare.'

'He slept with the curtains open, anyway,' said Georgie.

Hazel did not ask Georgie how she had come to know this. The narrow room felt small, with three grown women standing in it. Hazel went to the window and looked out across the tops of the trees towards the river. It felt like a small miracle, to be standing where he'd stood, all those years ago. She'd been a schoolgirl on the other side of the world, when her brother had inhabited this room. She wished their mother was still alive, so she could describe the view to her. It was a lovely view.

'Could I just take a minute?' she asked.

'Of course,' said Cass, touched. 'We'll see you back downstairs. No hurry.'

Once they'd gone, Hazel sat down on the bed. She lay back, careful not to put her shoes on the bedcover, and closed her eyes and then opened them, imagining what it had been like for him, waking up in this place. She touched the door and the dented brass door knob and then went again and stood in the window. She touched the wooden window frame and the metal catch. She stood and looked at the trees and sky.

At the table Cass spoke to Hazel about her memories of Stephen while Adam talked about politics with Dawn and Georgie. Cass said what a thoughtful person he'd been; sweet-natured, gentle.

'We weren't used to the accent. Cornwall felt much more remote, in those days. I don't know that we'd ever met an Australian person before. We used to love it when he came out with funny little phrases. We'd all say them. Everyone liked him, who met him.'

Hazel was really pleased. She'd heard nice things about Stephen today. It was a huge relief to her that he'd been mostly OK, while he was out here. It had always frightened her, to imagine him being miserable and getting sick. The thought of his loneliness was hard to bear, even now. And there were repercussions for her, for her sister, for their families. She had fretted that it could have been a genetic predisposition which brought on Stephen's illness; she'd worried for her children. She still did. She knew that it was the same for her sister Karen. That was why Karen fell over herself to accommodate her daughter Ginny, because she was terrified that suicide might be something that could run in a family, like hair colour. Whereas she had dealt with her own fear in the opposite way, by encouraging her children to be independent. If they were in the habit of self-reliance, then they'd always have that to draw on. That's what Hazel believed and had tried to live by.

After dinner, as they were leaving, Hazel had asked if they could convene for a brief talk, the following morning, before she and Dawn drove north. They agreed to meet at ten o'clock.

'Do you want me to sit in, for support?' asked Dawn, after breakfast.

'That'd be great. Thank you. I know what I'm going to do, but it just feels right to include them, let them know about it.'

Cass was feeling slightly anxious. 'You don't think she's going to try and sue us, or something? About Stephen, I mean?'

'Don't be daft,' said Georgie. 'What could she sue us for? I expect she just wants to know what happened, you know, how it was that he had to leave the farm. We only talked about the nice stuff yesterday. I didn't even mention the accident, did you?'

'No. I hardly said anything. I don't even know if she's aware of the accident.'

'Well, there you go,' said Georgie.

'It may be nothing to do with Stephen,' said Cass, doubtfully. 'She might just want to tell us more about her genealogical research.'

'It'll be fine,' said Georgie.

Adam put together a tray with coffee and they took it into the sitting room.

'What I wanted to talk to you about is the Victoria Cross,' Hazel began. 'I've got a plan about what would be best to do with it and I wanted you to know first, as we're all descended from William Gale.'

Cass gawped. She felt her mouth fall open, like someone overacting in a sitcom. What was Hazel talking about? They'd searched the whole house from top to bottom and still no one had been able to find the medal. All they could do was hope there was some hiding place they'd overlooked and that it would turn up eventually. And now this woman thought she'd just walk in and arrange its future, when there could be no plan, because no one could lay their hands on the wretched medal. Things could be about to get very awkward. She raised her eyebrows at Adam.

'I've been thinking for the past couple of years about what I might do with it. They're actually pretty valuable now. I think this one would fetch a lot, because it's an early one. William Gale won it early on in the campaign, I mean. At Alma.' She doubted that Cass and Georgie were familiar with the battles of the Crimea, so she was trying to keep it simple.

'Yes, we're well aware of all that,' said Adam, testily.

'Wait, hang on,' said Cass. 'When you say you've been thinking what to do with it, what do you mean?'

'That's what I'm coming to,' Hazel smiled. 'Like I say, it's been on my mind for a while now. Me keeping it in a drawer in my house, it's just silly. Paying hundreds of dollars a year to insure it when no one's getting any enjoyment out of it. And it's not serving the memory of the man who won it.'

It was dawning on them what Hazel meant. 'What are you saying, in a drawer in your house? You can't have got it!' said Cass.

Georgie began to laugh, whether from amusement or nerves the others couldn't tell.

'I beg your pardon' said Hazel. Why was Cass raising her voice like that?

'Well, we've been hunting for that medal for some time. It belongs here, you see,' said Cass.

Hazel said nothing. Cass went on explaining. 'It lived in a special table, a table with glass-topped shelves. With his other medals. It belonged to my mother. It's ours. You can't have got it.'

'I didn't know you didn't know,' said Hazel. 'Look, your mother gave it to Stephen. Not that we realized that, for quite a while. It took my mum some time to twig that it was there, among his things. She couldn't look at his cases, his room, not for ages after he died. When she got to it, the medal was still in his duffel bag, from England. She got a little envelope for it, so it wouldn't get scratched. She reckoned it was because Stephen was the only boy descendant. She thought that was why your mother had given it to him. Because medals and such usually go to the males in a family.'

'But that's impossible,' said Adam.

Hazel looked from one to the other of Cass and Georgie. 'I thought your mother would've told you.'

'It just isn't the sort of thing that Celia would have done,' said Adam.

'Well, she clearly did,' said Hazel. 'How else was it going to be in with Stephen's things?'

No one spoke. Eventually Cass broke the silence in the room.

'He must have taken it. I'm sorry to accuse someone who can't defend himself, but that is the only possible explanation. Celia would never have given away a family heirloom like that, it just wasn't in her nature. Stephen must have taken it.' There was a catch in her voice, as if she was about to cry.

Hazel looked at her levelly.

'Are you accusing my brother of thieving?'

Cass was unable to meet her gaze.

'I'm not saying he knew how valuable it was. He may just have taken it as a sort of souvenir. But our mother set a lot of store by her ancestry. He was a teenager and, let's be honest, he was pretty hopeless. Even if she'd wanted to give him something, there would've been no guarantee that he wouldn't have lost it. She just wouldn't have entrusted anything to him. He must have taken it.'

At this Dawn stood up abruptly, high spots of colour in her cheeks.

'You need to watch your tongue, young lady. Hazel here is showing you the courtesy of including you in her plan for the medal and you're offering nothing but baseless accusations. We don't speak ill of the dead, where I come from; but you don't seem to have heard about that. She's come a long way for this and you need to hear her out.' She turned to Adam. 'I reckon we could do with another cup of coffee, if you don't mind? Give everyone a moment.'

Everyone looked shocked by the force of her outburst, Dawn included. Adam stood.

'I'll come and give you a hand,' said Cass.

Dawn excused herself and left the room to get a breath of air. Hazel and Georgie stayed where they were. Georgie looked at the woman sitting across from her. It was inevitable that she should have been thinking about Stephen over the past couple of days, as she tried to summon memories to share with his sister. It was all such a long time ago. She'd struggled to create anything like a viable account out of what impressions she retained. And what she hadn't told Hazel, could never tell her, was what she remembered best: Stephen in the narrow wooden bed at the top of the house, his long pale limbs, the tender sweetness of him in the dark. How beautiful he had been and how unaware of that beauty. He hadn't been her first lover, but sleeping with him had been her first experience of making what had felt like actual love. Abandon. Whispering into his ear. The different tastes of him. The smoothness of his arms and chest. Once, when they'd finished, they'd both lain back and giggled from the sheer exhilaration and joy they'd given each other. All her life she had carried the warm, secret memory of those nights inside herself. And here was his sister, someone she would once have considered to be an old woman: someone with grey hair and wrinkles and a thick waist. Someone dowdy, even frumpish, with sensible, ugly shoes. Someone who was in fact several years younger than herself.

When Stephen had been there, when she was a girl, she'd thought it would always be like this. The nights with him would be just the beginning of her lifetime of adventures in the realm of pleasure. And there had been others, although not so many as she'd imagined there would be. And never so innocent, or so free. That was what she could not have foreseen. He hadn't been the person she'd loved the most in her life, and yet those times with him she had been enraptured, giddy with the sudden possibilities of what bodies could do. She understood she would never experience that again, not now. No one would ever make her feel like that, so tingly and alive; so completely at home in her own skin. She might never be naked with someone again. She would never except in memory be that girl in the high room, naked and filled with new longing. A stranger, sitting opposite her in a train or at a dinner table, would see her just as she saw Hazel. Old. Not ancient, but old: old enough to be a grandmother. If they troubled to see her at all.

Adam came back into the room with more coffee. Dawn reappeared. They all waited while he handed out the cups and passed round a plate of biscuits.

Hazel spoke. 'I'm going to be frank with you. There wasn't a lot of love lost concerning your mother, as far as my family were concerned. She wasn't very kind to Stephen, throwing him out on to the streets. The traffic accident wasn't his fault: that other car came out of nowhere. We knew that: after the funeral Dad wrote to your father, to get it clear in his and Mum's minds, and your father wrote back acknowledging that Stephen hadn't been responsible. I read the letter just before I came over here, as a matter of fact.'

'We weren't sure that you knew about the accident. That's what tipped our mother over, as far as having Stephen here was concerned,' said Georgie.

'Yes, well, there's nothing we can do about that now. You were probably aware that Stephen had some mental health issues, that's why he'd dropped out of school. Why he was travelling. He was vulnerable, you'd call it now. And your mother, she chucked him out. Wrote him a pretty horrible letter. The one nice thing she did was to give him that medal. So I wouldn't be in too much of a hurry to take that away from her, if I was you. At least giving him that showed she'd welcomed him into the family. For a while, anyhow.'

'She wasn't easy,' said Georgie. 'I didn't find out he'd gone until it was too late to say goodbye. I was broken-hearted when she made him leave.'

'Right,' said Hazel.

'Hazel, would you like to finish telling us what your plans for the medal had been?' said Cass. She had recovered her composure. She and Adam had clearly been conferring in the kitchen and decided that calm was a better strategy than shouting. 'I'm imagining that the three of us may want to talk privately about it, afterwards. But at least if you've outlined your idea we'll have something to go on, when we talk to a lawyer.'

The look Dawn fixed her with was one of undisguised contempt.

'It's a very odd situation, this,' said Adam. 'I think we'd have to come to some kind of consensus.'

'Seems pretty simple to me,' said Hazel. 'I've got it. It's been in my family's possession for the past forty years. Unless you've got documentation to prove otherwise, there's not a lot of discussion needs to take place. Quite honestly, I'm only telling you what I propose to do with it just as a formality, because William Gale is your blood relative too. I thought you might've welcomed the chance to honour his memory. But my mind is made up. And I should let you know at this point that I can be a pretty determined individual.'

At this Dawn's face broke into a smile. Hazel had spoken without raising her voice. Georgie could see that she must have been a good teacher. She certainly wouldn't have been in any danger of losing command of her class.

Adam and Cass looked pained. They'd searched through Celia's will in their earlier hunt for the medal – and Celia's mother's – for mention of the Victoria Cross, in case the legal documents might uncover some information, some clue as to where it might be, and there was none. They knew there wasn't any paperwork. No evidence of their ever having owned it.

They also knew, as did Georgie, that an act of spontaneous generosity would have been most out of character for Celia. She had given hospitality, when it had amused her to do so, but she had guarded her possessions jealously. It had been one of the paradoxes of Celia's nature that she had affected not to be interested in possessions, while never attempting to divest herself of any.

Hazel spoke.

'Look, none of yous seem too interested in the history of it. But the Crimean war was pretty ground-breaking, actually. It was one of the first wars to have a newspaper correspondent reporting on it. A lot of people think that's why the Victoria Cross was brought in because, for the first time, the people back home were able to find out what went on at a battle front. And that's how they discovered that it wasn't only the Officer class who showed exceptional courage. The VC was the first decoration that the ordinary, non-commissioned men could win. Oh, and Leo Tolstoy was there and wrote about it. Here in England, Karl Marx reported on an anti-war march, where people threw snowballs in Trafalgar Square. It was the last time soldiers' wives were allowed to accompany them on a campaign . . . There's a lot of stuff. It's pretty interesting. I've found it really rewarding, my research into it all.'

'Are you trying to tell us that you know more about its history and that gives you some sort of moral right over the VC?' asked Adam. 'Because you don't have the monopoly on the history. You haven't mentioned Mrs Seacole, for example.' His eyes glittered with triumph for a moment.

'I'm sure it's all very fascinating, but what's all that got to do with our medal?' asked Cass. She sounded worn out.

'It puts it in a context. A historical context. It means it's not just about one man, or one family. It's bigger than that. It deserves to be remembered. He does,' said Hazel.

'So, you'd better tell us your plan,' said Cass.

Hazel told them. She told them that she'd talked it over with her children and her sister and they had all agreed. Some things were beyond price. Not to be forgotten was one of them. When she'd finished speaking the room felt uncomfortably airless, as if her idea had taken up all the available oxygen. Cass and Adam sat in silence, thinking.

'May I speak, for a minute?' said Georgie.

'Oh, here we go. I was wondering when you were going to pipe up,' said Adam.

Georgie shot him a look. 'Well, I just want to say that I think it's wonderful that Celia gave the medal to Stephen,' she said. 'He had just as much right to it as we did, we're all apples from the same tree, when it comes down to it.'

Even as the words came out, she doubted very much that what she said was true. But she had been trained as an actress, after all. The fact was, none of them would ever know how the medal had come to be in Stephen's things. He wouldn't have stolen it, of that she was certain. But what had really happened was anyone's guess.

To Georgie now, it seemed more important to say the right thing. The right thing had to matter more than the true thing, whatever that was. The words *just right* came into her mind: what Hazel intended to do was right and it was just. This stranger with whom they shared DNA. Whereas, when Cass and Adam had discovered the value of the medal, they had not wanted to dispense it justly.

'I'm sorry to say that Hazel isn't wrong, our mother wasn't kind to Stephen in the end,' Georgie went on. 'He was bundled away with almost indecent haste, none of us had the chance to say goodbye. I really regret that. I'm sure you do, too, Cass. I was angry with my mother for years, about that. I'm glad she at least did one generous thing by him. Nothing can make it up to you and your family, what happened to your brother. I can't imagine how harrowing it must have been for you all. It must've been devastating for your parents. But what you're proposing is lovely. It's the best possible solution and I want you to know that I'm right behind you.'

Hazel's eyes had filled with tears.

'We'll be taking legal advice, whatever you say,' said Adam.

'It won't get you anywhere,' said Georgie. 'And I'm not going to come in with you on this.'

'Thank you, Georgie,' said Hazel.

'Lord knows, you're welcome,' said Georgie.

20.

Before they left Cornwall, Hazel had asked Georgie if she'd like to come to Wales with them. But Georgie was contracted to voice coach on a film set in Romania, so it would be just her and Dawn, after all.

Neither of them spoke much in the car. There had been such a lot of talking at Stony Hill Farm; they were glad to be quiet in one another's company. Georgie had followed them out to the car that last morning.

'Keep in touch, won't you? I'd love to hear how you get on in Wales,' she said.

'I will do,' said Hazel.

The atmosphere between Georgie and the others had been frosty, once the visitors had gone. It had been a relief to get on the train and away from their reproachful looks. Even so, she had found herself unable to sleep that night, her mind racing. She'd suddenly remembered that her father had made a drawing – maybe more than one – of Stephen. The following morning she rang Hazel and promised that she'd go through his archive and search it out for her, next time she went to the farm.

'Not that I'm expecting an invitation in the immediate future. They're not thrilled with me, at the moment.'

'Will it be OK?' asked Hazel.

'Yes, they'll get over it, eventually. Cass will, in any case.'

'You should keep the picture, if you find it,' Hazel told her. 'He was a part of your life, too.'

'Well, at least I could scan it into the computer and send that to you. It may not be any good, of course. Dad's talent was uneven, to be honest. I think he was planning to make a head, too, but I don't know if he ever got around to it. Cass may re-member if he did.'

'I appreciate that, thank you. I was thinking of making a memory book about Stephen, for me and my sister's children. Your dad's picture could go in there.'

'Like a photograph album?'

'Like that, but with other bits and pieces in there too. Some of his sketches, letters . . .'

'If you come across a photograph of him, from around the time we knew him, do you think you could send me a copy?'

'Of course I will. You know, Mum always thought Stephen had feelings for one of you girls,' said Hazel now. 'She sort of guessed, from his letters. I'm glad it was you.'

Even at this great distance, Georgie could not prevent herself from a little flutter of pride. This, at least, she had won.

'Cass isn't as . . . I know she can come across as a bit hard, but she isn't a bad person, in her heart.'

'I know,' said Hazel. 'Families don't always bring out the best in people.'

The two women drove north through the Snowdonia National Park. Dawn had spent some time in New Zealand and was struck by its similarity to the Welsh landscape, although the light struck her as different. The light in New Zealand was like clear water in a glass, whereas here it was as if an artist had rinsed an ink-tipped brush in that same water, leaving just a trace of black. They stopped at a steamed-up café for a break and to swap around. Dawn had offered to drive for the final leg of the journey, so Hazel would be free to look at the scenery.

The landscape was majestic but not welcoming. Water spilled everywhere: cascading out of rocks, the white spume tinted yellow; or unravelling through the flat green pasture in wide streams, like polished slate paths. As they rose, the tall wooded hillsides gave way to bare rock and scree. Sheep spotted the distant slopes like specks of spilled washing powder. Now and again a level field of marram grass housed the little domes of bedraggled red and yellow and blue tents. There was something pathetic in their primary colours, as if their brightness could offer any protection up here in the cold unyielding mist. They passed the steep terraces of a slate quarry. Black residue had tumbled down below, covering the ground.

'Looks a lot like the stuff you have to clean off the floor of the oven, doesn't it?' said Dawn.

'You're right there,' said Hazel. 'Not a place I'd choose for my holiday.'

'Me neither,' said Dawn. 'Strange to think me and Owen's people originated here in Wales. I'm not feeling like I belong here.'

Caernarvon, though, was lovely. The darkness of the mountains gave way to a silvery marine light which washed across the little town. Their guest house was ablaze with hanging baskets: their rooms had loudly patterned carpets and colourful Welsh blankets on the beds. As soon as they'd dropped their cases they set out to explore on foot. Hazel was enchanted with the castle walls, the cobbles underfoot and the rows of pastel-painted houses. The Menai Straits seemed to glint at the bottom of every street and alleyway, sometimes greeny-gold, at other moments in a flash of unexpected blue. Hazel felt relieved that she liked the place so much. It would have been difficult to leave the medal somewhere less hospitable.

The VC had come to feel like more than a small piece of dull metal to her. She felt a kind of tenderness towards it, by now. She thought it would feel something like dropping your child off for their first day at school, to leave it behind. There would be a little bit of apprehension, but a sense of freedom, too.

'Cass's face,' said Dawn, once they were sitting down for supper. 'When her sister said you had her blessing. That was a picture.'

'I didn't want to look at her at that point. I could feel her glaring at me.'

Dawn sighed. 'I guess, the trouble is, by the time you're the age we all are, you know there isn't going to be a magic bean. When you're younger, you go around convinced that life will put one in your hand. That something amazing will happen and you'll get rich quick.'

'Like in Jack and the Beanstalk, do you mean?' asked Hazel.

'Yeah, like that. You know, you always half-think you'll win a lottery, or find something worth a fortune at a garage sale. But life goes on, and we don't. Our professional lives are behind us now and we didn't get to be millionaires that way. And our parents have died and bequeathed us some stuff, and we're grateful for that of course. But there's no tiaras in the attic. No one's going to get given that magic bean. Not now. I suppose Cass and Adam were banking on the medal being their magic bean. It's got to be hard for them, to give up that dream.'

'You're right. That's a good way of looking at it. That makes me feel more compassion for them,' said Hazel. 'Thank you, Dawn. And thank you for speaking out when you did.'

'I don't know where the words "young lady" came from,' Dawn grinned.

'Once a teacher . . .' Hazel shrugged.

They were due to meet the Colonel at the castle at ten o'clock the following morning. It wasn't open to the public on Tuesdays, but he was to give them a private tour before they went into the Royal Welsh Fusiliers Regimental Museum, which was housed there. They were joined by a former serviceman who worked as a curator at the collection. The two men received them at the main gate. Hazel and Dawn both wore the court shoes they'd brought with them for the evenings, instead of their usual walking wear.

The museum was spread over two floors of the Queen's Tower, with round rooms. 'We thought you'd like to see our Crimean collection, before we have some coffee,' said the Colonel.

He led them past a display cabinet in which stood a large taxidermied goat, in full regalia. Dawn looked taken aback. 'Our Regimental mascot,' the Colonel explained.

In the section devoted to the Crimea, soldiers' antique red coats were on display, along with swords and medals, old pamphlets and occasional portraits. Information boards described battles and some notable actions. The Colonel led them to a large square of fabric, mounted behind glass on the wall. It was very damaged, hardly there in places. There were big patches where no fabric remained. Single embroidered words were the best-preserved parts of it. Hazel recognized some of them: Alma, Sevastopol, Inkerman.

'The Colours,' said the Colonel.

'Is that the actual flag that was in the Crimean war?' asked Hazel.

'It is. It was the one which was carried into the Battle of Alma, where William Gale so distinguished himself.'

'So it's really been in the wars. To coin a phrase,' said Dawn.

'Very much so. Carrying the Colours into battle was an act of tremendous courage, because of course it was so conspicuous that it drew enemy fire. At Alma, the Ensign to the Colour was killed, and so his commanding officer took over. He, too, lost his life. A Sergeant Henry Smith carried it on and survived. This one was torn through by sixteen balls.'

The four of them stood in silence, looking at the remnants of cloth.

'There's rather a nice story attached to it,' the Colonel went on. 'Some years later, in the 1870s, the Russian Tsar visited England and came to review the troops at Aldershot. When he passed this he made a comment about its tattered state and someone present told him that it was dilapidated because it had been pierced by so many Russian musket balls. So he turned his horse around and went back to salute it. Have you been to the Crimea?' he asked Dawn and Hazel.

They said they had not.

'It's a fascinating place. Unfortunately our friend Mr Putin has made it rather difficult to visit nowadays. The Foreign Office has advised against travel there, since the Russians went in in 2014.'

'It's funny to think that all these men,' Hazel signalled the display cases with their silent red coats, 'went out there to fight against the Russian invasion. Gave their lives, a lot of them. And now the Russians have got it after all. There didn't seem to be so much as a whisper from the international community when they invaded, this time. I don't mean it's funny to laugh at,' she added, in case her meaning had been mistaken.

'No, of course,' said the Colonel. 'Shall we?' And he led the way out and down the stairs.

'Just one more room before we pause for refreshment,' the curator told them. He selected a key from a large ring and unlocked a wooden door. The room within was circular, perhaps fourteen feet across. From ceiling to floor, the walls were lined with glass. Rows and rows and rows of medals gleamed in the electric light. Every one had been highly polished, their bright ribbons creating a mosaic of colour above each sphere or cross of shining metal.

'We're extremely proud of this room, obviously,' said the Colonel.

'These go up as far as Bosnia,' explained the curator.

Hazel looked around her. It was a treasure trove, like something in a fairy-tale. She wondered how many of the recipients of these medals were still living. It felt right, that all their decorations should be assembled here, together, as the men themselves had been, side by side, when they performed the deeds whose awards these were. It was like an Aladdin's Cave of courage. Hazel felt a rush of something like gratitude, that she had been granted a glimpse of it. She was certain, now, that she was doing the right thing.

Coffee things had been set out on a table in a room below, alongside a couple of stiff cardboard boxes. A small square cushion – like a pincushion – lay next to the boxes.

'When you told us you were coming, we went into the archive. What you saw displayed upstairs is only a part of the collection: two-thirds of it is stored away, in Wrexham. Anyhow, we asked them to have a look and see if there was anything under the name Gale and, as you will see, we found some things which we thought would be of interest to you. I had them brought over for your visit.'

Hazel was touched and curious. They sipped at their coffee. Once their cups were empty, the curator lifted the lids from the boxes.

'We're supposed to make people wear conservation gloves, handling these. But I think we can make an exception, for you,' said the Colonel.

Within a cloud of tissue paper was a battered-looking winter fur cap. 'This belonged to your William Gale's younger brother. We think it must have been his sister who gave his things to the Regiment, a Caroline Gale?'

'Yes, that was William's sister. And his brother Algernon's, of course,' said Hazel.

'Well, this was Algernon Gale's. Officers in the Royal Welsh wore peaked forage caps, but many families sent out privately purchased fur caps, against the cold. This must have been one of them.'

He took it out and handed it to Hazel. It felt very light in her hand. She had expected it to be heavier, to weigh as much as the animal whose frame it had once covered. She didn't know what to say about it. It was a mothy old thing. If she'd found it in a cupboard at home she'd probably have thrown it out. After what seemed an appropriately respectful amount of time, she put it back into the box.

'This one is papers and personal effects, apparently,' said the Colonel. From the second box the curator brought out two small leather-bound books, a handful of letters and a little leather box.

'Please,' said the Colonel.

Hazel stepped forward and opened the books. One was a book of Common Prayer, with an inscription: *To Algie on the Occasion of his Confirmation, with love from his devoted Mama, May 1846*'.

'A great many soldiers took their bibles or prayer books with them. As a sort of talisman. There are stories of men surviving grapeshot because they had one of these books in a pocket and it took the peppering for them,' said the Colonel.

'Pity that didn't work in this case,' said Dawn, who had little truck with religion.

Then Hazel opened the smallest box. Inside was a gold brooch set with black enamel, a forget-me-not at its centre. The outer edges were of gold filigree, studded with minute blue stones which matched the petals of the little flower. She picked it up and turned it over. When she saw what was there, she could not stop herself from exclaiming.

'Oh, Dawn, would you look at this! His hair must've been exactly the same colour as Stephen's.'

She forgot, in that instant, that her sister-in-law had never met Stephen. But she had seen his pictures, she knew he'd had auburn hair.

'Ah, yes, a mourning brooch. Mourning jewellery became very popular, in Victorian times, especially after the death of Prince Albert. Queen Victoria wore several pieces after she was widowed. People would mount a lock of hair in a brooch or a locket. Sometimes a ring. This is earlier, of course,' said the curator.

'But how has it kept its colour?' asked Dawn, peering down at the object in Hazel's hand.

'The hair was always on the reverse of the decorated face of the piece, so the wearer would have it close to their heart, I believe. It wouldn't have been exposed to light, even when it was being worn.'

Hazel didn't want to put it back into the box. She wondered how this lock of hair had found its way back to England, from all the way across the Black Sea. It seemed such a fragile thing to remember someone by. It could so easily have been misplaced, something so small, so weightless: someone must have taken great care to get it to his grieving sister. Surely it must have been William who had brought it, got it safely home? Or had a kind friend sent it back, via the mail? Hazel supposed she would never know. She closed her hand around it, just for a moment.

'His sister must have donated this, to preserve the memory of him.'

'Yes,' said the Colonel. 'People were terrifically keen on memorials in those days.'

'We lost our brother, too. My sister and myself. He was far from home as well,' said Hazel.

'In combat?' asked the Colonel.

'Lord, no. My brother wouldn't have made a soldier. He was more of an arty type. Bit of a dreamer,' said Hazel. 'But the medal, the gift of it I mean, we'd like it to be in his name. As we discussed in our emails. We wanted to commemorate William Gale, obviously, but I thought it would be a nice way of memorializing my brother too. It belonged to him, you see.'

'Absolutely. You'll've seen the labels next to some of the exhibits.'

'We were thinking: Donated in memory of Stephen Nolan, the great-great-grandson of William Gale. Something like that.'

'Of course. We'll formalize the wording in writing. And consult with you. It's very important that it should be as you wish. We like to work as closely as we can with families. It's a shared honour.'

No one spoke for a few moments.

'Would it be OK if we took some pictures of these?' Dawn asked. Hazel looked at her gratefully. It had been so poignant to her, holding the brooch, that she had not thought to make a record of it. She'd be able to show Anna and David, when she got home. And send copies to Georgie and to Karen, too.

After they'd taken photographs, the Colonel stepped back and cleared his throat, as if he was about to address a crowd. The curator took the cushion from the side table and held it out in front of him, standing very straight. The Colonel spoke a little about the proud history of the 23rd Regiment. The earliest Victoria Crosses which had been awarded to Welsh Fusiliers, for actions during the Crimean campaign. The Gale medal would be a proud addition here. It struck Hazel that he knew more about William Gale than almost all of the man's actual descendants.

Hazel could barely listen to what was being said, for a sudden flurry of nerves that she might have forgotten the medal, or mislaid it. She had already decided not to put it in her bag this morning. She had instead zipped it into a money-pocket inside her jacket. While the Colonel was speaking, she pressed the place with her elbow until she sensed its hard little points against her ribs. It was a relief, now, to take it out for what would be the last time. The Colonel saluted, and she and Dawn stood in silence. Hazel wanted to feel something go click inside herself, some sense of a door being quietly latched. But she had lived long enough to know that moments of release came unbidden at the oddest times: when you were brushing your teeth, or walking back to the car with a bag of groceries. Ceremony was grand and stirring, but it didn't bring anything to an end. It didn't resolve anything.

Loss, grieving, they made a person tired. It took such a constant effort of will, to keep on your feet.

Hazel placed the medal upon the outstretched cushion. She thought of the words used on Remembrance Day: The legion of the living salute the legion of the dead. It had to be that way around, Hazel understood, but just in this moment she wished it could be otherwise. She didn't require a whole legion, just three. Her heart was something like that tattered flag behind the glass: battle-scarred, torn all away in places, but with certain names in silver thread still upon it. Her mother's, her husband's, Stephen's, stitched indelibly into the cloth.

Acknowledgements

This book could not have been written without the outstanding research of Diana O'Sullivan, whose *Rise and Fall of the Bell Family* was a key source. I am only sorry that she did not live to see the publication of the book she inspired. Diana is much missed.

Passages from the letters of William Gale in Part 1 were taken verbatim from the real-life letters of Lieutenant George Frederick Dallas, published as *Eyewitness in the Crimea* (Greenhill Books, London, 2001). I am extremely grateful to the editor, Michael Hargreave Mawson, for kind permission to quote. The Crimean War is much documented, but Dallas's account is among the most immediate and fresh.

William Gale's letters also draw on material recorded in the correspondence of Sir Daniel Lysons, published as *The Crimean War From First to Last* (John Murray, London, 1895); Betty Askwith, published as *Crimean Courtship* (Michael Russell, 1985); and Major William Barnston and Major Roger Barnston, published as *Letters from the Crimea and India* (Herald Printers, 1998).

Thanks to all scholars and friends at the Crimean War Research Society and the members of CrimeanWar@groups.io.

Michael Hargreave Mawson responded to hundreds of questions with patience and generosity. Dr Glenn Fisher, FRHS, was kind enough to look over an early draft of the Crimean section. Special thanks are due to both these experts and also to Inge and Michael Trevor-Barnston, MBE, and to Major Colin Robins, OBE, for their courteous assistance concerning the Crimean War and medals.

All historical inaccuracies and blunders within these pages are my own.

Huge thanks to Polly Borland and Katie Hadwen-Beck for their round-the-clock help with Australian idiom.

The letters of Alice Gale in Part 3 were taken in part from the diary of Ally Heathcote, held in the collection of Museums Victoria, Australia, and are quoted with kind permission.

Extra-special thanks to Bobby and Billy Alessi for kind permission to quote from their song, *Oh Lori*.

Thank you to Tim Jones for the tour of the Royal Welsh Fusiliers Museum at Caernarfon Castle.

Thanks to my first readers, Charles Hudson, Violet Bannerman, Nell Hudson and Gabriel Hudson, and to Polly Samson and David Gilmour for their help and encouragement.

Thank you to the dream-team of Felicity Rubinstein at Lutyens & Rubinstein, Mary Mount and Isabel Wall at Viking.

Annie Lee and Emma Brown, thank you for your brilliant editorial help.

The one and only John Byrne was wonderful and culled many commas.

In writing this book and *After the Party* I was greatly helped, encouraged and sometimes challenged by Fira Karimova. My profound thanks to her for her wisdom, curiosity, patience and sense of humour.